# THE CASE OF THE MISSING BRIDE

CARMEN RADTKE

*IN MEMORIAM*

*Marcus Cordts*

# CHAPTER 1

Alyssa Chalmers shifted her weight from one foot to the other. How long could it take to read out twenty-two names, match them each to a face, and tick them off a list? She watched Matron McKenzie's slow progress. If she kept on at this pace they might still be here at nightfall.

Black sateen rustled as Matron came nearer. 'Louisa Jane Sinclair?' A sparrow of a girl curtsied, brows nearly disappearing into her fair bangs as her eyes grew wide. *She shouldn't be here*, Alyssa thought with a pang. *She is only a child.*

'Where is your box? Nothing missing from the items on your list?' Louisa-Jane's eyes widened further, her pupils dark disks in the paleness that was her face. She bent down to rummage in the patched cardboard case she carried instead of the regulation wooden box. 'Yes,

Ma'am,' she mumbled. Matron made a note on her list before she called out the next name. 'Emma Sayce?'

By the time the pen scratched over the paper for the last time, the train station lay deserted, its outlines barely visible in the gaslights that illuminated Port Phillip.

Matron clapped her plump hands to get everyone's attention. 'Now listen, girls. No dawdling or gossiping on the way. We shall proceed speedily and as quietly as mice. I'll be in front, and dear Father Pollock will bring up the rear until he sees us safely off.'

The girls obeyed, trudging in silence towards a new life.

The air smelt of salt, dead seaweed and sadness, Alyssa thought, with the gulls screeching like banshees in the all-enveloping darkness. The sea, so full of promise for a better life and a fresh start by daylight, was nothing but a miserable graveyard at night. She shivered. She must be coming down with something. Otherwise there was no explaining this feeling of doom in someone as sensible as she was.

The girls marched on until Matron came to an abrupt halt. 'Ouch,' a girl cried out. 'Can't you watch what you're doing, you stupid cow?'

Matron turned around to confront the speaker. 'Be quiet,' she hissed. 'And watch your words, girl. I'll have none of that language, thank you very much – Nellie, isn't it?'

'What on earth is going on?' a weary voice asked.

'Nothing, Father,' Matron said. 'It seems we have arrived. There's a man waving a lantern over there. Can you make out the name of the ship next to the small barge?'

Father Pollock peered through his spectacles. 'I can't be sure, but it does seem to be made up of two words. Surely you can read it? You're much closer to it than I am.'

Alyssa suppressed a smile. Matron's eyesight must be less keen than she might care to admit. The name *Artemis' Delight* was written in large enough letters to be deciphered, with the gaslights casting their glow onto the ship's massive brown hull. The masts creaked with every movement, as if straining under the weight of the sails. A funnel drew Alyssa's eye. It looked out of place, as if a child had drawn a chimney onto an already finished picture. How very apt that the *Artemis' Delight*, like the girls, was a mixture of the past, with its sails, and the future in the shape of steam power.

'Stay here while I talk to the man,' Matron said after a moment's hesitation. 'If you could give us your blessing now, Father, we shall not detain you any longer.' He obliged and gave them all a fond smile before he vanished into the darkness.

Matron lifted her skirt, although it already fell two inches short of the ground. From her wrist dangled a black reticule, containing the list of names and other papers.

Alyssa wished she could see the man's face as this vision of elegance approached him.

The man signalled them with the lantern to come closer. One by one, the girls trudged up the gangway. Wooden soles clanked on the uneven boards. *Like hooves,* Alyssa thought. *That's what we are. Cattle, going to the highest bidder.* She forced herself to move on, her shoulders tense with the sensation of being watched every inch of the way. She shook herself mentally. She must not let her imagination run loose.

The man smiled as he observed the last girl enter the gangway. He felt an unexpected warmth towards them, as they so willingly travelled towards their new lives, which would bring him much fortune. He'd drink to that, he promised himself as he melted, unseen, into the darkness.

The girls' procession ended in a large room below deck. Four benches surrounded a long table laden with food. The girls stared at it with a mixture of awe and greed.

'May we sit down, please, Matron?' a gentle voice asked. Alyssa half-turned to look at the speaker. Emma, she thought, satisfied that she remembered her name from the roll call.

'Yeah, please?' added another girl.

'Very well,' Matron said. 'I shall sit at the head of the table.' She sniffed, as if something was tickling her nostrils as she went around to her seat. As the first girls joined her at a respectful distance, she opened her reticule and fumbled inside. 'Now where ...?' She put the reticule down, a look of dismay on her face as she glanced around.

Her gaze fell on Alyssa, as one of the last girls still not seated. She beckoned her over. 'Yes, Matron?' Alyssa asked as she avoided looking at the tempting food.

'It's Alyssa, isn't it? I need you to retrace your steps for a moment, I must have dropped my handkerchief somewhere in the passage. I remember using it after we came up the gangway.' She peered at Alyssa. 'I trust you to be back within a few minutes.'

'Yes, Matron.'

Alyssa rushed off on her errand. Above her head, heavy footfall made the planks groan. A single lantern dangled from the wall, casting the narrow passage into a gloom. She stared at the floor, hoping for the handkerchief to give its presence away. It was too dark to stumble around for long, and the strange noises from above were unnerving.

She climbed up the stairs as quietly as she could, when a male voice from above made her halt. 'How long have we been in the seafaring business together, Mr Kendrick?'

'Since May 1857, Sir. Going on five years now.'

'I tell you, this cargo is going to be a world of trouble. Give me cattle, or sheep, or a hold full of iron ore.' A heavy sigh. 'But no, we had to be landed with this. Why me? Why the *Artemis' Delight*, of all the ships in Christendom?'

Alyssa flattened herself against the wall, eavesdropping shamelessly. The other man replied, 'Well, Captain Moore, you're the best sailor I've had the honour to serve under. Our owners know that no one runs a tighter ship. If anyone can handle this cargo, it's you.'

'That may be, but I maintain we're headed for a storm. I can feel it in my bones. Forcing me to go into the petticoat business!'

A thump, like a fist hitting a wall, made Alyssa start. She jerked her head to the left. A glimpse of white caught her eye. Matron's handkerchief.

She heard the captain continue, 'It's time for you to go down and keep an eye on our cargo. Make sure they stay well hidden while I make sure that our fancy Dr Mark Bryson joins you for a quick look. I will not have them pestered by any man.'

'Aye, Sir.' Heels drummed on the planks.

Alyssa snatched the handkerchief off the ground and hastened back to her companions.

She dropped a small curtsey as she handed Matron the retrieved item, glancing around for a space on a bench, but she couldn't see a gap. She squeezed in at one end, next to a lantern-jawed, mutinous looking girl, who glared at the still empty plates in front of them.

'I've had it with waiting,' the girl said. She tossed her head and snatched a hunk of bread.

'Stop that.' Matron narrowed her eyes as she looked at the offender. 'You again, Nellie? You'd better learn to mind your manners, my girl.'

The girl scowled. 'But I'm hungry, and there's loads and loads of bread.'

'We haven't had nothing since breakfast,' another girl chimed in.

'My goodness, that won't do at all.' A pleasant looking man in his early thirties entered the room. 'We can't have you starving before we've even set sail, can we?'

Alyssa felt her empty stomach lurch as she recognised the voice. She gave him a quick glance from under her lowered lashes. Her companions felt less restraint. Half of them gaped at him with open curiosity.

Matron smoothed her dress as she took in the well-made figure in the spotless uniform and his regular features framed by black hair. 'If you are sure, Sir?'

'Absolutely.' He treated the girls to another smile that made the corners of his eyes crinkle. 'You must be Matron McKenzie. My name is Kendrick, and Captain Moore sent me to welcome you on board. I'm the first officer. Still to come is our surgeon, Dr Bryson.'

Matron inclined her head. 'We're delighted to meet you, Sir.'

'Can we have our grub now?' Nellie snatched another piece of bread.

'Certainly,' Kendrick said. 'There's bread, butter, honey and water, and our cook also has some cold meat and fruit ready for you. But now, you'll have to excuse me.'

Without a single moment's hesitation, Matron and the girls helped themselves to as much meat and bread as they could reach, while Alyssa still wondered how she could gain access to the rapidly dwindling rations. But at least she could help herself to the water jug.

She filled a tin cup and drained it in one go. She could hardly remember when she'd ever been this hungry and thirsty. 'Could you please pass me some bread?' she asked Nellie.

The girl her ignored her while she tore out a chunk of bread with her teeth.

Alyssa cleared her throat. 'Could someone please pass me the bread?'

'Get it yourself. You got hands, don't you? Or are you too fancy for that?'

'That is quite enough, Nellie.' Matron put down her slice of bread to point the butter knife at the girl. 'I'll have no more lip from you. How you ever came to receive a good character reference from anyone is beyond me.'

Alyssa felt waves of dislike rolling towards her as Nellie shot her a dark look.

She swallowed her pride. 'Please, Matron, Nellie does have a point. I didn't mean for anybody to wait on me. I only asked because I didn't want to disturb anyone by reaching across the table.' She put on what she hoped would be a disarming smile.

Matron nodded graciously. 'We'll let it go for now, girls. We're all tired and excited.'

Alyssa's eyes beseeched Nellie to leave it at that. 'Sorry,' she mouthed. The girl shrugged and crammed a wedge of cheese into her mouth.

Alyssa's stomach rumbled. There was another loaf of bread on the other side of the table. She swung her legs around to get up and help herself to food without drawing more attention to herself.

'Here, take this.' A plate with a slice of buttered bread and a cut up apple was pushed into her hand. A blonde, clean-shaven man in his early thirties, who might have been handsome if not for the faint air of superiority and boredom, stood in front of her.

'Thank you, but there was no need for that, Sir,' she said. 'I can take care of myself.'

The man raised his eyebrows in a blasé manner and strolled over to Matron. Alyssa made a deliberate effort to concentrate on her dinner.

'That must be the doctor,' a girl said. She was barely more than a child, with shoulder blades jutting out through her thin dress. 'He's ever so nice looking, don't you think?'

'Don't listen to Nancy,' another girl said. 'She thinks every man who still has teeth left is *ever so nice looking*.'

Nancy blushed as the girls giggled. Alyssa risked a

sideward glance at the doctor. How mortifying should he have heard. But he and Matron seemed engrossed in a chat.

'Already looking for a man, Nance?' The sharp-faced girl who'd started the teasing fluttered her lashes and pursed her lips. 'Oooh, you're ever so strong and handsome, Mister.'

Nancy's lips trembled. 'That's enough,' Alyssa said. 'You've had your fun.' She must have spoken louder than intended, because the doctor interrupted his talk with Matron.

Matron clapped twice. 'Hush now,' she said. 'You have three cabins to share, which is more than enough space to accommodate you all. We'll now be shown to our quarters and tomorrow you'll receive a medical examination, which is nothing to worry about, I promise. Afterwards I'll select three girls who will act as my helpers and take on responsibility for their roommates.' She raised her right hand to quell any chatter. 'I'll attend every examination, of course, and Dr Bryson will behave with the utmost decorum, as will all of you. Doctor?'

He gave them all a quick smile that stopped short of his eyes. 'There's one more thing I'd like to mention,' he said. 'Whenever any of you feels unwell and wishes to consult me, always go to see Matron McKenzie first. We must, at all times, observe propriety.'

How Alyssa hated that word. If not for the idiotic rules of society, she'd be free to go where she pleased and do what she wanted. The doctor had it easy. He wasn't forced to knuckle under to Matron's authority as their guardian, or to lie to secure passage on a boat. Frown lines wrinkled her forehead. She smoothed them away. Smile, she told herself, smile and soon I'll be free.

'That went well,' Kendrick said as Doctor Mark Bryson joined him in the passage that had been created by nailing together thin planks of wood.

'You think so? I understand why your captain is bellyaching over this lot. Some of them eyed me almost predatorily. I'll have to think of something to put a stop to that.'

'They all seemed very nice to me.'

'So, you'd let them loose on your captain?'

Kendrick fell silent.

'I thought so,' Mark said. 'But quiet, here they come.'

The cabins in the between-deck were allocated by alphabet. Alyssa found herself in a square space barely large enough to accommodate the four rows of double bunk beds that lined the walls. A faint smell of animals clung to the floorboards, reminiscent of the previous inhabitants of this converted space. A rug made of sacking covered scrubbed planks.

'Hey, that's not half bad.' Nancy let herself fall onto

the lower bunk. She gave it a tentative jiggle. 'Crikey, there's a pillow. That's what I call travelling in style.'

Her head popped out. 'You don't mind if I take the lower one, do you? Only you're much taller than me, and I'm no good at climbing.'

'Certainly.' Alyssa pulled herself up onto the stepladder that lead to her bunk. A mattress stuffed with straw, judging by its prickly feel, and a woollen blanket made up the bed. She wondered what Nancy's life must have been like if anything this basic put her into rapture. At least someone had rigged up curtains to provide them with some privacy.

'It smells like home.' Another head popped up. 'I'm Hannah Beale. Call me Hannah. There's no need to stand on ceremony, is there?'

Alyssa smiled. 'You're right. My name is Alyssa Chalmers, and I'm afraid I don't know Nancy's last name.'

'Alcock it is. Only don't expect me to ever sound as grand as our Alyssa here does.'

Alyssa felt blood rush into her cheeks. 'I don't intend to. Sound grand, I mean.'

'I think it sounds nice,' Hannah said. 'Maybe you can teach us all how to talk like proper ladies? Help us pass the time.' Her brown eyes twinkled. 'And then we can all put that blasted Rosie in her place when she plagues Nancy again. Honestly, that girl's tongue is as prickly as her name. Her mama knew what she was doing, calling her that.'

'You know her?'

'Yeah. Most of us lived in Tin Pan Alley or were at the orphanage together for a bit.'

'At least you're with your friends then.' Alyssa felt a prick of loneliness.

Hannah got out of her bunk and put a hand on Alyssa's shoulder. 'Don't worry, we'll take care of you. Fancy or not, you're one of us now, aren't you?'

The warmth of Hannah's skin seeped through the fabric of Alyssa's dress. It felt good, as if some connection was created between her and this dark-haired girl with her impish face and eyes full of laughter. 'Thank you,' she said. 'I'd appreciate that.'

'Cut it out. Only some of us would like to sleep,' a heavy-set girl scowled at them.

Alyssa frowned. 'But what about our luggage? It's still in the dining room.'

'Gosh, aren't we grand? Dining room, my foot. As for your box, suit yourself. But you'd better sleep on it, because there ain't hardly room enough for all of that stuff.'

The girl turned around to face the wall. Alyssa could see that she was still wearing her skirt and blouse. She stiffened. Surely, they wouldn't be expected to sleep fully dressed?

She looked around in search of a solution to that problem. 'I'd better go and see Matron McKenzie about that,' she said when no idea was forthcoming.

'Suit yourself,' the girl in the bunk said.

'That's Milly,' Hannah whispered. 'She isn't usually this grumpy so you pay her no heed. It's probably her nerves telling.'

Alyssa nodded, grateful to have someone to steer her through this unknown territory made up of girls she had nothing in common with. It made her feel less alone and vulnerable.

She took a paraffin filled lantern from the hook on the wall. The anchored ship rolled gently from side to side. She'd soon get used to the movement, she thought, as she steadied herself with one hand against the wall to tiptoe back to the big room, hoping to find some clue to Matron's whereabouts along the way.

Another lamp dimly lit the passage. The floorboards groaned under her steps, echoing loudly in her ears. She rose onto her tiptoes, but for one split second the echo rang out as loud as before, and she thought she heard faint breathing behind her. Alyssa stopped and strained her ears. Nothing. She must have been mistaken.

She crept on until she came to the mess. She opened the door, describing a slow circle with the lantern. No Matron.

'What on earth are you doing here?' a familiar voice rang out from behind her.

She nearly dropped the lantern. So, she had heard someone after all. 'I'm looking for Mrs McKenzie, Doctor.'

'Already?' He raised his own light and motioned

Alyssa to follow him. 'You don't seem poorly, but by all means let's get Matron and have a good look at you.'

She pulled her shawl closer to her throat. 'I'm perfectly well, thank you, Doctor. All I intend to do is to ask Matron when we can fetch our luggage, and to secure us a wash bowl.'

'Commendable, although you could have thought of that earlier,' he said with a hint of amusement in his voice. 'I'd better lead the way to your trusty chaperone, so we won't break the rules a moment longer than we have to.'

As she was at a loss for an answer, she opted for dignified silence.

He stepped out onto the passage, walked past Alyssa's makeshift cabin and turned left at the end of the passage. 'Behind this door you should find Mrs McKenzie safely ensconced,' he said without bothering to look at his companion. He rapped on the oak door.

'Yes?' Matron sounded surprised.

'I've brought you one of your charges, Matron.'

'Oh, it's you, Doctor. One moment please, until I am decent.'

The wait was interminable until Matron opened the door. 'You'll have to pardon my dressing-gown, but I was getting ready to settle down for the night,' she said as she tied the ribbons of a pink nightcap dripping with frills.

'We'll try to make it as quick as possible, madam, so we can all get our well-deserved rest,' the doctor said, showing off his even white teeth to his advantage.

Alyssa stepped forward. 'We need some clothes, Matron,' she said, curtsying in the same moment as the ship leaned to the side. Her shoulder collided painfully with the door. She bit back a small yelp. 'We also need some facility to have a wash in the morning.'

Matron appeared surprised. 'Is that why you're here? Can't that wait, my dear? I'm already in my dressing-gown.' She gave the doctor a helpless look. 'Maybe you would be so kind as to arrange for the boy to take the luggage to the girls? He'd have to put the boxes in front of the door, of course.'

'Certainly,' he said. 'However, there still is this young lady. We can't leave her running around unattended.'

Matron stared at Alyssa as if she could propel her back where she belonged through the sheer force of her will. 'Whatever are we to do with you?'

Alyssa felt her cheeks turning hot. 'I did not intend to inconvenience you, madam.'

Mark said, 'These things should have been addressed earlier, and it was remiss of us to overlook all possible situations.' He gave Matron another charming smile. 'It seems our crew is not accustomed to having ladies on board. With your permission, to make up for our negligence, I'll take the young lady back to her quarters and you'll chaperone us from the sanctuary of your cabin, be it in spirit only.'

'If you think we could do that this once? These girls are my responsibility after all.' She sighed, shaking her head fast enough to set the rows of frills on her nightcap in motion. It looked like a sea of pink foam, Alyssa thought. 'Maybe I should get changed again.'

'But dear madam,' Alyssa said, watching the spectacle mesmerised, 'surely that would take longer than it would take me to get back to my quarters?'

The frills came to a standstill as their owner stared at her again. 'You appear trustworthy,' she said with a lack of conviction. 'And of course, if the doctor thinks it is appropriate, I shall make an exception. But only this once.'

'You possess a remarkable talent to stir up trouble,' he said as he steered Alyssa back, the geniality he'd shown Matron all but vanished.

She halted in mid-stride. 'What should I have done instead?'

'Waited until morning.'

'That wouldn't have done at all.'

'Everyone else seemed satisfied the way things are,' he said.

'Only because the girls expected things to be taken care of. And if someone falls ill at night-time, how are we to get Matron to fetch you if we are forbidden to venture out alone?'

He rubbed his clean-shaven chin. 'That is a question I can't answer tonight. But I'll make sure the luggage is taken to your quarters. I presume the boxes are clearly labelled?'

'They most certainly are,' Alyssa said. 'That is - I'd think so.'

'We'd better have a look, before I send some unsuspecting man out on a fool's errand.'

In the mess hall, he stooped to pick up a threadbare carpetbag. 'It is labelled,' he said, 'but I'll be darned if I can read that scrawl.'

'Let me have a look.' Alyssa held her lamp as close to the box as possible. 'Susanna Terry or Kerry, as far as I can make out.'

'And pray tell me, in which cabin would we find that fair damsel?'

'Oh. I've no idea.'

'You have no idea.' He sighed loud enough for Alyssa to feel stupid. 'Maybe you should grab your own things and leave it at that.'

Alyssa drew herself up as tall as she could. 'That would be quite unfair,' she said in her most cutting tone. 'I shall not avail myself to a single scrap more than anyone else.'

'Mrs McKenzie seemed to have no such qualms.'

'Mrs McKenzie is our Matron and as such, in a completely different position.'

He leant against the wall, hands in his pockets. 'As you wish. Are you ready to leave?'

Alyssa was glad he couldn't see her face, which by

now must have turned scarlet with indignation. She turned on her heels and walked in silence to her room.

Hannah lay still awake. 'Well, what did Matron say?' she asked.

'We'll receive our things in the morning.'

'That's all right, then, innit? We can sleep in our shifts.' Hannah closed the curtain again. 'Good-night.'

The man crept out of his hiding place and made for his own room. He congratulated himself. Following nothing but his instincts on a clandestine stroll, he now knew where to find distraction if he took precautions not to get caught.

# CHAPTER 2

**M**ark grimaced as the door closed behind the girl. Thus far his new medical post did not bode well. The only sympathetic people he'd met since his arrival were the first officer, Charles Kendrick, and the boy, Davies, who'd taken care of his belongings. These two should already be waiting for him, to enlighten him about his new surroundings. He glanced at his fob watch. The girl had cost him half an hour with her idiotic skulking around.

The door to his cabin stood ajar. Kendrick occupied the wingchair, while the boy jumped to attention as Mark entered.

'There you are, Doctor, just as I was going to summon a search party for you. Did you get lost on your way to your surgery?' Kendrick sank deeper into the chair.

'Side-tracked would be a better description,' Mark

said. 'I stumbled upon one of the maidens who felt herself unequal to spending the night without her things and escorted her back to her quarters.'

'Damn.' A shadow flitted over Kendrick's face. 'We'd better make sure nothing of that nature occurs again. Apart from you, only the ship's officers, cook and young Davies here are aware of the damsels hidden below deck. They must stay put, without exception.'

'I'd gathered as much from the captain's remarks when he greeted me,' Mark said, with a small nod and a sideway glance at the boy. Kendrick inclined his head the fraction of an inch and said, 'You can go and carry the doctor's medical gear to the surgery, Davies.'

'Take the trunk with my instruments first and then come back for the rest, please,' Mark said. 'Be careful not to drop it.'

'Sir.' The boy clapped his heels together and saluted hard enough for his fingertips to make visible contact with his forehead. 'Aye, Sir.'

'My, what an enthusiastic chap,' Mark said as Davies hurried away.

'He's a nice boy, if a bit overeager. He seems to think we're the Royal Navy.' He rose. 'I'd hoped we'd have time for a longer chat, but that'll have to wait until you've seen the captain again. We expected you earlier than a quarter of an hour before the girls arrived.'

'Blame the hansom driver. He got lost every time we turned a corner.'

'They all do, wherever you go in the world. But I won't keep you any longer now.'

~

'All done, Sir.' Sweat still glistened on the boy's forehead as he lifted his hand for another salute. 'Is there anything else needs doing before we go?'

Mark assessed the situation as he looked around properly for the first time. In addition to the bunk, his quarters offered the luxury of a folding table, two armchairs, a sea chest, a built-in shelf and two seascapes framing a porthole. 'Very plush,' he said. 'Let's get my things inside and then I'll have a quick wash before you take me to see our good captain.'

Davies led him to a Davenport desk that was placed snug against the wall. 'Watch this,' the boy said with obvious pride. 'You lift that lid and you'll find as sweet a wash-stand fitted inside as you'll ever see. Done by Mr Kendrick's instructions, Sir, and you don't have to be worried about the jug rolling every which way when it gets a bit rough-like.'

'Ingenious,' Mark said as he lifted the porcelain jug from the carved-out drawer and filled a bowl with it that had been made to fit another hole. Towels and soap were underneath in shelves. Several pigeonholes offered safe storage for letters, journals, pens and inkwell.

He snapped the lid of the smaller of his two trunks open and took out a silver backed comb and brush set.

Glancing into the wall mirror, he dampened his hair before running the comb through it. His hands received more attention. He worked up a good lather before he rinsed and dried them. Mark caught Davies giving him a quick once-over under half-lowered lashes. 'I hope I've scrubbed up well enough to see the captain now.'

'Yes, Sir.'

Davies led Mark four doors down the passage. A brass plate, mounted on the oak door, announced this as the captain's quarters. The boy knocked twice before calling, 'Dr Bryson is here to see you, Captain.'

'Show him in.'

Mark stretched his hand out again. 'Pleased to meet you, Captain.'

Captain Moore made no move to take the offered hand. The gloom on his face deepened. Dyspeptic, Mark thought, or suffering a touch of the arthritis judging by the painful grimaces he made. Apart from that he seemed to be in good shape for a man in his fifties who spent his life battling the elements.

Mark stood at ease, waiting for Moore to talk.

The captain glowered at him, 'You know what your post entails, Mister?'

'The same as every other medical post on board a ship, I'd say.'

'Hah. A bit of a ladies' man, are you?'

Mark stared in surprise. 'Pardon?'

'Look at you.' The captain pointed an accusing finger at Mark. 'If your fancy clothes have ever seen an honest pelting, I'll be darned. And your hands, soft and shiny as a baby's.'

Mark smiled. 'I'm a doctor, Captain Moore. If you should ever need a surgeon, better make sure he has clean hands or you might as well make your last will and testament straight away. As for my new clothes, I'm not sure you, or your first officer, would have let me set foot on board your fine vessel here if I'd worn my old rags.' He let his gaze wander across the cabin, taking in the heavy velvet curtains and the thick Oriental rug that muffled any sound. 'After eighteen months in an Australian mining town you hardly qualify as a dandy.'

'A mining town? Digging for gold as a side-line, eh?'

Mark's patience began to wear thin. 'I was patching people up. Do you know how easy it is to die out there in the wilderness?'

The captain stroked his silvery beard. 'Then what made you take this job?'

Mark paused for a heartbeat before he replied. 'It happened to suit me.'

Captain Moore's face darkened again.

Mark sighed. 'Your ship suits me, or rather your destination which brings me as close to home as I can hope for, while the United States are at war. My patients had nothing to do with it, if that's what worries you. Romance is the last thing on my mind. Will that be all?'

'Aye, Doctor.'

Mark turned towards the door. As he put his hand on the handle, he stopped. 'I nearly forgot to present you with my credentials, Captain.' He pulled a wallet out of his overcoat. 'My Certificate of Registration, handed out to me in 1853 back home in Boston.'

Captain Moore barely glanced at the document before he put it on the side table, securing it with a paperweight. 'Very good.'

Mark held out his hand. 'Shall I take it along to your office? Or to whoever takes care of the paperwork? Otherwise I'd rather keep it.'

'By all means. Or hand it over to Mr Kendrick.'

'Thank you, Captain.'

Davies still waited outside the cabin. 'Shall I show you around, Sir?' He saluted again.

'Only if you manage to keep your hand down,' Mark said. 'I may have signed on here, but I'm still a civilian, not one of your superiors in uniform.'

Davies' hand shot up again, only to be stopped halfway through the motion. 'Yes, Sir.'

'That's better. Now, lead me to my place of work.'

The surgery was as well appointed as the rest of the ship. It had shelves, two cupboards with glass panels in the doors and solid locks and a large table on which to make up pills and draughts. A desk, two cane-backed chairs and an upholstered armchair in case he wanted to rest his weary head were grouped closely together. A bamboo screen hid a bed.

Rain lashed the porthole that otherwise might afford him an outlook over Port Philip. Mark sat down on the bed. He fingered the thin woollen blanket. It smelled freshly laundered. 'This will do very well, Davies,' he said. 'If you could run along to my cabin and fetch the stack of medical journals from my trunk, I'll set up shop without delay.'

He took stock of the sparsely stocked pharmacy. Half a dozen brown bottles were crammed tight enough into the first cabinet to prevent them from falling over in rough seas. Mark greeted them like old acquaintances. Laudanum, three bottles of bicarbonate of soda, and two filled with arnica. He pulled out the stoppers, sniffing the contents before shaking a few grains out of each bottle to make sure the label was correct.

A knock on the door interrupted him. 'Come in,' he said. 'Put it next to me.'

'I would if I knew what you're talking about.'

Mark put the stopper back on the arnica bottle. 'I didn't expect you, Mr Kendrick. I sent the boy to fetch my journals.'

Another knock.

'There he is,' Kendrick said, as the boy entered. 'It's all right, Davies. You may go to bed.'

He strolled over to Mark. 'Everything to your liking? Otherwise just say the word.'

'Everything is fine, thanks. Compared to my last practice this is sinfully luxurious.'

'I can imagine. A mining town in the back of beyond, the captain told me.'

Kendrick lowered his tall frame onto a cane chair.

'What else did he say? We didn't exactly become bosom mates. Is your captain always this tetchy or did I do something to arouse his dislike?'

'He'll come around once he has time to get used to the new situation.'

Mark doubted that, from what little he had seen of the morose captain. He looked at Kendrick. A nice fellow, with an easy manner and a humorous glint in his dark eyes. He decided to be frank. 'What's eating away at him? Or is it too much of a liberty to ask?'

Kendrick shrugged. 'You're entitled to know as far as I'm concerned. Captain Moore, and may I say that to a certain extent I share his sentiments, is highly allergic to our new cargo and to the fact it is supposed to be kept hush-hush for reasons of safety.'

Mark raised his eyebrows. 'You don't make sense. What cargo?'

'Well, that's what the girls are, when it comes down to it, isn't it? Twenty-two females without family, to be rescued from poverty in Australia and duly delivered to be married off to the more prospering Canadians. I don't have to spell it out for you what could happen to their virtue if they ran loose, with all these lonely men around, do I? You can't blame the captain for being tetchy, with this responsibility forced on us.' Kendrick hoisted himself off the chair. 'In case you want to take a stroll onshore before dinner, this is as good a time as any. The rain has eased.'

'When are we departing?'

'That I can't say. It could be the day after tomorrow, could be later. We're still waiting for an inspection, and if there's one thing I have learned, it's that you can't hurry a man with a badge.' He glanced at Mark. 'Does it matter? We'll give you ample warning if you want to take a proper last look at the fair Melbourne.'

'I'd appreciate that. I'd appreciate it still more if you could spare me a man tomorrow, preferably one who knows his way around. It wouldn't hurt to stock up on a few things for the surgery.'

Kendrick took off his hat to smooth his curls. 'I'll be at your service if the captain agrees, and show you some sights. That is, if we have enough time and you don't intend to visit every apothecary in the city.'

'One ought to do, if he carries a wide array of drugs. We've got a long journey ahead and the stock here is quite Spartan for a ship of this size.'

'The captain doesn't believe in poison. Unless it comes out of an oak casket.'

'A man after my own heart, after all.'

A sharp knock at the door roused Alyssa from a heavy sleep. Gentle snoring filled the room, overlaid with the rustle of straw whenever one of the girls rolled over on her mattress.

'I brought the water,' a high-pitched voice said from the other side of the door. 'Mind you don't trip over the bucket, Miss.'

She reached for her dressing gown, until she remembered it was in her box. She drew the makeshift curtain halfway until it got stuck. 'You can stay in bed while I get the water,' she said to whoever might be awake, fumbling to get into her skirt.

'I don't mind if I do.' Milly snuggled back under the blanket. 'It's ever so much fun watching you.' A slow smile spread over her freckled face.

After a moment's hesitation, Alyssa returned the

smile. She tucked her blouse into her skirt. 'How do I look?'

'Honestly?' Hannah propped herself up on one sturdy elbow. 'I only hope the poor lad has legged it or he might scream. You're a sight, with your hair all over the place, and your lovely stockings all muddy. Not that he'd be likely to see them.' The girls giggled.

'I must have stepped into something on our way from the train. The sooner we get at our things, the better.' Alyssa dangled her legs over the bunk. 'Be careful not to move, Nancy. I'm climbing down. Watch out so you don't get mud on your blanket.'

The boy had brought two cans of water and two empty tin ewers. Soap and a clean towel completed the washing arrangement. Alyssa took care to prevent spills as she carried the cans. She might be muddy, but she drew the line at resembling a drowned cat.

When the basins were full, she rolled up her sleeves and scrubbed her face and hands, wishing she had her handheld mirror so she could tidy her hair. One more reason to insist on access to her box. She rolled down her sleeves and emptied the ewer into the other one so she could refill the first with clean water. 'Who wants to be next? Matron ought to be here soon to fetch us for breakfast.'

Alyssa's group was the last to enter the big room, but

judging from the bedraggled appearance of the others they were also the only ones who'd taken the trouble to scrub up.

Once again there was bread, butter and, oh joy, a pot of marmalade. Alyssa hoped to be lucky enough to get one of the apples or oranges that lent a festive touch to the table. Once they were at sea, it would be nothing short of a miracle to have such luxuries as fresh fruit.

'Attention girls and sit down. After you have finished your breakfast we'll have a roll call before we proceed with the medical examination.' Matron took the list out of her reticule and held it up for everyone to see. 'You'll be split up in three groups, one per room, and the doctor and I will decide who of you will be the most suitable sub-Matron. Every day one of you will go to Cook to fetch our ration. We will also take turns with our cooking, cleaning and laundry. In addition to that you'll receive instruction in needlework, housekeeping and basic reading, writing and arithmetic.' She sat down in a sweeping motion. 'Let's now thank the Lord for what we are about to receive.'

'Amen.' Captain Moore finished saying grace in the spacious officers' mess that now accommodated a variety of landlubbers in addition to his men. Either his mood had improved considerably since the girls had been safely stowed away, thought Mark, or the master of the *Artemis' Delight* took immense trouble to show the world and the saloon passengers in particular a brave face. There were five of them, wide-ranging in personality, but all agreeable fellows as far as he could tell. He looked forward to their company.

'Scrambled eggs.' Jack Parsons, a wiry man in his forties, lifted the lid off a china dish and inhaled the aroma. 'And sausages as well. You spoil us, Captain.'

'Enjoy it while you can,' Captain Moore said. 'We'll soon enough be reduced to eating bread and hard biscuits if we strike it unlucky.'

'In this case we all better make a note about this feast in our diaries,' Parsons said.

'Surely you have ample provisions for your crew and our lot?' Edward Dawkes, the youngest of the lot, added two sausages to a mound of eggs.

'If everything goes smoothly, yes, which it should, now that we have steam in addition to our sails,' the captain said. 'But the sea is its own master, and that's the only certainty.'

'If that's so, I'd better have another sausage.' Dawkes reached for the dish again. His white teeth gleamed in his bronzed face as he smiled. His moustache met his sideburns in such a precise fashion that Mark wondered how long he would be able to sustain this elegance once they were at sea.

'Mr Osborne hasn't had any yet,' barrel-chested Henry Turnbull said with an air of quiet authority.

'And that was the last one I took. I'm tremendously sorry. Have one of mine.' Dawkes offered his plate to his neighbour, a slight man whose low voice and inoffensive manner made him easy to overlook.

'It was my own fault,' Robert Osborne said. 'I should have been quicker.' He blinked owlishly. 'Really, I am perfectly well supplied.'

'When shall we be on our way?' Grizzled Thomas Harris tapped with his fingers on the table, as if to release some tension. The whole man resembled a tightly wound coil, Mark thought. It would be interesting to see how he would cope with the enforced idleness of a voyage halfway around the world.

'This afternoon with the tide, I hope,' Captain Moore said. 'Gentlemen, excuse the doctor and I. We need to get everything ready for the final inspection, and then we'll be good to go.

Captain Moore paused in the passage, stopping Mark. 'I couldn't very well ask you in front of those gentlemen, but what are you going to do, and what shall I tell the inspectors? You know how they are, always eager to cause you more and more paperwork.'

'It should be pretty straightforward,' Mark said. 'You'll need to show my certificate of registration, I presume, and a signed note from me that I have inspected and sampled our provisions and can vouch for their good condition. I'll also provide a written declaration that I have examined the girls and can vouch for them as well.'

'Are you sure it won't be more than that?'

'As far as I'm informed that will be all. A formality, especially since none of the girls struck me as a potential health risk.' He grimaced at the memory of one girl. 'Some certainly could do with less vitality and energy.'

'Pardon?' The captain stared at him.

'I was talking to myself, Sir.'

'When do I get the documents? I don't want to miss the tide if we can help it.'

Mark made a quick calculation in his head. 'Three hours for the girls' muster? I'll bring all the necessary documentation, if you tell me where to find you.'

'I'll show you.'

The office, like everything else on the *Artemis' Delight*, was neatly furnished, with a roll-top desk, a chair and a padlocked cabinet. Ledgers weighed down letters strewn across the desk.

'Should I happen to be somewhere else when you come around, put everything you've got here. We always do.' The captain opened a hefty ledger, which contained an astonishing number of loose documents in no discernible order. Mark decided to hang on to his own precious certificate by whatever means it would take.

'One last thing,' the captain said. 'I presume that your conduct of the - shall we say, inspection - of the, ahem, cargo, will be above reproach? I will not have anything undesirable happening on my command.' He looked him in the eyes, with enough force of personality to make Mark understand how Moore had risen to his rank, despite his current discomfort.

'I shall treat these young ladies exactly like I would any other patient,' he said. 'And to set your mind at ease, on no occasion shall I be left alone with one of them. Matron McKenzie will attend any examination without exception.'

'I gather she is a sensible person?'

Mark thought of the nightcap with its frills, and the air of vagueness that was at odds with the sharp glint in Matron's eye. He stifled a smile. 'Why else should the church have selected her for this position? Keeping these brides in check is not for the faint-hearted.'

Captain Moore pushed his lips outwards as if tasting that idea to see if he liked it. 'Off you go then, Doctor. We don't want to waste any more time.'

At least he didn't call him Mister anymore. That was progress.

He put his hands in his pockets as he ambled to his surgery. The task shouldn't be too demanding. A good look at the skin, pulse, eyes and general appearance of the cargo fulfilled all the requirements. No, not cargo. Mark mentally slapped himself. They were girls, not wool clips or iron ore, for goodness sake, however questionable their reason for being here was. And, let their moral standard be what it may, he ought to be grateful. Without them and the need for a surgeon to accompany the *Artemis' Delight*, he'd have been hard pressed to secure a berth on a ship that would take him as close to possible to his home and the battlefields. As it was, it could still take him three months to reach his destination.

He shook off his gloomy thoughts as he sat down and pulled out pen and paper.

'Ready, Sir?'

'As ready as I'll ever be, Davies. Tell Mrs McKenzie to bring her young charges along and send them in, in alphabetical order.'

Matron entered alone. 'I've told the girls to wait outside until I've talked to you for a moment,' she said, her pale blue eyes fixed on the wall behind him.

'By all means. Take a seat. I hope you have recovered from last night's interruptions.' Her colour changed slightly, he noticed. Up close he put her age higher than her clothes and demeanour suggested. He breathed a sigh of relief. She must be at least his own age, which was thirty-two, and the older, the better suited for her duties, as far as he was concerned.

'You must have thought me very foolish last night, I'm afraid.' She leaned close enough that he could smell lavender water. 'But I must admit that I was exhausted, and some of the girls were not quite what I had been led to believe.'

He leant back. 'I see.'

'Not that there is anything wrong with them,' Matron said. 'I'm sure they are all perfectly nice and well bred once I get to know them better. But that's not what I meant to say.' Two pink spots appeared directly under the rosy, if artificial bloom of her cheeks. 'If you give me a brief outline of what to expect, I might calm down my girls. As you can imagine, the thought of being attended to by A Man - ' She actually talked in capital letters, he thought, amused. ' - is deeply unsettling for them. I have some experience in that respect.'

'I thought as much.'

'I used to volunteer at the Royal Hospital for Women, until my husband passed away. So you see my medical experience and my widowed state make me a suitable travel companion for these poor girls. Most of them will never have spent a minute alone with a man other than a relative. Their reputation is all they have.'

'Sure,' Mark said. 'If we could begin? Five minutes should be ample for each girl. You can tell them there is nothing to cause them discomfort. Any physical contact will be conducted by you.'

He should have expected his, he thought. Even new countries like Australia were infected with a sense of female modesty that left women to die in agony because they would rather die than let a man properly examine their body.

'Thank you, Doctor.' Matron opened the door. 'Milly Adair!'

A big-boned girl edged into the room.

'How do you do?' Mark said. The girl dropped a small curtsy but remained silent.

'Move closer, my dear,' Matron said. 'Don't be shy, the doctor won't bite you.'

'Take a seat, Milly,' Mark said. 'You don't mind if I call you Milly, do you?'

She sat as stiff as a post at the edge of the cane chair.

'I'll ask Matron to check your heartbeat,' Mark said in his most gentle manner. 'All you need to do is to give Matron your wrist, and she'll count the beats she can feel.'

While Matron took Milly's pulse, Mark circled them. The mousy hair could have done with a wash, but the girl seemed reasonably clean and healthy. She would run to fat in a few years' time, but for now her solid body seemed to be mostly muscle.

'You can finish, Mrs McKenzie. How many beats did you count? 130 in two minutes? Excellent,' he said. 'Now, Milly, that wasn't too bad, was it? If everyone is as healthy as you are, I'll find myself twiddling my thumbs for the next few months.'

'Thank you, Doctor.' She jumped off the chair and curtsied again.

Mark leant against his desk. 'Send in the next girl. Just give me a minute to get ready.' He waited until she had closed the door before he jotted down her name and a few notes.

A knock announced the next girl, a brittle blonde with calculating eyes. 'Take a seat,' Matron said, studying her list.

'Thanks, Ma'am.'

At the sound of the voice Matron looked up. 'You're not Nancy Alcock.'

'No, ma'am. It's Rosie Thatcher. Nancy let me have her turn, because I was all aflutter, like.' She half-turned to Mark, putting her hands on her hips.

'How do you do, Rosie?' Mark pointed at the chair. The girl gave the seat a quick wipe with her hand before she sat down. 'I don't want to get my dress dirty,' she said when she caught Matron's quizzing glance. 'It's ever so nice, and you never know who sat down there before you, do you?'

She let her wrist dangle in front of Mark. 'You can take my heartbeat now.' She watched him from under her lowered lashes like a cat stalking a bird. Even her teeth reminded him of a feline, sharp and pointed. He'd have to make sure that none of the girls got any silly ideas about him, or his situation could become very awkward.

He regarded her in as off-putting a manner as he could muster. 'Matron will do it.'

'Ouch!'

Matron smiled at Rosie. 'You'll find it much easier if you co-operate and hold still. Then I wouldn't have to yank your arm, would I?' Mark circled the girl. Slim, but not malnourished. He gave Matron a sign to let go of Rosie's wrist. 'You may send the next in.'

The girl hesitated.

'Well, Rosie? Haven't you heard what the doctor said?'

Rosie's face turned crimson. 'Yes, Ma'am,' she mumbled. 'Yes, Sir.'

'That's better.' Matron dismissed her with a flutter of her hand.

As soon as Rosie had left, Mark said, 'You certainly put that young lady in her place.'

Matron smoothed her skirt. 'Girls of her class need a firm hand. Most of the girls will behave as they ought to. Otherwise I'll have to give them a reference that won't reflect well on them, and who'd risk not finding a husband over that? You'll see, the others won't give you any trouble.'

'I trust you're right.'

His hopes were dashed while his words still hung in the air. Striding into the room with an almost mannish gait was the dark-haired girl from last night. She curtsied stiffly.

'Sit down.' 'Matron peered closer at Alyssa. 'Oh, it's you,' she said. 'I hardly recognised you with your hair neatly arranged. That is so much better.'

Alyssa clamped her jaws so tight it hurt while the doctor slowly scrutinised every aspect of her person. Matron held her wrist tight enough to make her squirm. She felt like a butterfly pinned to a corkboard while still alive; treated with the dispassionate interest one shows a curious object. As soon as Matron let go of her wrist, she rose. 'May I leave now?'

'Certainly,' he said. 'Unless, of course, there is something you wish to discuss? You had a lot of urgent questions last night.'

She forced herself to keep her gaze on the wall.

He moved closer; she could feel it. 'Well? Last night you weren't that shy.' She turned around, to see his lips curl up in amusement.

'Now, Doctor. That is enough. You're making the poor girl blush.' A plump hand patted hers. 'It is all right, my dear, the doctor doesn't mean to tease you.'

Alyssa bit back a reply.

He bared his lips in what at first glance might have passed for a smile. 'As you are obviously at a loss for words, you may go. Should you find your speech again though, I'd suggest you do it at an appropriate time.' He was mocking her again. This time Matron must have noticed, because Alyssa had to endure another pat on her hand. She pulled her hand discreetly away before she turned to fully face the doctor.

'If the necessary arrangements for our well-being had been made, there would have been no reason to bother anyone.'

'I didn't know that the lack of a wash-basin constituted such a hardship.'

Alyssa took a deep breath. She would not give that man the satisfaction and rise to his bait. Instead she addressed Matron, as one woman to another. 'Surely you, Madam, understand how important it is that we do not convey the wrong impression.' She held out her hand in what she hoped would pass for a shy gesture towards Matron. 'The doctor may not grasp the importance of cleanliness and propriety for a female, but you do, don't you?'

'Of course, my dear. You did quite right.' Matron moved closer, as if to shield Alyssa from male ignorance. 'You will talk to the captain about it, I hope, Doctor.'

'I don't want to cause any trouble. But I really shouldn't take up more of your precious time.' A shy if insincere smile and she was gone.

Matron and Mark both stared after her.

'Where on earth did you find that girl? She's cut from a different cloth than her companions, I'd say.' Mark looked at his notes. 'She's older than most, at twenty-two.'

'She'd make a good sub-Matron,' Matron said. 'I don't know much about the poor girl, apart from the fact that she comes from an excellent family. Orphaned, of course. Her father was a senior official in her Majesty's service in Melbourne. I seem to remember there was some talk about him, but he's been dead and buried these four years at least, and his wife passed away a few months ago.'

She frowned. 'One does wonder what a girl of Miss Chalmers's class is doing among this lot, but of course she is on her own, and if she has fallen on hard times...' The sentence trailed away. 'She should prove invaluable as a teacher. Her manners and character are above reproach, and she appears very resourceful.'

'Oh yes,' Mark said, heart-felt.

Another knock interrupted them. 'Back to work,' he said. 'Let's see what surprises your other charges have in store for us.'

With Matron and the last of her charges dismissed, Mark loosened his collar before it choked him. Thank God that was over. It was understandable that the girls were jittery, but he'd been subjected to more startled glances and girly shrieks than any man should have to bear. He could almost admire Alyssa Chalmers' forthrightness. Exasperating as she was, at least she didn't suffer from a surfeit of nerves.

A hollow feeling reminded him that, although he'd duly inspected the rations first thing after breakfast, he hadn't eaten anything since.

'Davies?'

Either the boy had a knack for turning up whenever he was wanted, or he was under orders to dog his footsteps, Mark thought, as he looked up from his desk and faced the boy less than a minute after he'd called out. The boy held a box filled with pens.

'Care for a pen, Sir? Before I take these to Mr Parsons and Mr Dawkes?'

Mark took two. 'Thank you, but what I really wanted to ask for is a bite to eat. I'm half-starved but I'd better finish my papers for the captain. Bread and cheese will do.'

He bent his head over his notes. Nobody could accuse him of taking short cuts with his documentation. He made one copy for himself, in case the other one got lost in the captain's disorganised office.

The creak of the floorboards announced Davies' return.

'Put the tray on my desk, and then you can tell the captain I'll be with him shortly.' Mark dipped his pen into the ink well. A nice flourishing signature always lent conviction to official documents, even if, like this one, they stated nothing more than the correct number of flour sacks, potato bins and bacon sides plus observations about their condition.

He put down the pen and reached for a hunk of bread. Substitute girls for sacks, and the rest would read the same. The only information needed according to the hiring agent, were the correct number and their general state of health. Hardly a demanding task, making working off his passage a mere trifle. He should have more than ample time to read and reread every single scrap in his medical library.

He sobered up as he stared out of the porthole. They had three months at sea ahead of them, if they were lucky. The Lord only knew how many men had to die for want of a doctor in the war that was tearing his country apart, while he was stuck here chitchatting with the saloon passengers and catering to a gaggle of females on the prowl for a husband.

Mark picked up his pen again. 'Twenty-two female emigrants duly inspected,' he wrote. 'Three mild cases of malnourishment, no signs of infectious diseases or consumption. Signed on this 17 April 1862. Mark Hepburn Bryson, M.D.'

'What took you so long, Doctor?' Captain Moore wiped his forehead. 'Muggy,' he said. 'I'll be glad to see the last of Melbourne.'

Mark handed him the papers.

'I reckon these are for me?' A rotund figure pushed himself up to his feet. His belly strained against the buttons of his faded coat. 'Johnson's the name, inspection's the game.' A guffaw accompanied the joke. Captain Moore's face was a mask of quiet pain.

'How do you do, Sir. I'm Dr Bryson.' Mark shook Johnson's sweaty hand. 'I hope you didn't have to wait unduly long?'

'No worries, doc. The captain and I've been having a chinwag. Makes a nice change, to have real gentlemen to deal with. That's what's wrong with this fair country, if I may say so among us gentlemen. Too many crims and blacks once you leave Victoria.' He stuck two yellow-stained fingers into his mouth to extract a wad of chewing tobacco.

Moore treated him to a glacial stare.

'You don't have a spittoon, do you?'

Mark grabbed the nearest container he could lay his hands on, a marble ashtray bearing an engraved brass plaque.

Captain Moore closed his eyes until the spitting ceased.

'Is there anything else we can help you with, Sir?' Mark said.

Johnson squinted at the papers before he rolled them up and put them in a shabby brown satchel that already contained a few squarely folded sheets. 'Everything in order, you say? Nothing that demands my attention?'

'Absolutely nothing,' Mark said, putting a reluctant hand on Johnson's grubby shoulder to steer him away from the captain. 'Upon my word, if every vessel was equal to our good *Artemis' Delight*, your duties would be a picnic.'

'Nice soft berth you have here yourself, doc. Well, I won't keep you any longer.'

'I'll have you seen off board.' Captain Moore nearly tripped over his own feet as he rushed to open the door.

'Obnoxious fellow.' Moore stood at the rail, until Johnson was out of earshot.

'I hope you're not talking about me.' Henry Turnbull stepped out of the shadow. 'Harris and I hoped to catch a last glimpse of these fair shores and couldn't help but overhear.'

'That creature,' Moore pointed an accusing finger at the rapidly disappearing figure, 'could wear out the patience of a saint. Ask the doctor what I had to endure, if you don't believe me.'

'Not quite the ticket, was he?' Turnbull raised a bushy grey-speckled eyebrow.

Captain Moore's face took on a purplish hue. 'That sorry excuse for a human being overstepped the mark from the moment he opened his foul mouth. Among us gentlemen, my word! If I were a betting man I'd take any wager that his family came to Australia less than two generations ago on our Majesty's expense, and good riddance to them. Would you believe that I found him pawing through my ledger when I entered the office? I only thank the Lord that I keep nothing of value there that would have fit in his grubby pockets.'

Mark started to fear an apoplexy. He said, 'You got rid of him pretty smartly. Odds are you won't have to see that fellow ever again.'

Turnbull turned to Mark. 'We missed you at luncheon, Doctor. A delicious leg of lamb with all the trimmings.'

'I hope you saved some for me, considering that I toiled away making sure that there will be no shortage of food once we're at sea.'

'What a conscientious man you are.'

'Would you prefer me not to be?'

'I rather wish there were more of your kind. But I seem to have lost Harris. Nice talking to you.' He strolled away.

'Don't leave the ship,' the captain called out. 'We'll be on our way any minute now.' He pulled a whistle out of his uniform jacket and blew it.

'Captain.' The first officer saluted.

'All men to their stations, Mr Kendrick. It's time to bid Australia farewell.'

Mark and the saloon passengers watched the crew from a respectful distance. The sailors' movements resembled an intricate dance as they swarmed all over the deck, he thought, with every step rehearsed and precise in its execution.

'Hoist the main sail!' shouted the bosun. 'Hoist the main!' Another man picked up the cry, until every command formed part of a chorus performed to the sound of heavy footfall. Gulls circled overhead like so many airborne critics.

He wondered for an instant how the girls fared, with all the strange noise echoing in their cramped hide-away. It couldn't be easy, but he hoped they'd soon get used to it.

'Shall we go inside and toast our imminent departure

with a brandy to ward off the chill, Doctor? Surely even Mr Parsons must have seen enough to fill his diary with a charming account. We should ask him to act as our communal voyage diarist.' Dawkes turned up the collar of his dinner jacket as the *Artemis' Delight* gathered momentum.

'It's not cold, man,' Turnbull said. 'Only a nice breeze to fill our sails.'

Dawkes shuddered in an exaggerated manner. 'Pray, Mr Osborne, what do you say? Or do you agree with our hardy Scottish friend?'

Osborne shrank further into the shadows.

'My medical advice is to toast a safe voyage with whatever you prefer, gentlemen. Or rather, with whatever we can choose from,' Mark said.

A smoking-room had been created within the saloon by the means of two lacquered screens, thus giving the illusion of privacy. Easy chairs were scatted around two round tables and a carved walnut desk complete with writing paraphernalia that would not have looked out of place in a gentleman's home.

Dawkes opened the door to a cabinet hidden behind the chairs. 'If my usually unerring instinct doesn't fail me, we should find something of interest here.'

Harris looked over Dawkes' shoulder. 'If you hand me that tray with the glasses and a decanter, I'll put them on the table if you like. Or should I call the steward?'

'I'm afraid so, yes.' Dawkes shut the doors of the

drinks cabinet. 'Nothing palatable here, except for port and that is hardly a suitable drink for this time of day.'

'I'll take care of everything.' Mark was grateful for an excuse to leave the room. As expected, the boy was close at hand.

'Davies? Could we get some light refreshments, please?' He lowered his voice. 'Give the captain my compliments and tell him that the best time to talk to the ladies would be before dinner, when our passengers withdraw to their cabins to attend to their attire.' He peered down his shirtfront, spotting a splash of ink. 'I don't envy whoever does the laundry.'

A slow grin spread over Davies' freckled face. 'Poor old Soapy. He never knew we'd have so many people along, and toffs among 'em with more trunks than her Majesty herself.'

'Poor Soapy indeed. I'll try to give him not too much trouble.' Mark was happy to see the boy this animated, but Davies became self-conscious again, his fair skin flushing violently. 'I'm sorry, Sir, I don't know what came over me to talk that freely.'

'I'm the one to blame.' He gave the boy a reassuring pat on the shoulder. 'And I've got to warn you, I'll probably need a bit of your help, if I don't want to run afoul of crew or passengers. Just knowing what's what does help in that regard, you see.'

Davies' colour changed back to normal. 'You ask me anytime, Sir. There's not much me and my mates don't know, if you get my meaning.' He gave Mark a conspiratorial wink.

'I knew I could rely on you. But I'd better let you get our tea before we have a mutiny on our hands.'

'Come in, Doctor, and close the door. We don't want our two hothouse plants here to wither and perish.'

For a fleeting moment Osborne smiled. 'You will have your little joke, Mr Turnbull,' he said. 'But you must admit that it is cold. What do you think, Doctor?'

Mark shook his head. 'I'm New England born and bred, Mr Osborne, so Australia will never be cold to me. But I did notice that Mr Turnbull had the foresight to wear his native tweed, which ought to keep him considerably warmer than our lightweight suits.'

'Do I detect an envious note in your voice?' Turnbull said, raising his eyebrows. 'Just wait until dinner. It's a pity there are no ladies present whom I could dazzle with my impeccable evening dress and my charming conversation.' Mark's gaze was drawn to the door. No, it was impossible that anyone could have overheard him or someone else talking about the hidden set of passengers.

'Whoever said that your countrymen had a reputation for being strong and silent, certainly never met you,' Harris said, his shrewd eyes twinkling in his weather-beaten face.

'You should read my reports to head office. We Scots are also renowned for our business sense, and that entails certain social skills. Having an Irish mother also helps, of course. I was born with the gift of the gab and an eye for opportunities. But here come our refreshments, to a certain extent. We do seem to be deprived of anything of a spiritual nature.' Turnbull lifted the lid of the two pots. 'Tea and coffee. Who shall be mother?'

The first entry since they'd boarded the ship. He dipped his pen into the inkwell.

*'It amuses me to think that it is another man's bad habits that so easily enabled that paid tool J to smooth the path for our new venture. A list of names, written on paper of low quality, that is all to establish existence. All it needed was a little sleight of hand, to ensure it's gone from the ledger, and with it, all proof of my hidden jewels.'*

He could almost feel the weight of gold in his pockets. What a pity that he could not contact his agent while on board. He'd be best to advise whether this precious cargo should be sold wholesale, or if a few of them would merit an auction. With any luck, he would manage to get a good look at them, not just the glimpse from afar that he had in Port Phillips.

He smiled to himself. Life offered so many opportunities to those bold enough to grab them. How easy it had been to discover the girls' accommodation.

Laughably easy. The dark-haired girl had led him straight to her room, with her lantern. He could have reached out his hand and touched her, or the doctor. But they were both blind. Most people were, which made his life so much easier. Twenty-two white girls, at his disposal.

*'I wonder if there is another man alive caring so much about their welfare on this journey. It would be devastating should their well being suffer during this journey. I shall say a special prayer at night that all of us on board shall reach our destination in prime condition.'*

He chuckled as wrote the words. What a pity he could not share his wit with anyone, but every businessman had a few regrets.

# CHAPTER 5

Below deck in the girls' mess excitement, mingled with fear, suffused the atmosphere. Most of the girls sat huddled together in one group. Their eyes were huge with anxiety, and they clamped their ears shut to drown out the hoarse shouts and clanking noises that reverberated throughout the ship. Matron's reassuring smile stopped short of her eyes. She must be as frightened as the other girls, Alyssa thought, despite her efforts to mask it.

Alyssa herself longed to be outside, in the daylight. If only she could say good-bye to Melbourne on her own terms, she might regain the sense of freedom she ought to feel as they left the past behind. Instead she was cooped up in a dim barn of a room with a herd of strangers, at the mercy of people she did not know. All they had in common was this ship and the hope for a better future once they reached Canada.

The noise of indistinct commands and shrill whistle blows from the deck, and the constant heavy footfall that sounded as if coming from directly over their heads, made any conversation very hard, but she had no desire for talk anyway. There was no one she could have confided in without creating a sensation. No, she had to keep it secret that the last thing she intended to do was find a husband. Canada was only the first step on her voyage which would take her back to England by whatever means necessary. Her few remaining relatives there surely would not fail her in her orphaned state, however remote the connection was.

A pang of anxiety shot through her. If only she could be sure to find her mother's cousins. All she had was an address found on old letters, the last one dated from 1859. So much could happen in three years, people died, or left – but she must not think of that.

On impulse, she went to the screen that hid the pile of luggage. Her fingers itched to unlock the drawer of her box and put her hands on the novels hidden inside. It would be enough to touch them to calm down her nerves. She wouldn't take them out, only draw comfort from their presence. But that was impossible, or she might create a rush if the girls were led to believe they'd be allowed to get at their belongings.

Alyssa took a deep breath and forced herself to return to her old place. The noise outside the world of the hold subsided while the ship's movements found a new rhythm. They were truly under way.

'If you follow a few simple rules, you will find your voyage as pleasant as can possibly be.' Captain Moore's hands were folded behind his back. One look at his immaculate uniform and rigid posture were enough to stifle any chatter.

'As you may have noticed we have done everything in our power to provide you with clean, comfortable surroundings. Any complaints will be addressed to Matron McKenzie in the first and the doctor in the second instance. I shall be the last port of call, and may I remind you, that on this ship I am the law. Whatever is brought to my attention will be dealt with in an official fashion, so you should consider every action twice. Bear that in mind.'

He let his words sink in before he softened his tone. 'May I say that I am convinced that nothing untoward will happen. I realise that being kept out of sight will be difficult to achieve, but it is in your own interest, to avoid unwanted attention.'

Matron's enthusiastic nod let the dark ringlets peeking out from her bonnet dance.

'The doctor and Mrs McKenzie will now inform you of the details.' Captain Moore touched his hat. 'Have a pleasant time.'

Nervous giggles signalled his retreat. Matron clapped her hands. 'We're not done yet.'

'Could've fooled me,' Rosie muttered, but a sharp ribbing with an elbow quieted her.

'First of all, we can assure you that you are the very

picture of health, all ship-shape you might say.' More nervous giggles; Alyssa rolled her eyes. 'I, and the three girls who will serve as my sub-Matrons, will make sure you have fresh water and soap. The girl in charge of your room will send one of you to collect our daily rations from Cook. Food and water will be regularly inspected by the doctor.'

Matron showed the first signs of unease. 'Remember that Cook is a man, so no dallying, please. Keep in mind what the captain said. Under no circumstances shall we have any sort of consorting going on. Any transgression will be severely punished, and it will be mentioned in your character reference. I hope I need say no more.'

'Whatever does she mean, consorting?' Nancy sounded confused.

'Striking up a, well, friendship,' Alyssa said after a brief hesitation. Nancy blushed.

'Will the following girls step forward, please? Alyssa Chalmers, Harriet Jamieson and Susanna Terry. The rest of you may go to your cabins now.'

Alyssa put her hand up. 'Excuse me, Matron, when can we take our boxes?'

'Doctor?' Matron appeared at a loss. 'I hope you did address that problem with Captain Moore? Or do I need to arrange a meeting with the Master?'

He pinched the bridge of his nose between thumb and finger. 'There is not enough space to bring all the luggage along, but it should be sufficient to take along one change of small clothes each, and clean stockings.'

At least he had the grace to look slightly uncomfortable at the thought of female undergarments.

Alyssa smiled. 'But what about the rest?' someone behind her whispered.

She put her hand up again. 'What happens to the rest of our belongings? It may not occur to you, Doctor, but for most of us all our worldly possessions are in those boxes.'

'Matron and I will personally supervise the removal of the garments and make lists of the remaining contents. If anything vanishes, the offender will be punished.' He locked gaze with Alyssa. 'Is that good enough for you?'

'When can we begin?'

'I've got two hours before I'm required elsewhere. Will that time do?'

'I'll try my best,' Alyssa said. 'But we wouldn't dream of inconveniencing you. Surely you have better things to do than counting shifts and aprons?' She smiled as sweetly as she could. 'If I could be supplied with pen and paper we might be able to do some simple stocktaking ourselves.'

'It would be more proper,' Matron agreed. She moved close enough to the doctor to whisper, 'Some girls might be offended by having A Man touch their intimate belongings.'

Alyssa caught the words, and the resulting exasperated headshake, as he said, 'I'm sorry. Do I presume the esteemed Miss Chalmers shares your sensibilities?'

Alyssa's sympathy vanished. She said, 'I would, Sir, if it weren't for a simple fact. You are not A Man,' she imitated Matron's bashful whispering in capital letters, 'you're a doctor. May I have pen and paper, please?'

Mark rested his elbows on the rail. Already the city had lost her identity. Soon the land mass, growing more obscure with each passing mile, would be nothing but a distant memory. He wondered if anyone else shared his exhilaration. What did the girls below feel? Did they comprehend that this was final? There was no way back for them.

'Half an hour until mealtime, Sir,' a voice behind him said.

Mark turned around with a start. 'Good Lord, Davies, you certainly seem to be everywhere. Aren't you ever off-duty?'

Davies grinned. He'd shed his original shyness with the ease of a snake shedding her skin, Mark thought.

'Only dinner to serve and then deliver ink and paper to Mr Osborne and help with the dishes, that's all for tonight, Sir.' The boy peered into the rapidly expanding dusk. 'There she goes, and I never saw one of them funny animals. Hoppin' mad they are, Mr Kendrick said.'

'Kangaroos, you mean? Maybe next time. They're a sight not to be missed.'

'Maybe, if we stay on this route,' the boy said. 'Do you think I'll see some redskins? Only, everyone back home said how it'll be one adventure after another.'

Mark smiled. There was something appealing about the boy, or maybe it was the simple trust he showed him that made Mark give one of his rare promises. 'I cannot guarantee you a Red Indian, but if we gain permission to go onshore in San Francisco, I'll take you to Chinatown. I've got friends there, natives. Would you like that?'

'Oh, Sir!'

'All right. But I'd better get myself in a presentable state for dinner.'

He checked his appearance one last time in the large mirror. He would do, he decided, but that would be about it. At least his chin was clean-shaven for hygienic reasons, and if his curly hair was cropped closer than he preferred, that could be attributed to the foresight of a man who knew he'd have to live without a barber for a long time.

His suit was black and of a well-enough cut, and it was new, like the grey and the navy serge that were folded away in his sea-chest. When Mark ordered the suits and half a dozen shirts from a small outfitter's off

Flinders Street he thought them almost too elegant for what lay ahead.

He chuckled. How soon perspective changed once he'd returned from the outback. If Captain Moore had harboured suspicions that he might be a bit of a dandy when they first met, he wondered what the good sailor made of the gentlemen in the saloon? The boyish Dawkes, energetic Harris and gregarious Turnbull shouted the words bespoke tailor with their immaculate evening dress, complete with ruffled shirt-breast and silk waistcoat that showed off their figures to advantage.

He straightened his cuffs. 'Just a doctor,' he said, grimacing as certain words came back to his mind. 'Poor bloke, whoever wants to court that gal.'

The pen scratched over the paper.

*'We have hardly left Australia behind, and already the company palls on me. How much better one could while away the hours in the presence of the fair sex. What irony to think that only a few feet below us is all the female charm and softness to keep a man satisfied. But, to be sure, unsullied commodities fetch a much better price. So, I shall not complain, as hard as it is not to sample the wares.'*

# CHAPTER 6

'My compliments, Captain.' Turnbull helped himself to a glass of port after the last course had been cleared away and the company had retired to the smoking-room. 'The *Artemis' Delight* is more like a gentleman's club than a ship.' He relaxed into one of the armchairs. 'Cigar, anyone?' He presented a slim silver case.

'Thanks,' said Captain Moore, as he took two cigars and handed one to Kendrick, who had finished his watch. 'You should have seen us eighteen months ago, with only sails to speed us along, a hold full of cattle, and nary a piece of soft furnishing in the mess.'

'That's hard to imagine.' Harris surveyed the ankle-deep oriental carpet and the gleaming oak panelling with new appreciation. 'Someone has spent a pretty penny.'

'More like a pretty guinea.' Dawkes nursed a large

scotch in his hands. A boyish grin spread over his face. 'Not that I want to complain. I must admit I wouldn't have cared too much for a spot of rustic living on a long journey like this. As for the smell of cattle –'

Harris said, 'There's certainly none of that here. Bit of the other extreme, if you ask me. I caught a whiff of lavender once or twice.'

'So did I.' Dawkes leant forward. 'You don't have a secret wife stashed away, Captain?'

Captain Moore choked on his cigar smoke.

Mark jumped in. 'Nothing so romantic, I'm afraid. I asked the apothecary to mix something into the soap to soften the stench, and he overdid it. Although it is in keeping with the opulence of our surroundings.'

Kendrick drew in the smoke of his cigar. 'That's exactly what the owners of the *Artemis' Delight* intended, when they decided to change the direction of their enterprise. What you see before you, gentlemen, is a ship that was rigged out to satisfy the most discerning of gentlemen of a botanical inclination. That is why our *Artemis' Delight* was fitted with a steam engine and a funnel in addition to our sails, so we are not completely at the mercy of the elements.' He blew out a perfect smoke ring. 'Although there is no denying you'll probably see us praying for wind every day. These engines are hungrier than a whale.'

Mark's curiosity was stirred. 'An expedition ship? Hence the name?'

'From being the livestock and mineral carrying *Pride*

*of Penzance* we became the *Artemis' Delight*, ready to follow in the footsteps of many a now wealthy and famous man, bringing the rarest of flowers and most exotic of plants home to Queen and England. The hold is still slightly rough, but I hope that our passenger cabins leave nothing to be desired on our first voyage since the alterations.'

Dawkes leant forward. 'How exciting you make it sound! But unless I have been grossly misled, we are not going on an expedition into the wilderness?'

'Not at all,' Captain Moore said. 'It's all the way to Port Victoria from here, with a stop to re-supply coal and rations in San Francisco.'

'What happened to the original plans?' asked Dawkes. 'I thought there is still a small fortune to be made from procuring exotic plants plucked from the jungles of the Americas.'

'There is. Our hold was about to be fitted with compartments to transport whatever the scientific minded gentlemen would have cared for,' said Kendrick. 'But then your country happened.'

'Excuse me?'

'The War between the States, Mr Dawkes,' Mark said. 'Who can tell how far this madness will spread? Running the risk of getting caught up in our bloody mess wouldn't exactly make an enticing business venture.'

'But surely that war must soon be over?' Osborne stuck his head out a little bit, like a greying turtle emerging from its shell, Mark thought.

Turnbull raised his glass. 'Here's to that. Although, if there is one thing being said in every war, it is it'll soon be over. It never is, gentlemen. It never is.'

'We've nothing to worry about,' Captain Moore said. 'However horrible, we'll be far from the war, and as you see, nothing has been spared to make your journey enjoyable.'

Dawkes smiled. 'I'm certain it will be. And I promise, I'll keep my peace with our doctor and ignore the sorry fact that he is a lowly Yankee and I'm a gentleman from North Carolina.' He winked at Mark with good humour.

Mark raised his glass in a silent toast. His first impression had been right. All these men would be good company.

Kendrick said, 'What brings you gentlemen here? Australia and the Canadian frontier-land aren't the usual haunts of the Quality, as our less well-educated friends are wont to say.'

Turnbull re-filled his glass. 'Nothing mysterious about that,' he said. 'I'm a mining engineer, and Australia and Canada both have an abundance of easily accessible wealth if you know what to look for. Harris has mining interests as well.'

'That's right,' Harris said, helping himself to a cigar.

'There's a lot of money to be made if you do it by the books,' Osborne said. 'You must know that you find me on the other side of the fence, so to speak. I'm in the banking business.' A fleeting smile appeared on his face.

'Ah,' Turnbull said. 'I'd better be nice to you, in case I need a backer.'

'I'd be happy to see you anytime,' Osborne said. 'Although I'm glad to say I'm only scheduled to spend one or two years in Canada, training staff. Then it's home for good.'

'How long has it been since you last saw Greenwich?' Turnbull asked.

'Far too long,' Osborne said. 'I spent three years in Melbourne, and I won't mind admitting I never got used to the seasons being topsy-turvy.'

'Three years!' Dawkes exclaimed. 'To think I found a mere six months tedious.'

Captain Moore glanced at the padded coat, the scarlet scarf and high collar, and said, 'That does not astonish me. You must have appeared exotic to the colonials.'

Dawkes laughed. 'You are making fun of me, but what do you expect? The mater would have an apoplexy should I turn up on the doorstep with corks dangling from a wide-brimmed felt.' His good humour was infectious. 'She'd send me to sleep in the dog-house.'

'So, you weren't dispatched in disgrace to these fair shores?' Kendrick knocked ash from his cigar.

'Perish the thought. No, like all the others I must confess to have purely pecuniary interests in Australia. Since becoming head of the family, I've tried to spread our interests a bit. This country with its mineral wealth sounded promising, so I thought a visit might be profitable.' He grimaced. 'Not that it did me any good. It'd be foolish to sink money into a place teeming with convicts and their offspring if you don't have anyone absolutely trustworthy in place. Still, it never hurts to look for opportunities.'

Harris nodded. 'It's a sound principle to walk away if you can't keep an eye on things yourself. Agents can be a rum lot.'

Dawkes puffed on his cigar, blowing a string of smoke circles above his head. 'True, so I've decided to look at Canada and maybe go into the skin-trade instead. Regrettably, we Southern gentlemen must make our money somewhere, like everyone else.'

'What about you, Doctor?' Jack Parsons broke his silence for the first time.

Mark shrugged. 'I came here in the name of duty, when two cousins of mine with more brawn than brain decided to try their luck on the goldfields, and their parents implored me to tag along. My mother in Boston backed them up, saying a son practicing medicine in Australia was no worse than having me work in San Francisco.'

He grinned. 'The cousins returned home a year ago, healthy in body and wallet, while I stayed behind. Then I received news about the war, and here I am, on my way home to offer my services as a field surgeon.'

Moore regarded him with new respect. 'That's the spirit. Nothing worse than a man who shirks his duty or gets stuck in a rut before he's worn out his first pair of long pants.'

'Then you shall find us all to your liking,' said Turnbull. 'Although I'd wager that Mr Dawkes is the only one among us who's still on the right side of thirty.'

'Barely, Mr Turnbull,' Dawkes said. 'Barely. You aren't exactly as old as those hills that you dig into yourself. The mater would classify you as an eligible bachelor, and you'd soon be snapped up if you were to put yourself in her hands.' His eyes held a speculative look. 'Unless it's happened already.'

Turnbull's face lost its jovial expression. 'My wife died in childbed two years ago, and our son with her.' He pushed himself up. 'It's getting late. I think I'll call it a night.'

Alyssa's hand ached as she finally put down the pen. All that was left to do was take her own garments out of the wooden box and list the remaining contents. She bent down, holding her skirt with one hand. Although the floor was as clean as one could hope for, it was obvious that it used to hold greasy fleeces.

Her navy everyday dress would be best suited here, she decided. She hung it over her left arm. One cotton shift, and a nightgown, toothbrush and comb, her novel, and she was ready. She locked the drawer and pushed the lid of the box down to snap it shut.

'Are you done, my dear?' Matron asked.

'Almost. If you wish to retire, madam, I'll write up my list in the morning.'

Matron shook her head. 'Always finish the task, my husband used to say. If you hand me your bundle, you'll have the list done in a jiffy. I've never seen anyone write so fast.'

Alyssa reluctantly relinquished her belongings. Her bundle looked embarrassingly luxurious, compared to the other girls' belongings. Louisa Jane's shifts' and blouses and especially Emma's, had obviously been passed down through one or more hands until the fabric had worn as thin as a linen handkerchief. Pity mixed with anger filled her; surely the girls should have been sent out with more than a few rags to their name.

'Alyssa?'

She picked up the pen again, reading out aloud while she wrote, so Matron could make sure everything was correct. 'Alyssa Chalmers, half a dozen cotton shifts, three lace-edged shifts, three cotton nightdresses, one woollen dressing-gown, three flannel blouses, three flannel skirts, three flannel petticoats, one woollen dress, two cotton dresses, six pairs of stockings. Also, five guineas, two novels, a diary and a silver-backed hand-mirror plus tinned food in the locked drawer.'

'How did you ever manage to cram all that into one box?' Matron frowned. 'I only hope that you know what you let yourself in for. I can't make exceptions for you.'

'I won't be any trouble.'

Matron's face softened. 'I'm sure you won't be. I only wish I could improve your situation. A nicely brought up young girl like you shouldn't be all alone in the world and reduced to this.' She sighed. 'You remind me of myself in my younger days, when my family was forced to leave Scotland and seek our fortune in the colonies.'

'Why, that can't have been too long ago,' Alyssa felt compelled to say. 'I only wish I was half as pretty as you are.'

Matron touched her cheek. 'Little flatterer. Bedtime for you. Boy!' She poked her head outside. 'You accompany Miss Chalmers first. I'll wait.'

Matron settled in a corner and closed her eyes. This was harder than she had expected, with no one to turn to for comfort or counsel. But she'd made the right decision. Who better to take care of these girls than one who was so much more world-wise, and herself bereft of family? Her husband would have wanted her to go. She could hear his voice in her head, guiding her. He'd always had faith in her. She would not disappoint him, or her charges.

If only she could trust them not to stir up trouble. Rosie's face appeared unbidden in her mind. She'd be more than happy to hand her over to a husband.

Matron's eyes flew open as she heard Davies' footsteps. How awful if he had found her half asleep. She righted her bonnet and went to meet him at the door.

Alyssa crept into the cabin. She'd have to rig up some

sort of curtain in a corner, so they could wash and change in privacy.

She hung the lantern on its bracket. Everyone else was already asleep, despite the jolting. Alyssa braced herself. For someone who'd always had a bedchamber to herself until yesterday, the noises her seven roommates made in their sleep were a trial. Add to that the incessant creaking all around her, and she wouldn't sleep a wink.

'Wakey wakey! Time to get our grub.' Someone shook her hard enough to make her wince.

Alyssa pulled her blanket up to hide behind it. With her right hand, she reached for her shift and dress. 'If you draw the curtain, I'll be ready in a minute.' She turned towards the wall to protect what modesty she had left.

'Better hurry,' Milly said. 'Or there won't be anything good left to get from Cook. I bet you Susanna sends Emma, and she only needs to simper at a man to get something extra.'

Alyssa struggled with the last two hooks. 'You should be happy, then,' she said. 'All the rations will be shared equally among us lot. Has anyone fetched the water yet?'

'I have,' Nancy said. Her eyes sparkled with happiness. 'And we've been given a chest of our own, with eight drawers, for our clothes. We put the jug and ewers on top of it.'

Alyssa wanted to hug her. Maybe this voyage would be tolerable after all. 'Thank you.'

$\sim$

'Slop's here.' Nellie wrinkled her nose as she dumped a cauldron on the big table. 'Mugs and bowls are over there, on those brackets.' She sniffed the porridge. 'It smells better than it looks,' she admitted. 'There's also bread and butter.'

'And flour and currants and lard,' a pretty girl said in a soft soprano. Golden curls framed her heart-shaped face. 'Cook promised he'd let us make a suet pudding later.'

'Sweet on you already, Emma?' Rosie purred. Alyssa half expected her to slide out claws any second. Emma bit her lip.

Alyssa scanned the room for her chaperone. Surely Matron would interfere? There she was, busy slicing and buttering bread, oblivious to anything else.

It was up to her, then, to keep peace. She began to feel like she was treading on quicksand. 'I love a good pudding,' she said, stepping between Emma and Rosie. 'If anyone here knows how to cook it we'll appreciate it.'

Rosie scowled while Emma gave her a grateful look.

Alyssa filled her bowl and nursed it in her hands when she felt a sharp poke in her ribs. Porridge slopped over the bowl as she flinched, spattering onto her sleeve.

She drew in her breath, pretending nothing had

happened. As she dipped her spoon with her left hand into the porridge, she watched her neighbour from under lowered lashes. As soon as she sensed movement, she brought down her elbow, trapping Rosie's arm.

'Ouch!' Rosie hissed. 'Let go, you stupid cow.'

'Sorry. I hope I didn't hurt you. I wonder how that could happen?'

Nellie giggled. Emma and Nancy gave her admiring glances.

'Watch out,' Rosie said. 'If you think you can lord it over me with your fancy airs, think again.' Her eyes narrowed. 'You don't belong here. Don't you forget it.'

Alyssa's hand shot out and clamped Rosie's wrist. 'You watch out, Rosie. I'm not afraid of you, and neither is anyone else. We're stuck here together, so we'll better make the best of it.' She gave Rosie's wrist a slight squeeze. 'You don't have to like me, simply leave us all in peace. Or would you like me to ask Matron to make sure of that?'

Thankfully Rosie fell for the empty threat. Hatred gleamed in her eyes but she nodded.

'Good,' Alyssa said with more conviction than she felt. She gave Matron a quick glance. On one hand, she was thankful that Matron let them fight their own battles, on the other hand she needed to exercise her authority to keep them on a tight leash. Otherwise these would turn out to be the longest weeks of Alyssa's life.

∼

Three weeks, and the diary entries resembled each other like the days on this ship.

*Patience is fast becoming less of a virtue, and more of a penitence. I amuse myself with admiring the mature, but obvious charms of the good Matron from afar. I flatter myself to be the only one smiling about the doctor's explanations for lavender scent in the air. Dear me, how anxious the boy is to steer anyone away from certain parts of the ship! But the good lady has nothing to fear. Although I wonder if she wouldn't make a useful addition to my goods. Conjuring up an ingenious plan how to spirit her away as well, when we arrive at our next port, might at least help ease my boredom. But for how much longer? Sometimes I wonder if I should rely on my luck and ingenuity. After all, how easy is it in a flock of twenty-two for one little goose to go astray? I think I have already, in my frequent vigils, spotted a likely bird who likes to spread her wings in forbidden quarters.*

# CHAPTER 7

These were without a doubt the longest days of Alyssa's life. The only improvement thus far was her growing adjustment to the ship's movements. Where the first days and nights had inflicted new bruises all the time, when she was caught unawares by the rolling of the ship, she now had found her sea legs. If only the same could be said about her spirits.

She had never been this downcast before. Her days were divided between eating bland meals, herding her little flock, receiving needlework instructions from Matron and giving reading and writing lessons herself. The worst was the lack of daylight. She felt as if the nearly constant twilight they lived in drained all her energy.

They were all growing short-tempered, penned together as they were. Rosie did her best to keep her distance from Alyssa, after that first encounter, but others weren't as lucky. That girl sailed as close to the wind as she could, although, if not for her, Alyssa would not have struck up a fast friendship with Hannah and Emma.

They had sought her out one evening, while she was tidying away the books she used for her lessons.

'Ask her,' Hannah said, nudging Emma closer. 'Alyssa will help you, right?'

'If I can. What's the matter?'

A single tear slid down Emma's cheek. 'It's my shift. I was doing the laundry, with Hannah and Rosie, and Rosie caught my shift and my petticoat with the plunger, and tore a gaping hole in both.' She held out the damaged items. 'She says it was an accident, but I only have these.' Her eyes pleaded with Alyssa. 'Hannah said you might think of something to mend them. You always do!'

Alyssa took the garments and turned them over. It wasn't a miracle that they had torn so easily but that they hadn't fallen apart of their own accord. They were past mending. Poor Emma; by rights she should have had a second set at the least, but one only had to look at her ill-fitting blouse to realise that she had to make do with whatever she was given.

'Come with me,' she said. 'I'll ask Matron for permission to get a change of garments, and you'll have some of my things.'

'But -'

'I have more than enough.' Alyssa smiled at Emma.

'Oh, Alyssa, thank you!'

'And I'll have a word with Matron. She should remind Rosie that she needs to take better care when doing her chores.'

But these days even Emma's undemanding company wasn't enough to calm Alyssa's nerves.

The only relief she had, was while the saloon passengers sat down for luncheon. Only then, weather permitting, did the second officer, Mr Wainwright, herd them for an all too short interlude up the companionway to the deck. Twenty minutes of whooshing spray and wind, salty air and sunshine! Alyssa made sure to be the first one up and the last one to return to their prison below, while Matron found enough to chat about with their gallant escort.

Alyssa smiled to herself. Whatever it was they found to talk about, it brought a light into Matron's eyes, and Mr Wainwright's as well. Matron must feel very lonely sometimes, Alyssa thought. Although the older woman made a habit of talking more freely to Alyssa than she did with the other girls, there was no one her equal on this journey, and the responsibility weighed heavily on her.

Alyssa wondered how long Matron had been widowed; she clearly enjoyed male attention and company.

Alyssa herself craved nothing more than those few moments alone and the view of the vast emptiness surrounding the ship. Without these precious moments, with the scent of freedom filling her lungs and the rough wind to feel on her face, she'd go insane.

She even appreciated the doctor's daily muster, because it relieved the tedium a little.

Luckily for her, the strict hygienic rules she insisted upon paid off. Alyssa shuddered. She would be mortified if one of her mess was found with nits in her hair, as had happened with Rosie the day before. Alyssa instinctively touched her hair. It still stank of the paraffin they all had to rub in as a precaution after the doctor made the nasty discovery.

To be fair, he had been surprisingly nice. Instead of cutting off Rosie's infested tresses, he told Matron to ensure Rosie treated her hair with perchloride of mercury.

Rosie had taken to her bunk afterwards, but that came as no surprise. These days Matron let her sulk and only made sure Rosie went without dinner.

Alyssa wondered if anyone else shared her restlessness. Probably not. For most of her companions it was the height of luxury, sitting idle for a spell. She couldn't begin to imagine what hardships these girls had endured, to go with such good spirits towards an uncertain future. One had to admire them for that.

Sometimes she feared for them, especially Emma and Nancy, because they were so very trusting. If only she could shake of this horrible feeling that something was wrong, and there were eyes in the dark.

'Alyssa, are you daydreaming? And do sit down, dear,

when I'm talking to you. It's not your fault you're so tall but it is most uncomfortable having to stare up at you.'

She felt the blood rise in her throat. 'I'm sorry, madam. I did not intend to be rude.'

Matron patted her hand. 'It is your turn to read to us, before our lunch.'

She obediently took Mrs Beeton's Book of Household management, which was all the rage in all corners of the Empire, and opened it on the marked page. 'In giving a character, it is scarcely necessary to say that the mistress should be guided by a strict sense of justice. It is not fair for one lady to recommend to another a servant she would not keep herself,' she read aloud, disliking Mrs Beeton and her sanctimonious tome more and more.

Matron said, 'Thanks. That will do. I wish you all to keep these words in mind.'

'Not blimmin' likely that we'll have servants ourselves, is it?' Rosie sneered.

'In your case, very unlikely, Rosie. Which is why you ought to mend your ways before it's too late. You've been unsatisfactory right from the start.' Rosie opened her mouth in protest, but Matron went on regardless. 'I remind you all that I will be required by the Church and by your prospective husbands, who in their generosity have paid for your voyage, to give you a reference. A second character reference will be issued by the doctor. I do not need to remind you how fatal it would be, to arrive in Canada with a stain on your reputation.'

Rosie's face was a mask of frozen fury but she

clamped down on her lip. Matron gave her a look of pure triumph. 'I see that we understand each other. And now, let us hear what Mrs Beeton has to say about restoring the natural beauty of furniture.'

~

'Mean old trout!' Rosie banged the bowls with salt pork and rice on the table, her feet planted wide to stabilise her against sudden movement of the ship.

Harriet said, 'You spill our food and you'll be in the dog-house with me as well.'

'Oooh, I'm so scared. Giving me a bad reference as well?'

Harriet rolled her eyes in despair. 'You're really begging for trouble. Do you want to ruin all your chances of getting yourself a decent husband?'

Rosie slid her tongue slowly over her lips and pulled her blouse tight over her well-endowed chest. 'You want to save your worrying for yourself.' She rested her hands on her hips. 'I reckon I know what a man likes, and believe me, it ain't reading references.'

Harriet muttered something under her breath and rolled her eyes heavenwards. A sly smile spread over Rosie's face.

She looked very pleased with herself these days, Alyssa thought. But surely Harriet, as her sub-Matron, would know if Rosie was up to no good. Still, she couldn't help a sense of trepidation, which worsened, when a fight broke out between Rosie and her only friend Nellie, over a mug of spilt tea. 'Watch it.' Nellie dabbed with her sleeve at her wet skirt.

'Watch it yourself,' said Rosie, pushing her in the chest. Nellie fell with a cry against Emma, who stumbled and fell. 'Clumsy cows, both of you.'

Matron rushed over to help up Emma. 'Are you all right, my dear?'

Emma nodded, lips clamped together.

'Alyssa,' Matron said, 'I want you to sit with Emma until we can be sure she is unhurt. As for you, Rosie,' her voice took on a strident tone, 'you'll go to the scullery and wait there. And later you'll scrub the floors, for the rest of the week. Should there be one more incident, it will go down in your character reference.'

Rosie stalked off, muttering under her breath. Blimmin' Matron, always picking on her. And Emma, thinking how she was so pretty and sweet. Well, they'd all be surprised.

Rosie calmed down. Served them right when she got her man first. She crept out of the back door of the scullery, the way she'd done twice before.

She didn't hear the soft breathing a few steps away, but despite the gloom a golden gleam on the floor caught her eyes. A coin.

Rosie suppressed a triumphant cry as she bent down to pick up the money and slide it into her shift.

A gloved hand clamped down on Rosie's mouth. Her breath caught in her throat. She tried to wriggle free, but a second hand grabbed her throat, jerking her up. A body pushed her with the face against the wall.

Hot tears prickled under Rosie's eyelids. She let herself go limp, the way she'd done when she was fourteen, at the orphanage.

The hand on her throat released its grip to slide down her bodice, caressing her.

Her pulse quieted down. She'd give him what he wanted, and then, she prayed fervently, he'd leave her alone. She pressed herself against his body and moved her hips, to indicate her surrender. Her hands slowly hitched up her skirt.

Please, she thought, let him finish before we get caught. She spread her legs and prepared herself for the inevitable. Tears welled up in her eyes. She stared at the wall, concentrating on the dark groove in the panelling, where a lantern bracket had been.

The pain shot through her body. She concentrated harder on the groove, tracing it with a finger. Something warm trickled down her legs. His breath filled her ears and her whole head, until a male voice rang out from upstairs, loud enough to pierce through the fog in her head.

The hand released Rosie. For a few heart-beats she stood there, frozen, before she caught a grip. She smoothed down her skirt and snuck back into the scullery. She took a towel and wiped off her sticky legs. There. All traces gone.

She'd put this incident out of her mind. No-one

would believe her anyway. Or care. Nobody ever had. All that would happen was that she'd get punished for sneaking off.

~

The pen rested above the page.

*This was almost too easy. My prey, although eager to co-operate, left me wanting for more and better sport. I wonder how many other men before me have enjoyed her assets. She certainly did not give up her virtue for the first time, so this brief encounter has not diminished her market value.*

*The greed with which she picked up that gold coin! She can consider herself well paid then; I doubt that any other customer henceforth will show himself so generous in return for her services.*

*If the opportunity presents itself again, I shall no doubt allow myself another intimate moment, but otherwise a more alluring catch of equal parts innocence and charm should be better suited to relieve my tedium. Patience and restrain shall guide me, if and when I make my choice.*

*How bitterly I miss soft, perfumed skin and the company of experienced women who know how to please a man of refinement. But we all must make sacrifices and I shall not complain.*

# CHAPTER 8

Three weeks without anything on the horizon but the sea. There was something soporific about the sound of the water lashing against the hull and the ever-changing orchestra of the wind. Once he'd gotten used to the narrow confines of the *Artemis' Delight* and the constant bustle on deck, Mark had settled down into a routine that was as comfortable as a pair of old slippers. So far, his medical skills hadn't been taxed further than lancing a boil on the neck of one girl and pulling three rotten excuses for a tooth out of another girl's mouth.

With all this time on his hands he might be able to recall all their names before they made landfall. But then again, with any luck there would be no need to do so.

He had established an easy rapport with Matron, who, as he had suspected, hid a maternal soul under her youthful mask, and Captain Moore's original distrust had gone. He spent most afternoons and evenings playing chess with Turnbull, if the other man wasn't similarly occupied with the captain, or enjoying a game of cards with Dawkes, Harris and Parsons, if they could be found in the saloon. Osborne rarely joined in, but studied instead his well-thumbed copy of Charles Darwin's contested work *On the Origin of Species* or busied himself with a notebook that he otherwise kept locked. Mark found him a surprisingly good conversationalist, with an abundant knowledge of the natural world. In fair weather, they sometimes went outside together and looked out for seabirds and whales. His preferred company though was Mr Kendrick.

He was also catching up nicely with new medical ideas and treatments.

Mark reached out for one of the gallon-sized jars he kept his leeches in and took a closer look. There they were, like orange slugs with black spots, doing nothing but feed and rest. Strange to think how beneficial these little creatures were, to an extent that they were getting rare in some places because of the high demand.

He tapped at the jar, watching two leeches crawl over each other. All in all, it was a perfect interlude, at least if he managed to brush aside all thought of the war.

He strolled to the saloon. Halfway along the passage he took a deep breath. The air smelled decidedly spicy.

He entered, to find everyone else already assembled.
'Well, Dr Bryson?'

Mark sniffed again, before he raised his hands, palms outwards. 'I must confess I'm stumped. All I can say is, whatever cook is dishing up today makes my mouth water.'

'That's what you said yesterday. And the day before.' Turnbull tapped a smudged finger on a scorecard borrowed from a whist game. 'We've been playing our little game for over a week, and thus far you managed once to identify a dish by the smell, and that time we all did.' He shook his head. 'Sometimes I wonder if you take this seriously.'

'What can I say?' Mark said. 'Blame my occupation. Come into my surgery and we'll see if you can tell lamb from a Yorkshire pudding if you've had a nose-full of ammonium.'

Dawkes crinkled his nose in mock distaste. 'Do take Mr Osborne along, then, I implore you. I still trail him by one point.'

'You'd better make your minds up fast what's for luncheon.' Kendrick put his head around the corner. 'The captain asked me to tell you that we're starting the engine, and you'll get some whiff of the coal we're burning any second.'

A shudder went through the *Artemis' Delight*. Metallic clanking filled the room. Parsons listened with one ear cocked towards the floor. He pushed his chair back. 'Save something for me when our food turns up, will you, gentlemen? I'd like to have a look at this engine. She doesn't seem to be running as sweet as she should.'

'He's something to do with railroads, isn't he?' Harris' fingers drummed a beat on the tablecloth. 'Maybe he could arrange a tour for all of us. It would make a bit of a change.'

Turnbull said, 'Why don't we ask him when he returns? That is, if he ever returns. Once an engineer gets a professional bee in his bonnet, you can write him off as company.'

Dawkes said, 'Gentlemen, please. We have more pressing things. I believe I hear steps above the infernal noise of this contraption. I say, curried fish. What do you say?'

'Hell and damnation!' Parsons burst into the room. 'We need the captain!'

Mark said. 'What's the matter? Is anyone hurt? I'll get my bag.'

'I don't think you'll be needed, but the captain won't be happy when I tell him what I found.' He paused, his mood as black as his soot-smeared face.

Captain Moore came running. 'What in Heaven's name is this commotion about?'

'Stowaways,' Parsons said. 'You've got stowaways on board.'

'Stowaways?' The vein on Captain Moore's left temple throbbed visibly.

'Yes, Sir.' Parsons' mouth set in a grim line. 'And

there's worse to come. Better brace yourself – they're female.'

~

Matron twisted a lace-edged handkerchief in her hands.

'What do you have to say for yourself, woman?' Captain Moore stalked in an ever-decreasing circle around the stricken woman who had been summoned to the ship's office.

She burst into a flood of tears. Captain Moore came to an abrupt halt, looking startled. Female tears seemed to throw him off his stride, Mark thought. He sympathised with him; poor man. Moore looked around for help. 'Doctor Bryson?'

Mark put on his most cheerful voice as he coaxed Matron to sit on a chair. 'Now, now, my dear, calm down. We know it wasn't your fault you were discovered. Don't we, Captain?'

She sobbed louder.

Tiny beads of perspiration appeared on the captain's forehead. 'I'll get some cold water, shall I?' He mopped his face with a handkerchief as he bolted for the door.

'Wait a moment, Sir.'

Captain Moore found his escape route blocked by another female.

'What are you doing to poor Matron?' The voice could have cut ice. The captain stood in the doorway, blinking in a daze, until he felt himself brushed aside.

Alyssa knelt next to the chair. 'What have they done to you, my dear madam?' She glared at the two men. Matron threw herself into the girl's arms. 'Oh, Alyssa!'

Captain Moore tried again to escape.

'Sir!' Alyssa made an attempt to detangle herself from Matron's embrace. One look at her determined face, and the captain gave up. Matron's sobs turned to hiccups.

Alyssa shifted the focus of her fury to the doctor. 'I thought you were in charge of our good health? When do you intend to relieve Matron's distress? And you, Captain, don't stand there like a statue, fetch some brandy.' She took the handkerchief out of Matron's hand to dab the tears off her face.

Captain Moore stared at her open-mouthed.

'Eek!' Alyssa jumped up as the stench of smelling salts hit her.

'I'm sorry,' Mark said with relish, 'but you blocked the access to my patient.' He waved a small phial under Matron's nose until the hiccups subsided. 'That's better.'

He put the stopper back on the smelling salts phial and dropped it into his pocket. 'And here's our captain with a medicinal dollop of brandy. I know you don't drink but this is purely therapeutic.'

Matron's hand trembled, but she emptied the glass. 'Is there anything else we can do for you, Mrs McKenzie?' he asked.

Matron lifted her head and gave Alyssa a tearful look. She put her hand on Matron's shoulders. 'What about an excuse for your abominable behaviour? And I'd say you owe Matron an explanation what this is all about.'

'I'd say you owe us all an explanation.' Parsons and Turnbull pushed into the office.

'Here? And now?' The captain's temple still throbbed. Moore seemed to be on the brink of an apoplexy. It wouldn't take much more, and he'd have something a lot more serious on his hands than a simple case of female hysterics, thought Mark. He shot the girl a dark look.

'It is getting a bit cramped,' Mark said, forcing himself to sound relaxed. 'Why don't we all go to the saloon and talk things through like sensible people?'

Matron's hand clutched the girl's arm. 'You'll come with me, won't you? You are so good at explaining, and my head hurts.'

'Well?' A bear of a man with furrowed brows turned the tables on the captain, after he and his companion had swept a dazed Matron and Alyssa with them, presenting them to three other men in the saloon like explorers would two specimens of a hitherto undiscovered tribe. Alyssa would have loved to give them all a piece of her mind.

'I was under strict orders by our owners,' Moore said. 'Mr Kendrick and Doctor Bryson are my witnesses that I did not readily accede to them, but my hands were tied.'

'That's true,' Mark said. 'We were all not feeling exultant about the situation, but there was nothing we could do about it.'

The bear furrowed his brows another quarter inch. 'Does that mean, Sir, you were in cahoots with our captain here all along? You kept these unfortunate two stowed away like cattle ever since we went to sea?'

'Not quite, Mr Turnbull.'

'Good lord, what do you mean, not quite?' A weather-beaten man walked up to the little group. Not a bear this time, Alyssa decided, rather a well-trained watchdog that could spring into action in the blink of an eye. 'Explain yourself!'

The captain rubbed his beard hard enough to make a rasping noise. 'Not two, Mr Harris, but twenty-two, and Matron McKenzie.'

'Twenty-three females!' All the men were standing now, forming a semi-circle with the captain in their midst. That must be what a court-martial looked like.

For the first time Alyssa's conscience stirred. It wasn't fair. Surely the doctor would come to the captain's aid? There he stood, with just enough distance between himself and the captain to escape attention. His eyes met hers, and he raised his eyebrows in silent resignation. She turned her attention back to the captain.

'Well, Captain Moore? Or shall we all write a joint complaint to your managers?' The accusers closed in on their prey.

It was more than Alyssa could bear. She strode into

the centre of the room before her nerve would let her down. 'I'll have you know that Captain Moore has shown us nothing but consideration since we stepped on this ship,' she said, daring her voice to tremble.

Eight pairs of eyes gazed at her in amazement. The blood drained from her face, only to return in full force.

A meek man opened his mouth to address her, but was interrupted by the belligerent man whose unexpected appearance in the bowels of the ship was the source of all the trouble. 'Leave the interrogation to me, Mr Osborne. Now, my girl, who are you and what in tarnation's name are you all playing at?'

For an instant, Alyssa was taken aback.

'Don't badger the poor girl, Parsons.' The doctor's words rang false in her ears. 'Can't you see you are scaring the ladies?'

She clenched her fingers hard enough for the knuckles to hurt.

'Come on, my dear,' Matron whispered into Alyssa's ear. 'The gentlemen don't need us, and I must confess I need some quiet. I am feeling quite sick from this upset.'

She swayed as she rose. Alyssa bit her lip. This was not good. 'Doctor, please!'

To give him his due, he wasted no time to come to her aid. She sighed gratefully as he prevented Matron from collapsing with her full weight into Alyssa's arms.

'We'll take you straight to your cabin, and I'll prescribe you strict rest until dinner.' He steered Matron towards the door. 'Lean on me however much you like,' he said. 'No, don't say a word, you're light as feather. Are you coming, Miss Chalmers?'

They kept silent until Matron was safely inside her cabin. 'I feel awful,' she said. 'Do you think it was the brandy?'

'More likely an overdose of male arrogance,' Alyssa said under her breath.

The doctor gave her a quizzical look. 'What did you say, Miss Chalmers?'

She thought hard and fast. 'I was musing about the vagaries of chance, Doctor.'

'I see.'

She turned her back to him, concentrating on the patient. 'If you wish, I'll stay with you. Or do you want me to extinguish your lantern so you can rest your eyes as well?'

Alyssa felt herself pulled towards the door. 'Let sleep, that sweet restorer, do his work. That's doctor's orders. I'll make sure no-one will plague you any further, Matron.'

He nudged the door close. 'What on earth was going on?'

'I really can't tell you much about it. My mess of girls was already on deck for our twenty-minute turn in daylight, and Harriet's group was coming up, when Louisa Jane shrieked that a man was coming. The next moment the girls below hid in every nook and cranny they could find, until the captain appeared and frog-marched Mrs McKenzie away.'

'And you, of course, decided bravely to come to her rescue. So where are the rest of the young ladies? Still hiding?'

'Of course not. I made sure they are all safely in our quarters before I followed you.' She took a deep breath. 'At least I know where my duty lies, however uncomfortable it may be. Eight men, all picking on one woman! That is as reprehensible as it is improper.'

He was still searching for words when the ship jerked forwards, forcing Alyssa to grope for a hold. The doctor caught her by the shoulders. The corners of his mouth curled up. 'Are you done with your moving speech or is your eloquence sweeping you off your feet?'

She stalked off.

'Where have you been? And how is Matron?' Nellie, of all people, showed an amount of concern that was as gratifying as it was unexpected.

'She'll recover,' Alyssa said. She touched her head. 'The doctor told her to rest until dinner, and the same goes for all of us. Would you please do me a favour and tell the others? I've got a headache.'

Nellie said, 'No wonder, you poor thing. You were rushing away looking like you were about to horsewhip every single one of them.' She shook her head with grudging respect. 'I reckon they don't know what hit them.'

Alyssa stretched out on her bunk and closed her eyes. The sooner this incident could be forgotten the better. She shuddered. She shouldn't have behaved like a shrew, but she had been goaded beyond endurance. Her only solace was that she'd never have to encounter any of the men again, except for the doctor. She wished she wasn't that tall; then she could hide behind the other girls and never have to endure his sardonic smile again.

Captain Moore had calmed down. His was the stance of a man who had sailed within a hair of the centre of the hurricane and finally found himself in placid waters again.

He motioned Mark to sit down with the saloon passengers, while remaining standing himself. 'A few things, gentlemen, so we're all clear about the situation,' he said.

'We're listening.' Parsons said.

'To continue – and please keep your thoughts to yourself until I have finished – the Artemis' Delight does indeed have other passengers on board, in the steerage quarters on the between deck to be precise.' Captain Moore folded his arm behind his back. 'To the best of my knowledge, these girls, being all alone in the world, have been selected by clergy in Melbourne as brides for a number of god-fearing, prosperous miners in the wilds of the Canada. To keep the girls hidden from view was deemed a necessary precaution.'

'Good Lord, what do you mean?' Osborne blinked in confusion.

The captain pursed his lips. 'You may not realise it, Mr Osborne, but there have been certain repulsive incidents when innocent females lacked protection, on board of ships and on land. I hope you understand my meaning.' He cleared his throat. 'Although I detest subterfuge as much as the next man, we endeavoured to do our duty by these helpless girls.'

'You think they'd have to fear unwanted attention from your crew?' Harris said.

Moore walked up and down in front of the seated men. 'Possibly, although I would vouchsafe for most of my men. When you're confined together day after day, there isn't much you can hide after a while, but this journey is different.'

'Because of us? Do you believe we'd take advantage of these lasses?' Turnbull asked.

'And because I had to take on new hands. My men are all sailors, not engineers, gentlemen. None of them is equipped to look after this hulking big engine that you hear belching below your feet. To do that, I had greasers and stokers and a whole passel of other landlubbers forced on me.'

Parsons grinned. 'Railwaymen, the lot of them. They can be a pretty rough bunch.'

'Precisely. We are still doing our best to instil any sense of discipline in these men.' He paused. 'Do you have any more questions?'

Mr Osborne said, 'I do, Sir. Certainly, there is no need to keep those unfortunate ladies locked up below deck any longer?' His eyes pleaded with Mark. 'Don't you think, Doctor, that a certain amount of sunshine and fresh air is vital to their well-being?'

'I don't know about medical reasons,' Turnbull said, 'but I wouldn't wonder if those lasses could do with a bit of change. I presume they are all used to more than idle away their hours, and being cooped up, day in day out in the cavern of a boat wouldn't be to my liking.'

Mark said. 'Most of them weren't raised in mansions, if that's what you mean. But I agree, regardless of their station in life, more activity and especially more air and natural light wouldn't harm them.'

'That's settled then,' Harris said. 'We shall do what we can to make things a bit more agreeable for your little flock.'

'Doctor?'

'I'd say yes.'

'But what about chaperoning them? Matron McKenzie might find twenty-two females a bit more than she could be sensibly asked to supervise.'

'Surely there is safety in numbers?' Dawkes reached for the carafe in front of him. 'You could always nominate Mr Kendrick and Dr Bryson to act as our chaperones.' He grinned at Mark. 'If the little fury you went off with is a sterling example of this gaggle of brides, we could do with some protection. The Lord knows they have nothing to fear from us. Now, how about our little game?'

'Count me out,' Turnbull said. 'Too much coal fumes in the air.'

~

A drop of ink splattered onto the page.

*'What a singular evening. Later, when I've had time to reflect on how this might affect my plans, I might feel less sanguine, but for now my blood races through my veins. The secret is out, and we shall quite soon be able to mingle, hopefully freely enough to further an acquaintance without undue exertion. Although I will admit that a little challenge would add a certain spice to the situation. I think I speak for us all when I say that we are curious as to what kind of beauty, or lack thereof, awaits us.'*

He admired his own wit as he read over his last sentence.

*'To feast or not to feast, that is the question. Shall I help myself to a second taste from the soon available buffet? I wonder if my unpolished little friend misses my attentions.'*

# CHAPTER 9

'Silence, please.' Matron pressed her left hand to her temple as she toyed with her dinner of mutton stew and dumplings. 'You chatter worse than a flock of geese. And don't scrape your forks over your plates like that. My head still hurts.'

Nellie gave her a mutinous look. 'I thought we don't have to be gagged all the time now the cat's out of the bag. It's about time we had us some fun.'

'That's enough.' Matron threw down her napkin like a gauntlet and before Nellie had time to think of a reply the older woman loomed over her, jerking her up from the bench.

'Off with you, into that corner. We shall not suffer someone like you at our table until you have learned at least a modicum of manners.' Matron let go of Nellie. She picked up her napkin to wipe her fingers as if she had touched something dirty. 'And some tidiness, maybe.

As for fun, you'll do laundry duty for the next fortnight. That ought to keep you occupied.'

Nellie howled.

Matron righted her bonnet as she sat down again. 'Please, pass me the salt.'

'That should sort Nellie out once and for all.' Harriet looked at Matron with admiration as they all put down their forks. 'I couldn't do anything with her. Mind you, she'll be meaner than a snake, having to do the laundry. I'd make sure there's nothing valuable around that she could get her fingers on.'

'She wouldn't steal from us, would she?' Emma's hand went to her throat.

'Not stealing and such, not with the cat-o'-nine-tails hanging over us so to speak, but I wouldn't put it past her to do some damage if she thinks she can get away with it. She's not as bad as Rosie, but you never know.'

Harriet looked at Alyssa. 'You've got some nice things. Better watch out then. You aren't exactly our Nell's best friend.'

Alyssa's hand searched automatically for the golden locket she kept hidden underneath her dress.

Harriet laughed. 'There's no need to worry if it's your jewellery you're thinking about. I reckon none of us would be daft enough to take it. Mind you, it's probably best to keep it hidden, with so many strange people around. Doesn't do to be too trusting, my Mum always said.' Her pixie-like face shone with a mixture of worldliness and innocence.

'It probably wouldn't be valuable to anyone except me. It's a picture of my mother that she gave to me on my eighteenth birthday.' Alyssa pulled out the delicate golden chain that held her locket. With one finger she flicked it open, to reveal the portrait of a young woman dressed in a style that was fashionable a quarter of a century ago, and a curl of chestnut hair resembling Alyssa's on the other side.

Harriet stretched out her hand as if to touch the locket, but stopped in mid-air. 'Gosh, it's the loveliest thing I've ever seen,' she said. 'Mind you take good care of it.'

'I never take it off,' Alyssa said.

'No,' said Emma. 'I don't with mine, not ever.' She nestled out a silver filigree locket. Although of lesser quality than Alyssa's mother-of-pearl inlaid pendant, it must have cost a handsome sum. That was proof enough that Emma had been born to better things than the dismal orphanage where she'd ended up after her parents' untimely death. Alyssa wished not for the first time she had the power to help her friend.

Emma caressed the locket. 'My Mum gave it to me before she passed away, and she had it from her Mum.'

'Did you put a shamrock in it?' Louisa Jane asked. 'You won't ever fall on hard times when you've got a shamrock to bring you good luck, my granny used to say.'

'Yes. A four-leaf clover and a lock of Mum's hair.'

'If it's for luck, nothing beats a rabbit's paw.' Milly pulled something thin and furry out from underneath her skirt. 'I keep it in a pocket in my petticoat. Looks like we're all sorted for luck on this trip.'

The girls laughed. Matron joined in as well, although she sat too far away to take part in the conversation without raising her voice unladylike. Only Nellie sulked in her corner, and Rosie appeared subdued.

'We're pretty lucky already, aren't we?' the dainty red-headed Susanna said. 'Here we are, a boat load of orphans, on our way to a new place, where nice men with more than a few pennies jingling in their pockets await.'

'We might even catch the eye of a real gentleman.' Emma sighed, lost in a dream. 'Imagine we'd be real ladies.'

Alyssa took her hand and gave it a gentle squeeze.

'Now, now, girls,' said Matron. 'Don't get ideas above your station. That will only end in tears.' Her smile took the sting out of the rebuke.

'Yeah,' Milly said. 'Anyone'd think it's enough for the likes of us to find ourselves a nice feller who doesn't drink up his wages at the next pub and beats the living daylight out of us.' She stiffened as the last word was out, clamping her mouth shut with her hand.

Susanna moved closer to Milly, murmuring

something into her ear. She pointed at the rabbit's paw. Milly's face was still pinched, but she rubbed the paw nonetheless.

Matron clapped to get everybody's attention. 'It's time to clear the table and do the dishes, and then we shall retire quietly after this exhausting day. I only hope that we will not suffer this much excitement again.'

Louisa Jane said, 'I would die if I ran into a man again like that. I simply would.'

Matron soothed her, 'Now, don't get upset. We will not be disturbed again.'

'Excuse me, ladies?'

An eardrum-bursting shriek greeted Mark and the captain.

'Silence!' Moore struck his hand on the table.

Matron's hand flew to her mouth. The stillness caused by Moore's bellowing was so complete that Mark could hear her hasty breathing. Her startled gaze darted between her charges and the two men.

The captain slowly unfurled his brow. He folded his hands behind his back. 'That's better,' he said. 'I have something to tell you, and I do not intend to have to repeat myself. Do I make myself clear?'

With their heads lowered, the girls nodded. Only Alyssa Chalmers was brave – or curious – enough to risk meeting the captain's gaze, Mark noticed.

'As secrecy is no longer possible, you shall be allowed an increased amount of freedom. However -' Moore raised his right hand to stem any female volubility. 'However, propriety and discipline will be maintained at all cost. Under no circumstances will there be unsupervised contact with male members of the crew or passengers, nor will they have access to your quarters. Understood? I'll have anyone who disobeys this order clapped in iron.'

His stern face relaxed a little as he looked down at the startled girls. 'But I'm sure you'll be all good. The doctor and I will work out a schedule that will allow you to spend more time on deck and enjoy a few diversions.'

Hammering almost drowned out his last words. 'Do you hear that? You are lucky we managed to run away from a storm, into calmer water. Our carpenter and a few others have already started on a nice little shelter over the poop which shall give you some comfort in the weeks ahead. I wish you a good day.' He touched his hat with two fingers in a brief salute.

'That was a pretty speech,' Mark said as he followed Moore.

'I've done my part, Doctor. It's up to you to come up with something to keep them entertained.' He wiped his forehead. 'At least we no longer have to lock them up.'

Mark smiled. 'It seems your apprehension was unfounded, then.'

'Unfounded? We have twenty-three unprotected females on board, including Mrs McKenzie.' He narrowed his eyes. 'You'd better keep your wits about you, because you and Mr Kendrick will share the responsibility for the young ladies.'

Mark stopped in his tracks. 'What about your men? And the passengers?'

'There's no need to fret on their account, Doctor. I'll read them the riot act and make sure they're all fully aware that I will not tolerate any subordination on my ship. Nobody will dare put one finger on the brides. I'll have them flogged if they dare!'

'What do you expect from me?' The usually imperturbable Mr Kendrick nearly dropped the sextant as he stared in disbelief at his captain.

'You heard me,' Moore said.

'But I'm a very busy man. I'd have to neglect my real duties if you appoint me to chaperone the ladies. As you can see I'm still busy with our charts.' His fingertips drummed a short tattoo on his chest. 'What about our second officer? Mr Wainwright would be the most obvious choice, if you ask me. His task load is slighter than mine, and his experience as a married man would be invaluable. What's more, Mrs McKenzie and the girls are used to his accompanying them. I presume by now he is something of an uncle figure.'

Mark wished he had a similar case to make for

himself. It was one thing to be assigned as a doctor to a boatload of girls; quite another to act as their guardian.

'Doctor?' Mark gave a start, as Kendrick's foot made painful contact with his ankle.

'Well,' he said, 'it does certainly seem prudent to enlist Mr Wainwright to substitute for us. As he said, Mr Kendrick is a busy man, and as a doctor one never really is master of one's time.' He gave a rueful chuckle, hoping it sounded convincing. 'One moment you're twiddling your thumbs, and the next you're dashing from one sickbed to the next.'

'Davies!' The boy, who had kept a respectful distance, sprang to attention.

'Aye, Sir?'

'My regards to Mr Wainwright, and I'd like to see him straight away.'

Kendrick gave Mark an imperceptible wink.

Their newfound freedom made for happiness all around, as far as Alyssa was concerned. It didn't matter anymore that life still consisted mainly of household education as decreed by that wretched Mrs Beeton; they could venture outside. Doing nothing more active than sitting with their needlework under the awning that was put up over the poop to shelter them from the elements became a joy, and they sang and chatted with newfound pleasure. If only she could shake that sensation of frequently being observed that unsettled her more than she cared to admit.

They all were almost giddy these days, she thought, as she strolled over to the rail to look down at the sea. As much as she appreciated becoming more and more part of the group, she relished her snatched moments of solitude. This here was her place and hers alone. No-one else cared to be drenched by the relentless spray, or risk water stains on their dresses and a sunburned complexion.

Alyssa turned around, resting one hand on the smooth wood. Matron sat under the awning, winding wool with the aid of Mr Wainwright. She reminded her of a mother hen, guarding the chicks scattered around her.

She smiled at the image. Who should she cast as the fox? Not Mr Wainwright. Nobody could help but approve of him. His broad-shouldered presence and quiet manners gave them all a sense of security. Only the naivest girl could prefer a man like the sarcastic doctor to this quiet fortyish man with his kind blue eyes and slow smile or to the lively Mr Kendrick with his dancing eyes and ready smile.

Matron seemed to share this sentiment. Every so often Alyssa saw her exchange glances with Mr Wainwright, only to look away when she found someone else watching. So, who could be the fox?

'What are you doing?'

Alyssa found herself yanked to the middle of the

deck. Two pairs of eyes looked at her, one reproachful, the other concerned. 'Haven't you got the sense God gave a goose?' the doctor asked. 'One big wave, and over you go.'

She rubbed her wrist.

'The doctor is right, Miss Chalmers, even if he acted a bit rough,' Mr Kendrick said. 'A ship's deck can be a treacherous place. You should always stay away from the rail and stick with your friends.'

Alyssa wrapped her arms around her shoulders. The first officer was a nice man, and he was a seafarer, used to being on his own with nothing but an empty sky and the vast expanse of the ocean around him. He might understand.

'Have you ever been trapped in a crowd, without room to breathe, Mr Kendrick?'

'My mother took me to London once when I was but eight, to cheer for our newly crowned Queen Victoria.'

'Did you enjoy it?'

He paused, as if to weigh her question in his mind. 'The tiny part of me that wasn't scared stiff of all the people nearly crushing me and the incessant noise, yes. I'm Welsh, and nobody else in our village had ever yet been to London, so I had some tale to tell on my return.'

'You do understand then, don't you, that you can suffocate in a crowd if you can't step away once in a while? That you need to be on your own with nothing else but the sky and the wind and your thoughts?'

His face softened. 'In that case I'll stay with you for a while if I may.'

'Thank you. I appreciate that.'

They stood in companionable silence. Alyssa shaded her eyes with her hand, watching the foam-capped waves roll against the ship, when something disturbed their rhythm.

She drew in her breath. It looked as if an island was erupting, shooting a stream of water thirty feet high into the air, until it burst into a myriad of glittering drops.

Alyssa pressed her knuckles into her mouth. Nellie shrieked, 'It's a monster.'

'What kind of animal is it, Mr Kendrick?' Alyssa asked.

'It's a humpback whale,' he said. 'Magnificent sight, isn't it?'

'Yes,' she said. 'Oh yes. It's wonderful.' She watched the animal grow bigger and bigger as it arched its silvery body out of the water, only to dive back in. The sound of the impact dwarfed every other sound around them. Her heart beat a tattoo with happiness.

Another shriek made Alyssa turn her head. The other girls huddled ashen-faced under the awning. She paid them no heed, turning back towards the whale.

'You're not afraid at all, are you?' Mr Kendrick asked with something like respect. 'There's a lot of superstition surrounding all kinds of ocean creatures.'

'No.' She pressed herself as close against the rail as she could. 'I only wish I could stay here forever.'

A mournful sound interrupted her.

'Listen,' Kendrick said. 'The whale is calling out to its herd, or ... Good Lord!'

'She's calling her calf,' said Mark as he joined them. 'See its head poking out of the water! By the way, I've sent your companions below deck. They did not seem to appreciate this spectacle as much as you do.'

Alyssa looked back. She hadn't heard any movement at all, but the deck lay deserted. She drew herself away from the rail. 'There's nothing for me then but to follow their example,' she said, staring one last time at the whales. A small sigh escaped her.

'I'm afraid so,' Kendrick said. 'There will be other opportunities to enjoy yourself.'

She smiled at him. 'Again, I must thank you, Mr Kendrick.'

'Not at all. But please remember, you need to take care when you stand here, and watch out for rough weather.'

'I hope you don't think I have neglected my duty, Sir,' said Mr Wainwright, his hands still entangled in strands of yellow wool, as Alyssa and the two men joined him and the others in the girls' mess.

Kendrick dismissed the notion. 'We're here not to check on you, but solely on a diplomatic mission. Well, I am, the doctor just tagged along for want of anything better to do, and then we got distracted. Davies! Bring the surprise.'

The boy appeared seemingly out of nowhere, to put down blue, red and yellow rings made of rope.

'Now we can play deck quoits!' Kendrick beamed at Matron like a benevolent Father Christmas. 'Courtesy of our saloon passengers and the captain, who has given permission that the gentlemen may instruct you in the rules. You'll learn the game in no time at all.'

'Oh, Mr Kendrick, we don't know how to thank you,' Matron said.

'Don't thank me, dear madam, it is entirely the captain's doing. Weather permitting, we'll start right after the gentlemen have had their tea.'

'Did you see Wainwright's face?' Mark asked as the two men climbed down the companionway. 'You shouldn't tell such blatant lies in front of an honest chap like him.'

Kendrick shook his head. 'A most amiable fellow, our Mr Wainwright. His only fault is a certain lack of imagination. As important as discipline is, sometimes you have to bend the rules a bit.'

He wasn't the only one who'd had to adjust to the changed situation. It had been especially hard on the captain, Mark thought. Since the girls had been discovered, he found himself constantly interrogated about their wellbeing by the saloon passengers. Turnbull and, surprisingly, Osborne insisted on knowing their whereabouts and making sure the girls were as comfortable as could be.

In the end, Moore gave in. It was the only sensible option open to him, Mark mused. A ship did not lend itself to clandestine business. His only fear was that contact with the gentlemen might raise unfounded hopes among the between deck passengers.

'No. The captain knows what he is doing,' Kendrick said when Mark mentioned his doubts. 'There's no thought about damsels in distress or images of white knights once they meet in the flesh.' He grinned. 'Although I did get the impression that we just detected the tender buds of a sprouting affection. I should have known that something was up when Mr Wainwright declined my offer to relieve him occasionally on his escort duties.'

Mark dug his hands into his pockets. 'What if the captain has something to say to it?'

'Why should he, if no one neglects their duty. Anyway, who should tell him? You?' A warning edge crept into Kendrick's voice.

'Of course not. I was only wondering after all his admonishing, that's all.'

'Wondering, eh? Let me tell you a story, then.'

He led Mark into the surgery, shut the door behind them and perched himself on the edge of the desk.

'It's not a happy story, and I don't particularly want anyone to overhear,' he said. 'In the summer of 1860, we returned home to London after twenty months. Nobody knew when to expect us, because we had suffered a couple of delays, and we didn't have steam power yet. Nobody had come to meet us. The captain, Mr Wainwright and I, all live some distance from London, so we decided to put up for the night at an inn. We sent a messenger to the agent and looked ahead to a few weeks in the company of loved ones.'

He fixed his gaze upon the wall. 'The agent arrived the next morning, at breakfast. We were still wiping bacon fat off our chins when he handed Mr Wainwright a creased letter.' Kendrick shifted his gaze to Mark's face. 'It was about his wife. There had been some epidemic. By the time we came home to England, she was already dead and buried, and instead of returning to a cheerful fire in the hearth and the arms of a loving wife, Walter Wainwright was left with nothing but his memories and an undertaker's bill. If anything puts a smile back on his face, Captain Moore'd be the last to interfere.'

He stopped abruptly, listening to the ship's bell.

'Enough chitchat, Doctor. It's time to brush up and drink our tea.'

He paused over his open diary, took a coin and flipped it in the air. It spun around and landed on his palm. Heads up. He smiled.

·  ·  ·

*As for the business side, after many hours of deliberation I have decided that the new development in reality simplifies the situation. The documents are still gone, and the associates my agent has chosen will just ask for another medical inspection in SF. No need for clever subterfuge, to lure them out of hiding.*

*As for my own pleasure, as has been my habit in such cases, I let the coin decide. It said, yes. How considerate of the captain to arrange games during which I hopefully shall make my selection.*

The preparations for the deck quoits took so little time that the girls were still struggling to get in line next to each other when everything was ready. Three concentric rings had been drawn onto the deck planks, marked with a three in the central ring, a two in the middle and a one in the outer ring.

Kendrick picked up the rope rings and dangled them from his outstretched hands. 'The doctor and I shall give you a quick demonstration,' he said, 'and afterwards our gentlemen passengers shall each pick two of you ladies to complete their respective teams. You throw the ring like this,' he bent his hand and flung the quoit. It landed on the two. 'The players take alternate turns,' he said, 'one from each team, and the first team that reaches fifty points or higher wins.'

He went to pick up the quoit and handed the whole set to Mr Turnbull. 'Would those ladies, who wish to give it a try, step forward so the team captains can make their selection?'

A few of the girls blushed. Even Nellie and Rosie exchanged insecure glances until Matron said, 'There's no need to be shy, girls. I'm sure the gentlemen won't do anything to inconvenience you.' In a lower voice she added, 'I'll be watching the whole time.'

That resolved, a dozen girls stepped up, and the selection took place with remarkable speed. Not once did the gentlemen glance at the girls' faces, Alyssa noticed, but instead they seemed intent to pick the strongest. Plain-faced Milly beamed with pride to be selected first, while the acclaimed beauties Emma and Susanna stood ignored.

The girls, whether playing or, like Alyssa, observing, responded in likewise fashion to the gentlemen. They kept their eyes firmly on the rings, whooping with joy as they threw the quoits onto the marked fields or cheered on a friend whose throw had knocked an opponent's quoit in a worse spot with a heart-felt, 'Oh, well done!' The gentlemen themselves, who acted as team captains, were more interested in winning than in the charms of their female team members and kept a firm watch on their male opponents.

It worked so well that the captain found nothing to criticise, when he joined the party for a game after lunch. His relief went so far as to whistle as he flung his quoits with a precision that cheered him and put his team firmly in the lead.

Alyssa felt herself relax to the extent that she regretted not playing, but standing on the side line gave her at least a good glimpse of the male personalities. Altogether, she approved most of the affable Mr Turnbull and inoffensive Mr Osborne, who took everything in their stride, whereas Mr Harris and Mr Dawkes showed a fierce competitive streak, and Mr Parsons seemed only interested in the correct technique of the throws. She only wished that Mr Kendrick and the doctor would play; it would be interesting to see what they revealed about themselves.

The captain flung his third quoit, landing it on a 3 while at the same time displacing his opponent's ring.

'Is that sporting, Captain?' Mr Dawkes said. 'Is that nice? Shouldn't you, as the undisputed master of ship and game, be given some kind of handicap, to make it a bit fairer?' His side-burns and moustache gleamed almost golden in the sunlight as he took off his straw top hat. A dark stain on his index finger reminded Alyssa that she needed to ask for more ink, for her lessons.

'It's not practice you want, Mr Dawkes, but the ability to look ahead. But I shall be more than willing to give you a revanche game. But not today.' Moore shaded his eyes against the glare of the sun as he peered at the cloudless sky. 'Maybe not even tomorrow. Something's brewing. We've already had an unusually long spell of calm sea.'

'Are you sure?' Osborne asked.

'Yes, I am. As sure as any man can be.' He sniffed the

salt-laden air. 'Take a good whiff, gentlemen, and you can smell the difference.'

'But what about the ladies?'

The girls looked up without exception. Alyssa saw a puzzled expression on most faces.

The captain appeared to share their sentiment. 'I don't follow, Mr Osborne.'

'They can't be comfortable in the between deck in rough weather?' His face flushed as Parsons and Dawkes shared meaningful glances. 'The ladies should be invited to the saloon during the day should we encounter rough weather.'

A storm? Alyssa drew in her breath. A few girls gasped. Matron put a finger against her lips as if to remind the girls that they should not disturb the gentlemen talking.

'I agree,' Turnbull said after a glance at their white faces. 'Especially if that means Dr Bryson will be at close hand should we suffer the dreaded mal de mer.' He picked up the quoits. 'Let's not cry wolf. How many points to put the captain in his place?'

'What a lovely day.' Matron looked around approvingly as they ate their dinner. 'You were all behaving as nicely as one could wish, and I'm very proud of you.' She took a slice of bread and dipped it into her bean stew.

'Do you think we'll really be invited into the saloon, Matron?'

'It's possible, Nancy. But there's nothing to be afraid of. If you all remember to talk only when you're spoken to and keep your eyes cast down and your hands in your lap, you'll do fine.' She helped herself to another slice of bread. 'And should we be offered food, simply follow my example.'

'I couldn't swallow a bite if a man was watching me,' Louisa Jane said. 'Which gentleman do you think is the most handsome? Mr Kendrick or Mr Dawkes?'

'They're both ever so nice looking,' said Nancy. 'And what about the doctor? He's a proper gentleman as well. I only hope our men will be half as nice.'

'Yes, but he's got a young lady waiting for him already.' Louisa Jane sighed. 'Cook said, we'd better not get any ideas, because the boy told him yesterday that he'd knocked over the lady's picture when he was dusting, and broke the glass, but the doctor didn't get cross with him at all. He only told him to pick up the glass. That was nice, wasn't it?'

'Yeah,' Harriet said with a small toss of her head, 'but what cheek of Cook to think we'd get ideas about men. Why, we've got suitors waiting for us. Right, Emma? Alyssa?'

Emma's colour changed slightly. 'Sure,' she said after a brief pause. Alyssa frowned. Was Emma having second thoughts about her future? Maybe she should tell her the truth about her own plans. She had enough money to take Emma with her back home to England, and she would enjoy her company if the thought of marriage was abhorrent to Emma.

~

He sat idle, pen hovering over the diary. What nice surprises this voyage kept throwing up. A most delightful diversion, these girls.

*This business venture promises to be most successful, judging by what I saw today. Apart from my first acquaintance, who appears amply equipped for her new life, there were no less than three girls worthy of my attention, but I think I have made my choice. A fair-haired enchantress, with a voice like velvet and delightful curves lurking underneath her pitiful rags. After all, life can't be all work and no play.*

'Lobster.' Turnbull punctuated the air with his fork before he speared his lamb chop with it. 'You want to make money in these uncertain days, you're better off to invest in a fishing fleet than in the fur trade, Mr Dawkes. You wouldn't believe the money lobster fetches these days, and there is a limit to the number of furs a woman can wear, whereas we have to eat every day.' He chewed his meat with every sign of appreciation.

'Speaking of which,' Dawkes said, 'if Captain Moore's

predictions are correct and we run into foul weather, where do you suggest accommodating the girls, Mr Osborne? I suppose we could have the screen taken away to enlarge the room, but it still would be a squeeze.' He winked at Kendrick. 'You see, I do take the good captain's advice to heart and try to look ahead. Where is he, by the way?'

'Right here,' Moore said, as he entered the room while Dawkes was still speaking. 'Excuse my tardiness, gentlemen, but I had to sort out a few things between our bosun and our new engineering crew. They've never had to deal with anything but a gentle puff here and there until now.' Moore sniffed appreciatively. 'Lamb chops, is it? How is your competition progressing, if I may ask?'

'We had to put it on hold for a few days,' Turnbull said. 'That engine of yours may smell of roses to Mr Parsons, but is has fouled up the air for the rest of us to an extent that it would be unfair to carry on, especially now that it has become a two-horse race between Mr Osborne and Mr Dawkes.'

'Never mind,' said Moore. 'You have ample time before we make port.' A sudden jolt of the ship made the bowls clang together. The wind drummed against the sails with increasing speed.

Mark's hands shot out to hold on to his glass and his plate. His companions did likewise, their reflexes honed on patches of rough sea.

'You've got ink on your cuff, Mr Harris,' he said,

catching a glimpse of a stain peeping out from underneath the jacket sleeve. 'Better have the boy take care of it immediately.'

'How clumsy of me. Must be my old quill. I'll have to ask for a new one.'

The captain braced his feet against the floor and raised his glass. 'There she comes, gentlemen. Here's to hoping the hurricane has lost most of its bite on its way to meet us.'

'We'll never see land again.' A hand clasped Mark's wrist with surprising strength. The *Artemis' Delight* shuddered under his feet. Every plank creaked and groaned as if under an impossible strain. Mark had to struggle to keep his balance.

'Can you hold up your head?' he enquired. 'A few drops of brandy might help restore you.'

'Hold up my head?' Parsons' forehead glistened with sweat as he pushed himself up on his pillow, only to sink down again after the exertion of swallowing the brandy. His eyes bulged as another wave pummelled the ship. Mark hurried to hand him a bowl. 'I'll be back as soon as I can,' he said, 'but it might take a while, I am afraid. You're not the only one succumbing to seasickness.'

He knocked on Turnbull's door. 'Come in,' a faint voice answered.

'Please forgive the smell.' Turnbull's hand shook as

he leaned over the washstand. His knees buckled as the ship swayed again. He retched.

Mark nearly went down himself as he jumped to prop up the heavy man. The wind howled with an intensity that drowned out almost every other sound.

'Didn't intend to be such a nuisance.' A greyish tint spread over Turnbull's face. 'Should soon be over. Not much left inside of me.'

Mark lowered him onto his bed. 'Try to swallow this brandy,' he yelled, 'and see if you can keep it down. I'll send someone to look after you.'

Mark found Osborne in a slightly better state, although he seemed deeply agitated. His concern, though, was not for himself.

'How do the ladies fare?' His teeth chattered as he sipped his brandy.

'I haven't had time to see to them yet.' Mark dampened a towel in Osborne's washing bowl. 'Place this on your forehead. I'll soon be back.'

'There's no need to rush on my account.' Osborne's body shook so badly he had to hold on to the bedpost. 'I'll be fine. Go and take care of the other patients, Doctor.'

Mark spotted Osborne's cherished notebook lying in a corner. For once it was unlocked.

'Where do you want it?'

A spot of colour appeared on Osborne's waxy skin.

'Put it in the drawer, please.'

Harris seemed immune to the turmoil, so Mark

accepted his offer to take care of Turnbull without hesitation.

Dawkes was another matter. His eyes were bloodshot. His whole body went rigid as Mark dragged him into a slightly upright position. 'Have mercy, man,' he whispered. 'Can't you see I'm dying?' His head sank back.

Mark took his wrist, which dangled from the bed. The pulse was surprisingly strong and regular, a fact Mark could not explain until he noticed the empty wine bottle rolling around on the floor. He let go of Dawkes's wrist and got up. 'Here's a bucket in case you need it, but it's highly unlikely,' Mark said. 'I'll drop in again later.'

Dawkes groaned.

The ship lurched. Mark steadied himself on the bedside table, displacing a small leather-bound book in the process. Dawkes let out a small cry.

He struggled to get out of bed and grab the book. He swayed slightly. 'If you could send the boy with water I think I shall manage.'

'How bad is it?' Kendrick waited for Mark in the passage. As the ship gave another violent lurch his arm shot out to steady himself with one hand against the wall.

'It depends,' Mark said. 'They'll do for now, but the question is, how much longer are we to suffer through this storm?'

Another wave sent the ship sideways. Every plank groaned under the onslaught. Kendrick had to raise his voice to make himself heard.

'The worst should be over by morning,' he said. 'We've turned to the wind already and lowered the sails. All we need to do is ride it out.'

The ship's bow climbed upwards. Bile rose in Mark's throat. He blindly grabbed Kendrick's arm with the left hand, while he pulled the brandy bottle out of his coat pocket.

'Dutch courage?' Kendrick raised his eyebrows in sympathy.

'Medicine, Mr Kendrick.' The brandy burnt in Mark's belly, but it did the trick. The nausea was gone – for the moment. He put the bottle away. 'Give the captain my regards, and I'll now see to the girls, unless he urgently needs me somewhere else.'

'That's why I'm here,' Kendrick said. 'I'm under orders to act as your second.'

The screams were audible despite the fury of the hurricane. The stench of vomit hit Mark and Kendrick as soon as they yanked the door to the between deck open. Most of the girls lay huddled on the floor, praying or sobbing. The partition wall and one of the benches had come loose and were pushing relentlessly forward.

'Help,' yelped one of the girls, grasping Mark's ankle. 'Thank the lord you're here.' Alyssa struggled to hold a retching Nancy in her arms.

Kendrick hurried to relieve her. 'What do you want me to do, Doctor?'

Mark knelt next to the girl that still held on to him. 'Water,' he said. 'Lots of clean, cold water. And put as many mattresses and blankets in my surgery as you can fit.'

Kendrick lowered Nancy to the ground and turned back on his heels. 'That's too small. I'll give orders to get the saloon ready, and I'll get some help to secure the furniture before it maims someone.'

'Whatever you think best,' Mark said. 'But for heaven's sake get me water! And another bottle of brandy.' He gently patted the girl's hand. 'Open your mouth, that's a good girl. We'll soon have you clean and comfortable again.'

'Doctor!' A sudden lurch of the ship threw him sideways. Gritting his teeth, Mark crawled to the next patient.

'Watch out,' a girl called, rushing to get hold of the bench that was shooting towards him. 'Emma, no!' Another girl pushed the first one aside and threw herself between Mark and the bench. She cried out with pain as it hit her. Mark crawled towards her, but she shook her head. 'I'm fine, Doctor. Take care of the others.'

'Are you sure?' Now he recognised Alyssa.

She nodded. 'Just let me catch my breath for a moment, and then I'll assist you.'

~

Seventeen patients later, and he was still far from finished. With every new attack, the storm found another victim. To Mark, the battle became increasingly personal. Time after time he came crashing onto his knees as he administered to the stricken. He would have been lost without Kendrick and his female helpers. He didn't remember who they were or if it was only one and always the same. The noise deafened him, and salty sweat drops blurred his vision. There was nothing left in the world but the howling storm and the sickness, and he was losing his own battle. Any second now, and he'd give in to the punches that knocked the air out of his lungs and tore at his guts. Rest, he thought with the little bit of his brain that could still think, all he needed was one minute of peace and he would be ready to fight on.

'Doctor!' A witch shrieked into his ear, her fingers clawing at him, her eyes dark holes smouldering in their sockets.

The hands touched his face now, tearing at it, forcing his protesting mouth to open. Something filled his throat, burning and suffocating him at the same time.

He gulped. Salty wetness met his parched lips, sloshing into his open mouth. More wetness streamed down his face. Sounds fought their way through the fog that enshrouded him. Words began to emerge as the blood pounding in his ears changed from a roar to a whisper.

'Are you feeling better, Doctor?' Eyes of amber, marked with lines of exhaustion, looked down at him.

'For a moment you had us worried, my friend. I've never seen anyone turn pea-green around the gills that fast. You shouldn't do that, you know.' Kendrick put his arm under Mark's shoulders and heaved to get him back to his feet.

Mark attempted a weak smile. 'Blame your beastly storm for that.' He shook his head to drive away the remains of the fog. 'A breather of fresh air and I'll be as good as new. Is it safe to stick my head out of the companionway?'

'As long as you don't get in into your head to take a stroll on the deck, you should be fine. I'll come with you, just in case.'

'But my patients?'

'Can survive without you for five minutes. Miss Chalmers and Matron will see to that.'

# CHAPTER 10

The sea was calming down, but still the waves came up to a couple of inches below the rail. Cascades of spray washed over the *Artemis' Delight*. Ripped sails whipped against the masts. Mark inhaled as deeply as he could to fight down the lingering nausea. Although the ship rolled heavily from side to side, he found he could maintain his balance once he recognised the rhythm.

'Have another sip.' Kendrick offered him a silver flask. The smell was strong enough to mask the stench of sick that clung to Mark's clothes.

The taste lingered in his mouth. Mark handed the flask back. 'Thank you.'

'Keep it, if you want to. Plenty more where that came from.'

Mark's whole jaw hurt with fatigue as he attempted to smile. 'No thanks, or I'll end up in a state worse than this. You already poured enough down my throat to half-drown me.'

'That wasn't me. I had my hands full to hold you to the ground, so you wouldn't thrash around like a whirligig, while the young lady made you take your medicine.' Kendrick gave him an amused look. 'You make a lousy patient. You nearly slapped Miss Chalmers, and that after the poor girl threw herself in harm's way to save your skin, from what I saw when I returned. When there's time, you'd better find out how badly she's bruised.'

He signalled Mark to climb down again, while he pulled on a thick leather strap to close the hatch behind him. 'What now, Doctor? Back to the ladies, or shall we take a look at our crew?'

'You're positive Matron can handle things? Then let's see what damage this weather has done to your men.'

It could have been a lot worse, Mark reflected as, two hours later, he finally caught a break. Two decks-hands were laid up, plus the complete engineering crew, and the cook. They were admitted to one side of the saloon, together with the male passengers. On the other side of the hastily nailed together plywood wall the least sick of the girls rested on a pile of blankets. Mark counted himself lucky that Matron, though not spared completely, declared herself able to take charge of this makeshift ward.

The girls who were too weak to manage the stairs up to the saloon deck stayed behind in the surgery. Miss Chalmers, who admitted to a few bruises and sore ribs, but roundly denied any when he asked her, took care of them. Everything was under control.

Mark staggered back to his quarters to allow himself the luxury of a real bath. Usually he declined Davies' offer of lugging around copious amounts of hot water but today he needed that comfort. With every bucket load that was tipped into the tin bath his sense of contentment rose. He unwrapped the soft soap he had purchased in wise anticipation in Melbourne, hoping it would mask the smell of sick permeating the ship. It was with a sense of regret that he emerged half an hour later from the rapidly cooling water, to return to duty.

If Captain Moore noticed the cloying scent that clung to Mark's skin and hair, he hid it well. Marching in circles around the room, he seemed to pay more attention to the creaking of the planks than to Mark's report.

'Everyone ought to recover nicely,' he concluded.

'Granted; seasickness has never yet claimed a life. The only question is when will the men be back on duty?'

Mark said, 'That is beyond me to tell. It all depends on how much longer we are pummelled like a schoolboy who has stepped into the ring with a heavyweight, and on individual condition. All I can tell you is that every additional hour of agony prolongs the recuperation process.'

Captain Moore cupped his ear and listened intently to the moaning wind and the persistent drum of thunder. 'Twenty-four hours,' he said with an air of finality. 'By then the wind will have died down almost completely. Come breakfast, and you can hardly call it a good breeze anymore. Can you now give me a prognosis, Doctor?'

'If you don't expect me to put my neck on the line for its accuracy, yes. A day of complete rest, two at most, and they'll soon be able to dance a jig for you.'

'That long?' A crease appeared in Moore's face. 'Why did Sam Plover have to succumb, of all the people? You'd expect landlubbers to prove inferior to the elements, but he's been sailing since the day he was out of short trousers!'

Mark's puzzlement must have shown, because Moore gave him a dark look. 'The cook, doctor, our cook! My crew is accustomed to hardship, of course, but what shall I do about the passengers? I can hardly ask them to tuck into canned beans, rice and salt pork, which is among the best we have to offer while Cook is laid up.'

Another burst of thunder made Mark doubt the captain's prognosis that the storm was almost spent. He raised his voice to make himself heard. 'They don't seem to be a complaining lot to me, if that is of some comfort to you. Otherwise I can always prescribe them a diet of arrowroot and dry toast until they have fully recovered.'

'It won't have to come to that.' Kendrick entered the captain's cabin. He too was freshly scrubbed, his hair damp under his hat. 'Two of the ladies have volunteered for kitchen duty, Sir. All that's needed is your permission, and we'll be back to normal in a twinkle.'

'Let me guess,' Mark said. 'Our intrepid Miss Chalmers is not only the Antipodean version of Florence Nightingale, but also reigns supreme in all things epicurean.'

'You do seem to harbour a grudge against our heroine. Pure jealousy, I suppose, because she proved sea-worthier than you.' Kendrick dug his hands into his pockets, his feet planted wide to keep his balance. 'But rest easy. The ladies in question have been named to me as one Emma and one Nancy, if that is of any interest to you.'

'Not at all,' Mark said. 'As long as they don't poison anyone. I'd better make another round through the ward before I retire.'

A sudden lurch of the *Artemis' Delight* made him wince. His hand went to his stomach. 'You're certain these are the dying spasms of the storm, Captain Moore?'

He found the saloon silent. Only Wainwright, who had

volunteered to act as an orderly for the men, was awake. 'Everything is fine, Sir,' he said. 'Things quieted down pretty fast after you were gone.'

'Good. I'll see you in the morning.'

The surgery was also quiet, apart from some heavy snoring. The paraffin lamp shone low, casting the female form squatting against the wall in a half shadow.

Mark felt a twinge of guilt as he moved closer. Infuriating as she could be, Miss Chalmers' help had been invaluable. She must be shattered. Tomorrow he would insist on inspecting her injuries; tonight, she looked too exhausted to bother her more than he had to. He stretched his hand out to touch her shoulder.

The girl came with a start to wakefulness, dropping a book in the process. She bent down to retrieve it, but the doctor had already picked it up.

His expression was studiously blank as he handed her *A Tale of Two Cities*, after giving it a wipe with his handkerchief.

She said, 'I realise we're not supposed to enter the hold with our baggage unsupervised, but I presume I'm not the first to do so. There was no one to turn to in any account.'

'So of course, you took matters into your own hand.'

Tears welled up in her eyes. She hung her head, for once not fighting back.

He heard her uneven breath as he shifted his balance in accordance with the ship. He steadied her with one hand. 'Get some rest,' he said. 'You have already done everything in your power to see us through the worst. I don't want to have you on my hands as well.'

'But there is no-one to relieve me.'

'What a high opinion you have of me. I'm perfectly capable of looking after my patients. After all I am the doctor.'

She pushed herself up, swaying with tiredness. 'You'll wake me, should my help be required?'

'Yes, of course, but now off with you. Although I'd appreciate it if you would lend me your book. We're in for a long night, and Charles Dickens will help me stay alert.'

Without a word, she put the book on the table.

'Thank you,' he said. 'For everything.'

With a sigh of relief Alyssa rested her head on a scratchy hessian. For once she was too battered and weary to mind sleeping in her own filth.

# CHAPTER 11

'Rise and shine.' Alyssa forced herself up onto her elbows. She shook herself out of her stupor.

'The storm has broken,' she said, surprised by the stillness of the air around her. The snoring and moaning of the girls lying slumped on mattresses and sacking on the ground were the loudest sounds in the room. She shivered. 'We thought we were going to die.'

'It's not an experience I'd like to repeat,' Mark said. 'It's hard to believe, but one or two days of solid rest, and no one on board will be the worse for wear, God willing.' He stretched out a hand to help her up. 'How are your bruises? Not too bad, I hope. I could do with your assistance on my round. If you'd like, I'll ask Matron to inspect them, unless you'd prefer me to do it?'

'No,' Alyssa said with more force than she had intended, but the last thing she desired was to be made to lie around idle because of a few sore ribs. 'I'm perfectly fine, there's no need to waste time on me when there are so many patients waiting. Shall we start?'

He bent over each patient, measured their heartbeat and had Alyssa help him lift them into a sitting position. She hoped he didn't see her occasional wince, but he was too occupied with his patients to spare her more than a passing glance. Nevertheless, they worked well as a team, with Alyssa doling out arrowroot while he coaxed the girls to swallow. His behaviour was much less abrupt than she had come to expect from him. Today she could not help but approve of his manners, and his skill.

When he declared himself satisfied, she prepared to resume her vigil again. Instead, he nudged her towards the door. 'Your constant presence with the girls is not necessary now, and I might need your assistance elsewhere, with saloon passengers and crew.'

'But I can't do that,' she heard herself say.

'Why not?'

'They are men, Doctor Bryson. You yourself were reminding me of the strict rules of the captain, and of society.'

'Don't be absurd. This is not the time to rediscover your overblown sense of propriety.'

She bit her lip. How stupid she'd been to expect that he'd treat her with the same consideration he showed the others, and ceased finding fault with her every action. 'Very well,' she said as expressionless as she could, to hide her pain. 'I'll do what I'm told.'

The gentlemen in the saloon were still asleep. Mark

gave them a swift glance, commenting on the decreasing pallor and regular breathing.

He turned to Alyssa. 'We'll start on the other side of the screen,' he said. 'We'll rouse the gentlemen after we have finished there.'

Mr Wainwright was still standing guard, his silent presence a comfort. Matron slept. She looked small and vulnerable in her crumpled clothes, with her bonnet askew.

Alyssa knelt beside the mattress. 'Wake up, dear Matron.' She patted the limp hand. 'The doctor is here.'

Matron gave a small start. Her hand went to her bonnet. 'I must have nodded off.'

Wainwright smiled at her, with unveiled tenderness. 'No-one could have fulfilled their duty more conscientiously than you, Mrs McKenzie.' He stretched his legs as he rose.

'I do not doubt it,' Mark said. 'Indeed, all I need to do is look around me to see that everyone seems to recover nicely under Matron's care.' He gave her a quick smile. 'But it would be remiss of me not to insist that you get some well-deserved rest. Mr Wainwright will see you to your cabin, and Miss Chalmers can take over from you and look after the ladies. Mr Wainwright, you'll surely assist me with the gentlemen?'

'I'll be at your service, Doctor, as soon as I have seen Matron to her cabin.' He held out his arm, and Matron clung to it.

Loud words made it abundantly clear that good health, if not good will, were fast being restored on the other side of the screen in the saloon. Alyssa allowed herself to eavesdrop along with the other girls. Someone might take the doctor to task in a way that was impossible for her. Unfortunately, one of the men must have tumbled wise to the fact that they were not alone, because the voices dropped to a murmur.

Time to take stock. Of the six girls in the saloon, only two could in all honesty be described as seriously affected. Alyssa made a mental note to have Louisa Jane and Milly taken downstairs to the surgery. The other four, though weak, had regained enough strength to declare the enforced arrowroot diet insufficient.

They were not the only ones. 'Good heavens, Doctor, we are famished, and you tell us it would be ill-advised to eat too much too soon?' a pained cry rang out. 'Yes, we are aware that we are not the only casualties, but still we must have some food. Be reasonable, Doctor.'

The reply was too low for her to hear, but it seemed to satisfy the men.

'I'm done for the moment.' Alyssa flinched as the doctor appeared behind her back. She had concentrated so hard on catching the words from other side of the partition that she had not heard his steps.

'A couple of hours should suffice for most of the patients to gather enough strength to have a light meal,' he said. 'Two of your companions have been amiable enough to take over the kitchen. Is there anything else you would like to know?'

'Where shall we eat? This room should suffice if we take turns, but it needs to be cleaned. As for the between deck, a single scrubbing won't be enough to restore it to sweetness.' She lowered her voice. 'We also need a bathroom, where we can have some privacy.' The last words were hardly more than a whisper, but one or two of the girls overheard and broke into a nervous giggle.

'Certainly,' he said. 'Is there anything else?'

'If I could get access to my trunk? To get some necessities?'

'Granted,' he said. 'But it may be some time before I can take you.'

'Maybe someone else could accompany me, then? Or I could go by myself?'

He clucked in mock reproach. 'You can't be serious, my dear. That would be disregarding the rules, wouldn't it? As you made it so clear earlier on, where would we come to once we go down this treacherous path.'

'What was that about?' Hannah asked as soon as he was out of sight.

Alyssa tried to appear unruffled. 'The doctor enjoys making fun of me. Can you help me get the girls to the surgery? Once we are there we can start to get cleaned up.' She wrinkled her nose in disgust. 'I can't wait to be rid of that smell, can you?'

'It's worse than a pig sty in the wet,' Hannah said. 'If there's anything I can do to help, you'll let me know, right?' Her hand went to her mouth as the ship jerked. She retched. 'Oh Alyssa, I'm sorry.'

'It's all right. I'll get a cloth.' Alyssa gave her a reassuring smile. 'You take it easy, Hannah. I can cope.'

And she did. She had never been this busy in her whole life. When the doctor didn't need her help on his rounds, Matron had to get some rest from her nursing duties, or one of the girls needed reassuring that they were not doomed. She was constantly rushed and so tired she fell asleep as soon as she rested in her bunk.

But it felt good to do something useful. The other girls also rose to the occasion, with Harriet and Susanna in charge of the general household chores, and Emma and Nancy running the galley. Emma thrived thanks to the compliments they received for their cooking. Her cornflower blue eyes held a new spark, and she seemed to float on air.

If only they had time to talk, like they used to. It was not for want of trying, after the first three days that went in a blur for Alyssa, as rushed as she was. But everything conspired against them. It seemed as if Emma only had to say, 'Oh, Alyssa, can I -' for someone to call her away. One day soon they'd sit down and have a proper talk, she promised herself. But not now, while they were still struggling with the aftermath of the hurricane.

*'Honesty compels me to admit that my little dalliance proves to be the most delightful diversion. So far, we have not progressed further than a few chaste kisses on a slender hand, but it is the thrill of the forbidden that makes this so exhilarating. I need to use my powers of wit to snatch a few unobserved moments with my fragile beauty, but if there is one lesson this storm has taught me, then it is to seize the moment. I am three persons now, the businessman who does not want to lessen the value of this golden-haired rose, the sportsman who pits his wit against crew and passengers, and the lover. I am indeed feeling a stronger attachment to her than I'd thought possible. She is so enchantingly innocent and trusting, never doubting me for a moment. She is most helpful too, in understanding why our acquaintance must be kept as secret at all costs, to protect her reputation. What a pity she wasn't born under better circumstances, but that cannot be helped.'*

He blotted the page carefully. What a wonderful way of probing one's own mind keeping a diary was.

# CHAPTER 12

Seven days, later, and normalcy had returned to the *Artemis' Delight*. One good thing had come out of the misery of the last week, Alyssa thought as she finally could look up to a piercingly blue sky, dotted with crisp-edged clouds. She was now truly one of the girls. Even Nellie and Rosie acted less catty. She wiped a damp strand of hair out of her face.

'Are you daydreaming?' Hannah shaded her eyes against the sun. 'We won't ever get the laundry done if we don't get cracking.'

'I know,' said Alyssa, 'but it feels so nice to breathe fresh air again.' She let her gaze travel around. The awning that used to give them shelter still hung in tatters, but as soon as the sails were repaired, that would be seen to, Mr Kendrick had promised. The sail-maker and his helpers were hard at work. Hidden from her view by the bridge and the wheel house, the sound of heavy canvas flapping against the wooden planks mingled with the male voices singing a shanty.

She turned her attention back to the task at hand. Hannah pulled a face. 'Mind you, if these tubs keep on coming I might wish I'd be on a sickbed again.'

'Don't say that,' Alyssa said. 'I pray we'll never have to live through that again.'

'It wasn't all that bad.' Susanna winked at her. 'Especially with someone as nice as Mr Kendrick or the doctor holding your hand, although it is a shame he is already spoken for.' A dimple formed in her left cheek. 'Not to forget Mr Wainwright. Why, he could hardly bear to let Matron out of his sight.'

'Shush, or she might hear you.' Hannah dumped a new load of linen into the tub.

'Matron wouldn't mind,' Susanna said. 'She is nice, and so is he. Wouldn't it be lovely to have a wedding on board?'

'Can you do that without a priest?' Emma's eyes grew huge as she looked up from filling a separate tub with water and soap, before she put a definitely masculine white muslin shirt inside with as much care as if it was made of silk.

Susanna said, 'I wouldn't know. What do you think, Alyssa?'

'Remember when he told us that on this ship he is the law? It stands to reason that, if he can clap us in irons he can also officiate at a marriage.'

'Talking of wedding bells already?' Kendrick and the doctor strolled around the corner.

She wondered how long they'd been lurking around. Susanna covered her mouth with her hand, while Emma's pale skin took on a becoming shade of pink.

Alyssa said, 'We simply wondered about the power Captain Moore holds.'

'The answer to that is easy,' Kendrick said. 'A lot. If you think of a ship as a private fiefdom, the captain is lord and master, jury and judge all rolled into one.' His eyes held a merry twinkle. 'If there are any more questions, I'll be only too happy to answer them. No, there's no need to be embarrassed. After all you are supposed to be on a bridal voyage.'

Alyssa muttered a few words under her breath. Only the doctor was close enough to catch them and gave her a puzzled look. She'd said, 'More like going to the cattle market. But not me.'

Kendrick took the plunger out of Susanna's hand and gave it a tentative twirl. 'We're most obliged for the trouble you all go to on the behalf of the common good. You have gone above and beyond the call of duty, taking on other people's laundry like this. To thank you in a proper fashion, we have the pleasant task of inviting you to dinner tonight in the saloon.'

He let his words sink in, before he went on. 'Mr Turnbull's cabin is fitted out with a piano, and he has offered its use. Mr Wainwright and I both play the fiddle, and should we find a pianist, there might be what you might call a hop. Your servant, Mrs McKenzie.' He took off his hat in a sweeping motion as Matron approached, having finished her needlework.

Alyssa smiled despite her persisting annoyance. He was such a good-natured fellow, the very opposite of his acid-tongued friend, that he must please people. This voyage took on an almost pleasant air, especially now that she had finally rid herself of that stupid feeling that somebody was watching them.

Matron was torn. 'As much as I appreciate the nice feelings that prompt the captain's invitation, I cannot help but feel it may be unwise. Some of the girls might get ideas in their head which are not befitting their station in life. They might believe themselves too grand for the men waiting for them.' She sighed as she confided her worries to Alyssa in the privacy of her cabin. 'However worthy, any miner must by comparison seem rough, no matter how much gold he has in his pocket.'

Her expression grew so troubled that Alyssa felt compelled to cheer her up. 'I'm convinced the captain would not allow any unwise familiarity,' she said. 'If you would enforce a strict code of behaviour we should all be the better for this experience.'

'But how can I do that? In you I put my utmost trust, for you're almost too sensible for your own good, but the very thought of my other girls being swept off their feet in something very much resembling an official ball! Why, some of them are naïve enough to believe they are being courted, which of course could never happen. It does not do to mix with different classes. It could only lead to disappointment.'

'But surely it will be enough if you remind us all that this invitation is the simple means to thank us for our effort?'

'It should. But there is something so romantic about a dance. I met my husband at a ball, and from the first dance on he couldn't keep his eyes from me. But at least we were well matched when it came to our station in life, which is paramount for a happy marriage.' Matron sighed again. 'No, Alyssa, I have made up my mind. I shall go and tell the captain that we accept his invitation, but there'll be no dance.'

'A hop? What do you mean, a hop? I'm astonished to hear you utter that vulgar expression, Mr Kendrick. The only thing that astonishes me more is that you dare entertain such a notion.' Captain Moore was breathing fire into his first officer's face. 'I always maintained that nothing good would come out of this business, and now look at yourself. A hop, indeed. What next? Inducing our sail-maker to set up a milliner's shop?'

'With all due respect, Sir, Mr Kendrick is blameless,' Mark said. 'When the idea was first flouted, he expressed grave doubts.'

'Did he? Why don't you speak for yourself, then, man?'

'Because I'd have preferred to do so in private, Sir.' Kendrick moved his head a fraction to indicate Matron's presence.

Captain Moore's face took on a haunted look as he realised his gaffe. He nevertheless made a decent job of apologising, Mark thought, because Matron managed to curtsey and mumble her thanks before she fled.

Moore hastened to see her to the door before facing the two men again. 'What next, I want to know?' The vein on his temple throbbed. 'What next on this infernal trip?'

The girls accepted the loss of a dance with good grace. 'It wouldn't have been jigs and reels and such as we know how to do anyhow, would it?' Milly said. 'We'd only have looked like fools.'

Emma nodded. 'You'll make sure we won't make any mistakes, will you, Alyssa? We don't want the gentlemen to think bad of us.'

'Yeah, and we don't have to worry about not being dressed properly either, although Matron says we're allowed to get our best things out,' Hannah said. 'Do you think there'll be pudding? And things like fish knives? I wouldn't know what they are.'

'I don't know,' said Alyssa. 'Just wait until the gentlemen have picked up their cutlery and do the same. Now, when shall we get our dresses?'

They all were in a festive mood as they made themselves ready. Alyssa had decided on a garnet cotton dress, with a small bustle and cream-coloured lace cuffs that set off her dark hair and amber eyes. The matching lace collar graced Emma's pale blue dress. Harriet and Matron had helped taking it in at the back with a few stitches, and now it looked as if it had been made for Emma, instead of being another handed down garment. Matron wore lavender silk shot through with grey, and Susanna sparkled in Alyssa's green blouse with matching skirt. They all set off in an air of excitement.

Quiet decorum dominated the festive evening, to an extent that Alyssa prayed it would soon be over. Though the food was superb, now the cook had recovered, with a roast of lamb following a soup course and trifle for the ladies and cheese for the gentlemen to round up the feast, she would have gladly exchanged it for an hour of solitude on the deck.

Alyssa risked a sideways peep. Everyone else appeared happy enough, if very quiet. Because the gentlemen were heavily outnumbered, they melted into the background instead of taking their usual place centre-stage. The girls kept their gaze demurely fixed on the table, as Matron had told them.

The silence became almost oppressive. Every click of cutlery, every chink of glass rang in Alyssa's ears. She fiddled with her napkin, hoping for someone, anyone to speak. Her glance darted to Mr Wainwright. He seemed engrossed in the selection of cheese. She could not expect any action from him, then. What about Mr Kendrick? Or the captain?

'Stop fidgeting or you will knock over your glass,' Mark whispered.

Alyssa ignored him. That he of all the company was seated next to her had done nothing to enhance her pleasure in the evening, nor did the fact that his gaze constantly seemed to travel towards her face. It was unsettling.

'A toast,' Kendrick cried out. He stood up smartly and raised his glass, first to his captain at the head of the table, then to Matron, who presided over the other end. Alyssa breathed a sigh of relief.

'Splendid fellow, isn't he?' Mark said. 'I shouldn't get too impressed though. As far as I'm informed he's not in the market for a wife, with his being at sea for years on end. You might wish to warn your companions as well.'

Alyssa's foot kicked out before she could control herself. For once she was glad to wear cumbersome, wooden-soled boots. A startled yelp next to her bore that out.

'What is the matter, Doctor?' Captain Moore put down his glass again.

'Nothing, Sir. I had the misfortune to hit my shin in the process of rising. It felt like being kicked by a mule, so you will forgive my crying out.' Loud chuckles rewarded this admission of his clumsiness. 'But now, whom shall we toast?'

Kendrick said, 'Who else but Mrs McKenzie and her delightful charges? Without them, we would have been hungry and ragged, but instead we feasted like kings and were spoilt like kings, too.'

'I agree,' Turnbull said. 'Let's drink to the ladies. They have shown themselves equal to all of us.'

His words rang so sincere that Alyssa looked at him in grateful surprise.

'A toast then,' said Captain Moore, gripping his glass before anyone else could break into effusive praise. 'To the ladies' present at this table, and to our beloved Queen Victoria.'

'To our Queen,' Alyssa said. 'Long may she live and prosper.'

'To the Queen, and to President Lincoln.' Mark emptied his glass.

'Satisfied, Mr Osborne?' Captain Moore puffed away at a cigar after the ladies had retired.

'Very much so, Sir. It was all that one could wish for,

as a small way to express some gratitude after everything the ladies have done for us.'

'Indeed, Mr Osborne, indeed.' The captain raised his eyebrows. 'I only hope we won't have reason to repeat this experience.'

Parsons perched his head to the side to avert the smoke from his cigar stinging in his eyes. 'It went better than I expected. I've got to admit, when you came clean about those lassies, I thought they'd be a lot rougher around the edges. But they seemed quite presentable. Especially your ministering angel, Doctor.' He chuckled. 'I'll never forget the first encounter when she took us to task over our interrogation of Matron. A game girl, that.'

Mark stared at him in surprise. To be sure, Alyssa Chalmers had some sterling qualities, if one managed to overlook the nature of her reason for being here. Try as he might, he found it hard to forget that she was intent on marrying the next man who offered for her, regardless of affection. Whenever he found himself warming towards her, this knowledge hit him with a vengeance. Maybe he ought to warn Parsons. The man, good fellow that he was, showed lack of imagination that made him particularly ill-suited for the girl, especially when he had time to think about the situation. And he was much too old for her.

He forced his attention back to the conversation.

'Hand-picked by the church, so I was told.' Moore blew a perfect ring of smoke. 'You usually do find a better class of people in Victoria than in the most parts of Australia, from my experience. Not a lot of convicts and their offspring, but a great number of merchants, civil servants and squatters; the kind of people you'd wish for to build a colony we can be proud of at home.' He squinted through the smoke. 'All the gals had to come with personal recommendations as well, as far as I know.'

Dawkes tapped the ash off his cigar as the ship jerked again. He cried out in dismay as the ash settled on his jacket instead of the ashtray. 'We wish them all the best for sure, but I wish you'd taken a boatload of decent servants as well as your two dozen girls, delightful as they are. If this goes on, I shall not have a decent shirt to my name when we reach port!'

Turnbull leant back in his armchair. 'Why didn't you book a first-class cabin on a passenger clipper? Or better yet, take a valet along?' His lips curled up at the corners.

Dawkes rolled his eyes heavenwards in mock desperation. 'Pray, my good man, where should I find such a man in the whole of Australia? If there are half a dozen decent servants spread around the country, I'd be surprised.' He shuddered. 'No, Mr Turnbull, there is nothing for it but to suffer until we reach civilisation again.'

Turnbull clapped a hand on his shoulder. 'That's the spirit. Think of the adventures we can write about in our diaries.'

'Oh yes.' Osborne nodded. 'Any more excitement,

and I will run out of empty pages before we even stop in San Francisco.'

'I possess a spare notebook,' said Harris. 'A few short sentences, that's all I jot down about most happenings.'

'Your brevity must be commended.' Dawkes yawned discreetly. 'I must confess that the Samuel Pepys' school of scrutinising one's every move gets a trifle monotonous. What do you think, Mr Osborne, with your preoccupation with your notebook? Or do we by any chance harbour a novelist in our midst? Otherwise I'll help myself to the last of the ink here.'

'Don't mind me,' Osborne said after a moment's hesitation.

'I am very proud of you,' Matron said. 'You behaved just as you ought, every single one of you. Your grooms will consider themselves very lucky, once we are there. Now get changed and put your party dress back in your boxes. I'll meet you there.' She swept off, a serene smile on her face.

'Can you help me take off the collar, Alyssa?' Emma said. 'Thanks for letting me wear it.'

'Keep it,' Alyssa said. 'It looks as if it's made for you. We want you to be the bell of the ball in Canada as well.'

Emma's hand hung for an instant in the air. She sighed. 'I wonder –'

'Oh yeah?' Rosie swung around, bumping hard into

Emma before she could utter anther word. 'You better not get any daft ideas, missy, only because you're Miss High-and-Mighty's pet. The blokes might fancy you, but I warn you. If you do so much as look at my fella, I'll scratch your pretty blue eyes out.'

She gave Emma another hard shove, only to be grasped by Harriet and Alyssa.

'What fellow? Leave her alone,' Harriet said. 'We'll let it go this time but if you touch Emma again, we'll tell Matron and then you'll be sunk. Right, Alyssa?'

'If Emma agrees. And you'd better apologise to her.'

Emma nodded.

Rosie's gaze darted from one face to the next. 'Yeah, ta, Em, I'm sorry. Can I go now?' She sashayed out of the room.

Alyssa looked after her. 'She'll never change, will she?'

'Forget Rosie, she's hopeless,' Harriet said. 'Can anybody help me with the hooks at my back?'

Alyssa wished she could escape the morning muster. There was no reason for the doctor to have them all line up day in, day out for inspection like raw recruits when they all were the picture of health again. The muster was a waste of time, and, she admitted to herself, the less she saw of that man with his ever-changing moods the better. He unnerved her.

She went up to Matron's cabin to take the matter up with her.

'You do appear a trifle drained,' Matron said. 'But it would be most irregular, my dear. It never takes long, and it is our only opportunity to be informed about any plans or decisions concerning us.'

Alyssa smiled her sweetest smile, as she repeated her carefully rehearsed excuse. 'I cannot help but feel that your presence is all that is needed, and I've fallen woefully behind with preparing our lessons. I'd hate to let the others set up a home of their own without sufficient skills in reading and sums. It would only be too easy for unscrupulous shopkeepers to take advantage of them.'

Matron pondered for a moment. 'I will talk to the doctor about your argument, or it might be better to address Mr Wainwright, but until their decision is made I'm afraid you cannot be excused.'

'The girls on kitchen and laundry duty are.'

'This behaviour is unlike you, Alyssa. What has gotten into you?'

If only she knew. But she couldn't admit that. 'I'm sorry, Matron. But it seems such a shocking waste of time when nothing ever changes from day to day.'

Her words came back to haunt her, for the next evening

the wind changed its pitch to a shriek and the swells returned with bone-shaking intensity.

Alyssa had to use both hands to hold onto her bunk.

'Down to the floor, everyone,' she ordered in the first lull between two breakers crashing into the ship.

The girls huddled together, looking at Alyssa with fearful eyes. But she saw hope there too, and trust, as if she held the secret to their safe deliverance. She could not fail them.

'Stay here,' Alyssa said. She nodded towards the washstand. 'You know what to do in an emergency. I'll try and find help to get the surgery ready.'

She pressed a hand against the wall to steady herself as she half-stumbled along the passageway that led to the stairs. Every wail of the wind and creak of the planks was magnified and echoed, until she felt herself shaking all over.

It came as a relief when she reached the doorway of the surgery. 'What are you doing here and once again on your own?' Mark asked as she half-fell into the room.

'The storm's returning,' she said. 'I just wanted to make sure we are prepared.' The ship lurched sideways. Alyssa fell forward with a cry, only to find herself caught by Mark. 'It's all right,' he said. 'I've got you.' His jacket smelt of tobacco smoke and his shaving cream, nice ordinary smells.

Alyssa's breath steadied. She righted herself. 'I'm sorry if I'm acting silly.'

'Not at all.' He led her with a firm hand towards the

door. 'It's no wonder if your nerves are affected by this racket, although the wind seems to be dying down. But as you can see, we are prepared for all eventualities. I'd better take you back to your quarters. Again.'

She gave him a weak smile. 'Thank you.'

Her legs still felt unsteady, so that she was more grateful for his support than she cared to admit. Without him her nerve might have given way, unsettled by the still moaning wind and the strange sensation that each of her footstep was echoed somewhere along the passage.

Only a few bedraggled girls made it out of their bunks that morning. Alyssa had trouble keeping her eyes open after the events of the night. Breakfast would be a welcome interlude, if only because it afforded her the opportunity to sit in silence for a while.

'Alyssa!' Susanna tugged at her sleeve. 'I need to talk to you for a moment.'

Susanna's voice shook so badly she got a fright.

'Of course,' she said. 'What's wrong?'

'Not here,' whispered Susanna. 'We need to be private.'

Alyssa rose as quietly as possible. She followed the usually so sunny girl to the passage. 'Whatever is the matter?'

Susanna shook her head in a frenzied rhythm. 'She's

gone,' she said. 'I've searched and searched, but I can't find her, Alyssa. She's gone.'

A lump of ice formed in her stomach, making her shiver. 'What are you talking about? Who is gone?'

Susanna's face crumpled. 'It's Emma, Alyssa. Our Emma is gone.'

# CHAPTER 13

Alyssa sank against the wall. 'When did you last see her?'

Tears spattered down Susanna's face. 'Not since last night, I didn't. We were dead tired, with what all went on these last few days, and I dampened the lamp early. There were some rustling noises and such, but there always are in the dark and so I thought, someone had to go, and follow a call of nature, and then I nodded off.' She bit her knuckles. 'Do you think it was her?'

'That was before the weather turned bad?' Alyssa's mind went back to those echoing footsteps, but surely that had been later, and much closer to the stairs leading to the surgery and the men's quarters. No, there couldn't be a connection.

Susanna wiped her eyes with the back of her hand. 'Maybe an hour before, I think, but I also heard some rustling later. I didn't pay any real attention. You don't after a couple of nights, and when the wind howled again as if it wanted to swallow us alive, I was too scared to think. I simply told the girls to hold on to their bunks.'

'Did you see or hear Emma?'

'I searched and searched my mind, but I don't think I did. We were all so scared and sick, and it was that awful, I didn't do a head-count and I should've.' The flow of tears intensified, turning into a flood. 'Oh Alyssa, I think she's dead.'

Alyssa's chest tightened, making it hard to breath. She fought to keep calm, but her voice shook as she made Susanna take to her bunk. She was at a loss what else to do to comfort the poor girl. She only wished she could do likewise and pull the blanket over her head, willing the outside world to go away.

She gave herself a mental shake. All this nonsense and self-pity did not help. If ever she had needed to keep her wits about her, it was now. Emma had probably made a forbidden trip to the luggage hold, as she herself had done on occasion. She might be lying in a hidden corner, bruised and battered, for all they knew.

If only she could call for an open hunt for Emma, but she daren't. If her friend had disobeyed the captain's orders, the consequences would be grave. She must shield her as well as she could.

Alyssa went back to her place, deep in thought. Her absence had gone unnoticed, testament to the precarious state her companions were in. Usually any deviation from the norm led to endless quizzing and ribbing, but today everyone nursed the aches and pains resulting from being flung around in their bunks like so many rag dolls. Matron had been too unwell to rise.

Alyssa sprinkled salt on her porridge without noticing. The noxious taste made her eyes bulge. She pushed her bowl away, reaching for some bread. It might settle her stomach.

Matron must be told, a task that she did not relish, but it couldn't be helped. She would perceive how important silence was, with Emma's future depending on the character references the girls would receive. If only she could trust the doctor as well. He was sure to notice at the muster that Emma was missing, and she needed someone who could walk freely all over the ship to conduct a search, something she was unable to.

'You're crumbling the bread,' Hannah said.

She flinched. How stupid. She moistened a fingertip to pick up the crumbs.

'Come in.' Matron rose with difficulty. Another broken night had taken its toll.

Alyssa's conscience pricked her as she noticed how exhausted the older woman was. But she had no choice. If any pleading with the doctor had to be done on Emma's behalf, that task fell on Matron.

Her mouth fell open as Alyssa recounted the facts as she knew them.

'But I don't understand. She can't be gone. People don't disappear like that.'

Alyssa covered Matron's trembling hand with hers. 'That is entirely my thinking, but you see how important it is to keep this to ourselves until we have found her? And that the captain doesn't find out – at least not yet?'

'Doesn't find out what?' Mark bared his teeth in a grin as he suddenly appeared next to her, giving her a bad start. 'You must excuse me, but I did knock as loud as I could to announce my presence.' He put his black bag on Matron's side table. 'I don't intend to pry, but what is it you are so anxious to keep from Captain Moore?'

Getting a decent account out of Alyssa Chalmers resembled the pulling of teeth, Mark decided. The whole affair was messy, painful and, due to the girl's mulish resistance to the operation, excruciatingly slow.

He listened with growing annoyance. Anyone could see how badly that melodramatic tale affected the already exhausted Matron. He could have shaken that girl for her insensitivity. Instead it fell on his shoulders to soothe Matron, promising to produce the missing female without unnecessary ado.

It shouldn't be too difficult. A discreet search in the men's quarters ought to do the trick. He beckoned Alyssa to follow him, while he told Matron he would have the boy bring her a light meal, and to rest easy while he was conducting his search.

'Well, Miss?' He pushed the door to the surgery close with his elbow. 'How is it possible that, wherever there is anything remotely smelling of trouble on this voyage, I find you in the thick of it? Or are you so naïve that I have to spell out the obvious explanation?'

She opened her mouth to protest, but he pressed on. 'You see what an impossible situation you have created? Couldn't you have talked to me quietly, so Mr Kendrick and I could have inspected the men's quarters on the pretext of making sure everyone survived the night without harm? Once word reaches the captain, he's duty-bound to take official action.'

He paused, waiting for her to say something, but she didn't. 'The girl probably succumbed to the charms of a glib-tongued sailor and will creep back shame-faced any second now. We could have hushed it up if not for the fact that Miss Prim-and-Proper-Chalmers had to cry hullaballoo into Matron's ears and who knows who else's.'

She flinched as if he had slapped her, but she kept quiet.

Her stony silence exasperated Mark further. He had neither the time nor the inclination to deal with affairs of this sort or be forced to feel guilty by a prissy British maiden on a manhunt, as much as others might be taken with her charms.

He chose his next words with great care. 'You may

not be aware of it, but there are some females and some men who are prone to act on a, well, mutual attraction. It's not the end of the world, as undesirable as it is. Now if you would have the kindness to return to your companions, I have no doubt I'll be able to procure your friend in good time. I seem to remember her vaguely. Big-mouthed, blowsy and more at home in a scullery than a saloon?'

His words had the desired effect. The confounded girl broke her silence.

'Emma was nothing of that sort, Doctor.' The words dripped with contempt. 'I dare say you have ample experience with the type of girl you described so eloquently, but nothing could be further removed from the truth. Something horrible must have happened, and all you do is insult me and her.' Her voice became brittle. 'It was foolish to believe you would help.'

'Wait.' What was the matter with him? He usually prided himself on the skilled mixture of respectful sympathy and detachment he showed as a doctor, but these qualities eluded him when it came to Alyssa Chalmers. He touched her sleeve. 'I'll swear Mr Kendrick to silence and we'll bring her back. I promise.'

She looked at him with eyes filled with pain. 'You won't, not if she hasn't been found yet. I have realised it will already be too late.'

Mark shifted his weight from one foot to the other. Confound her, she could almost make him believe there was something amiss. Nothing in it, of course, but still …

'We'll bring her back,' he repeated. 'Now run along while I take care of things.'

'Doctor?'

Her calm tone surprised him. 'Yes, Miss Chalmers?'

'I want to remind you of one thing. This has nothing to do with your low opinion of me or someone else. This is about a missing girl.' Her eyes burned like torches in her white face. 'A sweet, pretty, guileless wisp of a girl, Doctor. Emma was only nineteen.'

Kendrick was in the wheel-house, a small shed-like room on the poop deck, fast losing his patience with the bosun.

'You arrive in the nick of time to settle a dispute, Doctor,' he said as Mark entered. 'Mr Smythe here is adamant that all the dirt from the funnel is invading our lovely new shelter, clogging up his insides while he's steering.'

'Aye,' said the bosun, a heavy, hairy-faced fellow with a permanent scowl. 'I've been coughing out me lungs ever since we got steam. Never used to trouble me before, me chest.' He moved a wad of chewing-tobacco around in his mouth. 'Stands to reason, doesn't it?' Yellow spittle dribbled into his square cut beard. The spectacle was as fascinating as it was repellent. Mark could not help but watch.

'Stands to reason,' Smythe repeated. 'It's no good

cooping a man up in the stink when he ought to be out on the poop, doing his job in fresh air like the Lord meant him to.'

'What's your opinion, Doctor?' Kendrick asked.

'It's an interesting point that you have there, Mr Smythe,' he said. 'From a medical point of view, I should like to examine you after you've been outside for a while and have another look later, when you've been inside for another couple of hours.'

The bosun perked up. 'Told you so, Mr Kendrick. Doctor says as I am right.'

'Yes, yes,' Mark said, nudging the big fellow to the door. 'Be a good chap, and do as I tell you.'

'Lucky for you we still have the old steering wheel outside in place. You can do your job from there, Mr Smythe,' Kendrick added after catching on to Mark's intention. 'Only make sure you don't startle the ladies should they venture upstairs.'

As soon as they were alone, his tone changed. 'What's wrong, Doctor? You seem to be labouring under some strain.'

'Emma Sayce is missing. One of the girls told me.'

Kendrick's cheerfulness disappeared faster than his features could register the change in his mood. His mouth still formed the shape of a smile after his eyes had grown grave. 'That's a fine spot of bother,' he said. 'Are you sure the girl hasn't got anything mixed up?'

Mark recalled the reluctance with which the story had

been told, and the palpable fear radiating from Alyssa. 'I was convinced there is nothing more to it than a clandestine rendezvous,' he said. 'But now - Miss Chalmers was adamant something is wrong, and as trying as she can be, I'd be a fool to dismiss her as overly fanciful.'

'Alyssa Chalmers, eh? I can't figure out what fault you find with her, but she is certainly not prone to hysterics.' The ghost of a smile crossed his face. 'We'd better do anything in our powers to keep her away from the captain. That first unfortunate encounter is still raw in his memory.'

'Where shall we start with our search?' Mark asked.

The men's quarters were almost completely deserted. Only the crew who shared the night watch enjoyed their slumber, snoring in their narrow bunks. A quick glance was enough to convince Mark that this was the wrong place to look. There was hardly enough space to swing a cat, and the lack of privacy made it impossible to hide a girl.

Kendrick closed the door. 'We've got to look somewhere else.'

'But where?' Mark tried to draw a map of the ship in his mind.

'She wouldn't be in one of our cabins,' Kendrick said after a heartbeat's pause. 'I'll take it on my bible oath that the captain and Wainwright are above reproach, and the three of us are the only ones of the crew who don't have to share their quarters. We are a bit more cramped than usual because we had to take on the engine crew as well.'

'Maybe Emma Sayce met with an accident somewhere in the bowels of the ship?'

'We'll have a look, but whatever would she been doing there?' The first officer looked gloomy. 'There's nothing for it, then, if we don't find her lying in a dark corner. We'll have to tell the captain.'

'What next?' The vein on Captain Moore's temple throbbed hard enough to make Mark fear an apoplexy. 'There's been nothing but trouble since we set sail.' He sank onto his armchair. 'Do whatever you have to, Mr Kendrick, enlist the doctor here and Mr Wainwright if needs be, but find me that missing bride — now!'

If she had to wait any longer for news she would start tearing out her hair. It was bad enough she had to appear unconcerned in front of the other girls when Emma's absence could no longer go unnoticed, but to be forced to do nothing was almost more than Alyssa could bear. It must have been hours since the doctor started the search.

Alyssa let out her breath in a hiss. Where was he?

Where was Emma Sayce? The three men had nearly exhausted the list of possible places. All that was left was the between deck, which they ruled out straight away because there could be no doubt Miss Chalmers would have found the girl then, and the saloon passenger's cabins.

Those cabins would have to wait until luncheon was served, they had decided. 'No point in raising the alarm if we don't have to,' Kendrick said. 'I'm pretty sure this is a wild goose chase, but if she's there we'll find her then. If not—'

Mark swallowed. There was something distasteful in the idea of entering another man's private sphere without permission, especially men of honour. He shared an uneasy look with Wainwright, whose discomfort could be felt a mile away. But still, it couldn't be helped. He turned his mind to practical things. 'How do we get into the cabins? Breaking and entering?'

Kendrick raised his eyebrows. 'How long did you say you lived among ex-convicts? They seem to have rubbed up on you.' He pulled a saucer-sized key ring out of his uniform pocket, sending half a dozen keys jingling.

'That's useful. Just entering then.'

The first officer shrugged. 'This is still our ship, Doctor, which means we are entitled to those keys. How do you think the boy can perform his duties?' He listened to the ship's bells. 'Half an hour until luncheon. We'd better not all miss it, for appearances' sake.'

'I'll conduct the search,' Wainwright said, a nerve twitching on the corner of his mouth.

Mark said, 'It had better be me, attending to the call of duty.'

Kendrick gave him a thoughtful look. 'Which patient?'

'The bosun. I'll take another peep at him, for the sake of verisimilitude. That way we can also be certain that none of the saloon passengers will feel obliged to hold his hand.'

'You do have a certain flair for subterfuge, don't you?' Kendrick handed Mark the key-ring. 'And you seemed to be such an upstanding man.'

He wasn't the only one whose appearance was deceiving, Mark thought as he closed the last door behind him. Only Turnbull's and Osborne's lodgings conformed to the mental picture he had formed of their occupants. Both were tidy, with personal touches kept to a minimum. In Osborne's case, they consisted of a well-thumbed copy of Keats' poetry with a faded velvet hair ribbon serving as a bookmark, and his diary; and Turnbull displayed metallurgist's books next to a leather-bound book carrying his initials on the spine.

The biggest surprise had been Harris and Dawkes. Harris, in particular, was a puzzle. It was hard to imagine that energetic, forceful man wearing a silk dressing-gown striped like a bumblebee. Dawkes on the other hand would have fit that image well, but instead the self-proclaimed southern dandy, made do with a single silver-backed brush and comb on his dressing table, leaving ample space to set out half a dozen photographs of what must be his family and the ancestral home, a sprawling mansion in classical Palladian style. A watch-chain dangled from a notebook bound in pale blue leather.

Mark sighed. Intriguing as these glimpses might be, they didn't help. All he could tell for sure was that he had found no trace of the missing girl. She had vanished.

'People don't vanish.' As soon as she had seen him, Alyssa had slipped out of the girls' mess, shut the door firmly behind her and met him in the passageway.

'You told me yourself you feared that we'd be too late and Emma is no longer alive.'

'Yes,' she said.

'You can't have it both ways,' he said. 'I understand you were very fond of her, and it is awful, but there can be no doubt she must have fallen overboard and drowned. Otherwise we'd have found her.' He regretted his harsh words as soon as she looked up to meet his gaze. The spark had gone from her eyes, he noticed, and she held her head as if every single movement cost her dearly.

'I know,' she said. 'But what you don't seem to understand is we need to know how it happened. And why.'

'That should be obvious enough.' He'd had ample time to think it through. 'It's not the first time that someone feels sea-sickness coming on when walking along a deck. She'll have rushed to the rail, to seek relief, and either she lost her balance on the slippery planks, or the ship heaved badly enough to make her fall overboard.' He took Alyssa's icy hand, chafing some warmth back into it. 'I'm truly sorry, Miss Chalmers.'

Her hand rested limp in his. She blinked back tears. 'It can't have happened like that.'

'Why not? Don't tell me it's impossible, because you weren't allowed to be out on your own. You know as well as I do that that hasn't hindered you in the past.'

'No,' Alyssa said. Her voice became more brittle. 'Because all the girls were scared witless after you and Mr Wainwright warned us away from the rail. And because Emma Sayce was afraid of being alone in the dark.' She paused. 'If it had been me, Doctor, your diagnosis would probably be correct. But not in Emma's case, and I can't do anything about it. Unless you help me.'

Her whole body started to shake. She was doing it again, Mark thought, making him feel guilty. He should have been annoyed, but instead it was quite – touching, somehow. She was mistaken when it came to her friend's fate, but that was natural, under the circumstances. 'I'll do what I can,' he said, still holding on to her hand. 'But not here, where anyone could see and hear us. We can talk in my surgery.'

~

Mark left the door ajar, in case anybody should come along. It would look infinitely worse if they were found together without Matron's supervision in seclusion, he said. Alyssa agreed. This was not the time to observe niceties.

He saw with satisfaction that some colour was returning to her face. He began to suspect that underneath her prickly façade was an altogether more vulnerable person than she let the world see. Although – every time he had formed a definite opinion of that girl, something had happened to knock it sideways. Mercenary, generous, prissy, unconventional – for a man with a scientific mind she posed a puzzle, an experience he disliked.

He needed a drink, and judging by Alyssa's pallor and ragged breath, she would also profit from a medicinal drop. Mark unlocked the drawer at the bottom of his Davenport desk.

'Very impressive. Your own private cellar,' she said with a wan smile.

'I prefer to be prepared for all eventualities.' He poured them both a generous dose of whisky. 'Down with it in one go. I promise you'll feel better afterwards.'

She gasped for breath as the liquid burned its way through her throat and into her veins. It helped to thaw her frozen emotions, though. She licked her lips as she eyed the empty cup. A second drink might offer some solace.

He snatched the cup out of her grip. 'You seem restored enough to tell me in sober terms what you suspect,' he said. 'The last thing I need on my conscience is the knowledge that I set you on the path of depravity. And try to be quick before someone else comes looking for me.'

She frowned, unsure what to say.

'You told me she was afraid of the dark,' he prompted her.

She nodded. Relationships had become easier after the first awkward weeks, with everybody loosening up a bit, she explained. 'You learn a lot about people when you see them day in, day out, whether you like it or not. After a while we were glad to talk. It helped to banish the ghosts, although no one else shared my apprehension about what lies ahead. They all looked forward to having a proper home, and the security marriage is supposed to offer.'

Their gaze met for an instant. There was a question in her eyes that he couldn't properly read. Mark shook his head mentally. He was getting fanciful. 'So, you talked.'

'You remember when you nearly bit off my nose for standing at the rail? The other girls were making fun of that, afterwards, and of the way I wished I could have a few moments of solitude, with only the stars and the night sky for company.'

Her voice got smaller. 'Nancy said that I was so brave, to wish for something like that, and Rosie said she wouldn't mind a spot of nightly entertainment, winking at me and making everyone blush.'

She swallowed hard. 'That night, Matron said I could go up for a minute, under Mr Wainwright's supervision, if I took Susanna and Emma along. We were tidying away the notes for the lessons that day. Susanna was overjoyed, and Emma beseeched me with those big, trusting eyes, and made me promise to be with her every second.'

She paused. 'You've seen the outback. You know how desolate Australia is, even a bare mile away from the towns, with nothing but bush. That's where Emma's parents were hoping to farm. Then, one day when they'd left her to go to town for supplies, a deluge cut off the road.'

She blinked back tears. 'Emma was only five, and she was left all alone for two days. There was no-one to turn to in the wilderness, no neighbours, nothing, and all around her, when night fell, she could hear dingoes and possums and all kind of beasts scarper through the bush. She told me she'd lose her mind if she ever had to go through something like that again, and I believe that. So would you if you'd heard her.'

'Maybe she fell overboard at an earlier time,' Mark said without conviction.

'No. Someone would have seen her. Someone always sees you on this ship.'

'That's true. No ill-fated nightly excursion then. At least not alone.' He tried to keep his voice level, hoping it didn't sound as if he was casting a slur on Emma's character.

'That's what I think. She might have been persuaded by someone else,' she said. 'Emma wasn't gullible, but she struck me as very biddable and obliging, apart from being so beautiful hardly anyone could keep his eyes off her when she walked past.'

'I don't clearly remember her off-hand, but I take your word for it,' Mark said. 'Some other girl might have gone for a walk with her, and something happened that the other one now doesn't want to be discovered.'

'Yes.'

Mark mentally let a series of faces pass. There were a few very pretty girls, yes, but none that had made such a big impression on him, when they filed up for the muster. He'd done his best to keep them at a safe distance to avoid complications. To be honest, only one girl stood apart, as far as he was concerned, but he'd be darned if he would tell her that, especially since he still struggled to make up his mind about her character.

'Emma Sayce.' He rifled through the pages of a notebook. 'Found her!' He smacked a page with the palm of his right hand. 'A very healthy girl. I never had any reason to treat her apart from that bout of seasickness we all shared. That should explain why I can't put a face to the name. I've got a shocking memory when it comes to that.' He broke into a grin. 'You were right, Miss Chalmers, all those weeks ago. It appears I'm not A Man, but only a doctor.'

The corners of her mouth curled up despite her obvious distress. 'Or you didn't notice her because she spent so much time in the galley after the cook got seasick.'

Mark whistled. 'That's who she was? I remember two girls wielding spoons. One nothing but a shy child, as far as I could see. But you're right, the second one, she was a vision of loveliness.'

'Yes,' she replied after a palpable pause.

Kendrick poked his head through the doorway. 'I gather there's a council of war going on? May I come in?'

'By all means,' Mark said. 'You're just the man we need.'

He summed up the facts in a few sentences. An uneasy silence settled over the room after he'd finished.

'What shall we do now?' Kendrick asked, looking first at Alyssa and then at Mark. 'What would you suggest?' said Mark

Kendrick rubbed a finger along the side of his nose. 'No offence, Miss Chalmers, but some proof might be called for, especially when it comes to Captain Moore. He is the law on board, but the law needs more convincing than your impression of the girl and a hunch.

It would cause immense harm if Miss Sayce were found under the wrong circumstances.'

He hesitated. 'Would it upset you terribly to join me in a search for clues, Miss Chalmers? If she is hurt, we might still find her, although I can't think of any more places to search. If she's dead and her body has gone, she must have gone overboard.'

'You're not upsetting me at all,' she said in a low, but firm voice. 'You think we might find something tangible on deck?'

'At least I can't think of anything better right now. Who knows, there might have been hair-pulling or something of that sort going on. You never know until you've tried.' He gave her another apologetic look. 'Some girls can get a bit nasty in a fight, and from what I've seen there are one or two hellcats among you lot.'

To Mark's surprise, she didn't balk at the picture. 'Rosie and Nellie,' she said with a puzzled tone on her voice. 'Yes, I see . . .' She looked at them with an unwavering gaze. 'Rosie had an argument with Emma, after the dinner party, because she was jealous. It wasn't the first, but this time she looked fit to kill.'

'I'm sorry,' said Kendrick.

'Yes.' Alyssa's breath was unsteady. 'So am I, if she is guilty.'

Mark said, 'We need to find proof. If the girls had a fight, there will be something.'

'If I can induce Matron to take the air with me before dinner, would you gentlemen and Mr

Wainwright be able to join us in as natural a manner as possible?'

'I'm afraid Mr Wainwright's help won't be that active under that circumstances,' Kendrick said. 'He might be busy tending to Matron's well-being.'

The ghost of a smile flitted over their face. 'I count on that.'

'You do, don't you?' He pushed the door wide open. 'Davies! You need to escort Miss Chalmers back.'

'Thank you,' she said. 'For both hearing me out, and for believing me that Emma might have been - murdered.'

# CHAPTER 15

'What a girl!' Kendrick said after she was out of earshot. 'I hate to say it, but I believe she's right; and not for the first time.'

'What I hate to say is that we still have to decide on what to tell the captain. And Mr Wainwright. If that girl is correct, which I'm not saying she is, who can we take into our confidence if a murder has occurred?'

'That's the crux, Doctor. I'm not yet inclined to tell Mr Wainwright the whole truth because it would pain him to have secrets from his good lady, and I trust Miss Chalmers has the good sense to hide her suspicions from Matron for the same reason. I wouldn't want them to feel forced to test each other's loyalties.'

Alyssa was deep in thought as she followed the boy. It all made horrible sense. She could easily imagine Rosie attacking Emma in a fit of spite. Her heart skipped a beat as an idea formed in her head. If Rosie was the culprit, Emma could still be alive. Rosie might be capable of a lot, but physically it was beyond her to lift a girl and throw her over board. 'Yes...'

'Sorry, Miss?'

'It's nothing, Davies,' she said, forcing herself to smile at him. 'I was talking to myself.'

All she had to do was ask a few discreet questions and find out if Rosie could have slipped out of her quarters during the night. Then they could confront her, make her admit what she'd done, and get her to take them to Emma. This was her only hope. She began to pray under her breath, because, if Rosie was innocent, that left only one explanation - a clandestine rendezvous. And who in all honesty could blame Emma if she had succumbed? Only the prospect of matrimony brought Emma on this ship, and if a decent suitor offered himself, most girls would be tempted.

She dug her teeth into her upper lip. She'd have told Mr Kendrick about her deductions, but only him. Her eyes narrowed as she recalled the doctor's whistle. She wouldn't put it past him to blame Emma for whatever had happened. Vision of loveliness! He'd made Emma sound – well, easy. As if any man could understand their situation.

She could almost see it, Emma's glowing face turned towards a shady figure, rough hands grabbing her and pulling her into an unwanted embrace, Emma's panic and subsequent attempt to flee from the faceless brute. Maybe she slipped or the ship heaved and the helpless girl toppled over the rail. Or – Alyssa's heart drummed against her chest – the man had pushed Emma, to hide whatever men of his kind would have to hide.

No. She shook off that picture. If Emma had been attracted to someone, she'd have told her. Rosie was the obvious suspect.

She shivered. If only there were someone she could confide in. She had never felt this lonely before, not even after her mother's death. It hurt almost physically. She, who tended to fiercely protect her privacy and her independence, found herself longing for someone to share the burden of her knowledge. But she couldn't.

'Are you all right, Alyssa?' Nancy asked. 'Only you were gone quite a bit, and you're all white.'

'Yes, thank you,' she said. 'The doctor has given me a powder against my headache.' She looked around. 'I hope we will never live through anything like this. It hardly bears thinking that these brave men have to venture outside in all weather and battle the elements.' She gave an exaggerated shudder. 'I'm sure we were all grateful to be safely in our bunks.' She let her gaze wander around to see the reactions. Nancy and Louisa Jane clung to each other. Harriet and Susanna gasped. Nellie gave Rosie a quick glance. In return Rosie glared at her, while she put a hand in front of her mouth to hide a small smirk, as good as confirming Alyssa's suspicions. She felt sick. Still, she couldn't give in to weakness.

'You look pale, too, Matron,' she said. 'The doctor has advised me that we are all in need of fresh air. Mr Wainwright should soon be here to accompany us.'

'Are you sure, my dear, that we ought to venture outside? I can't help but think we should all stay away from that horrible deck. I'll never be easy in my mind again in the open, with the responsibility for all you girls. I've already failed once.'

Alyssa touched Matron's shoulder. 'You didn't fail anyone, dear madam. Surely you must know that.'

'Indeed,' Wainwright said. Matron gave a start as he and Kendrick suddenly appeared in the doorway to the girls' mess. 'If you'd be willing to take my arm, we could all do with a turn in the air. Doctor's orders, and Mr Kendrick and I are here to ensure your safety.'

He bent towards Matron, lowering his voice. 'I know this is hard on you, but you must put on a brave face for everyone's sake. Please, my dear?'

Only Alyssa and Kendrick were close enough to overhear those words. They exchanged a knowing glance.

'I believe you were right,' Alyssa said as Kendrick led her around of the deck. 'What do I look for?'

'It could be anything, a strand of hair or fresh scratches on the planks, anything that looks peculiar,' he said. 'Don't look at me, keep your head down, as modest as you can, and tell me later if you've found anything. We don't want to attract any attention. Lucky for us that no-one else shares your well-established preference for being this close to the water.'

Alyssa focused her gaze in front of her feet. Her neck started to burn. 'I feel like someone is watching me.'

Kendrick said, 'Who isn't? This must be how a fox feels when he hears the tally-ho. I'm afraid my innocent attentions have subjected you to more scrutiny from your companions than I'd expected.'

Alyssa missed a step. 'Oh no. I'll never be able to make another move unobserved, and we need to be able to communicate.'

'I'm sorry. I wish I could rectify that.'

'But you can,' she said. 'Please, Mr Kendrick.'

He came to an abrupt standstill. 'Anything for you, Miss Chalmers, but how?'

'Ask someone else to walk with you, once we've seen everything.' Alyssa tugged at his arm to get him moving again. 'I'll take you to Susanna or Harriet, if you wish. They're both sub-Matrons like me, and I promise you they won't bite.'

'Excellent idea,' someone behind her said,

Alyssa and Kendrick both turned around. 'Doctor Bryson!' Kendrick said.

'I thought I'd join you. You didn't expect me to shirk my duty, did you? Until the dinner-bell I'm all yours. Which of our fair maidens should I ask for the pleasure of her company?'

Envious glances followed Susanna and Harriet as they were lead away. Only Matron seemed oblivious. She clung to Mr Wainwright's arm as he steered her around the deck.

Alyssa kept on strolling on her own, although it was hard to concentrate on searching the ground without appearing to do so.

Listening to the silvery peal of laughter the doctor elicited from Susanna made it harder still. He'd never been this charming when talking to herself.

Considering the circumstances, it could only astonish how quick Susanna had overcome her grief for Emma. One might be tempted to call it heartless, to flirt in such an obvious way. The doctor, of course, encouraged his pretty companion, touching the small hand on his arm every couple of steps, as if nothing bad had happened. Her head pounded. Who of these girls did she know, after all? Had she been asked about Rosie yesterday, she'd have been forced to admit that the girl was grasping, jealous and a trouble-maker, but she wouldn't have thought her to be as depraved as she'd proved herself to be.

Mark bent again close to Susanna, whispering something in her ear. Alyssa could only pity his fiancée who must credit him with more virtue than he possessed.

How much superior in every way Mr Kendrick comported himself, Alyssa thought. He managed to hold an easy conversation with Harriet while treating her with a distance that should preclude any suspicions of a dalliance. A worthy man, who might win any heart.

The thought still reverberated in her aching head as something shiny caught her eye.

Kendrick laid the silver chain onto Captain Moore's desk. 'There goes our hope of an accident.'

Captain Moore stared at him. 'What do you mean?'

'This chain and locket, Sir. They belonged to Emma Sayce. Miss Chalmers and I found them in a dark corner, less than five inches from the bow.'

Moore loosened his collar with two stiff fingers. 'She could have lost them.'

'No, Sir. See that?' Kendrick took the chain and put it on his outstretched palm. 'If you look closely, you can see there's one link broken.'

'Maybe it broke and slipped off her neck without her noticing.'

'I'm sorry, Sir,' Mark said. 'Mr Kendrick is right. She couldn't have lost it that way.'

'Why not?'

'Because -' Now Kendrick loosened his collar.

'Because Miss Sayce kept the locket hidden,' Mark said. 'She always tucked it in under -' The captain's discomfort rubbed off on everyone, he thought, feeling himself suddenly tongue-tied.

'Out with it, man.' Moore crossed his arms over his chest.

'Her shift. If she'd lost it, it would have gotten caught there. In her petticoat.'

'There we go,' Mark said as soon as they'd left the captain's quarters. 'Nice situation we've gotten ourselves into.' He turned around, half wondering if he should have left Moore in such a state. If the ashen face and the laboured breathing the captain had displayed after the last revelation were anything to go by, Moore sailed close to the edge. Definitely the heart, Mark thought. Maybe he should have tried harder to convince the captain to take a rest. He said as much to Kendrick, but to his surprise the first officer dismissed that idea.

'That wouldn't have worked,' he said. 'Not with Captain Moore. He's tougher than crocodile skin. No, what's really eating into him is that he feels responsible for the girls.'

They both turned towards the closed door of the captain's quarters.

'What do we do now?' Mark asked again.

'We follow orders,' Kendrick said. 'Find the culprit and lay Miss Sayce's ghost to rest.'

# CHAPTER 16

He turned the page, tearing it in his haste.

'This must not happen again. Even now I find it hard to reconcile myself to the fact that she is gone. This precious diamond, the one whose face could launch a hundred bids. How fragile life is, and how short. From now on I shall refrain from taking any risk with what remains from my goods.'

A deep groan.

'Why did she have to pry? When I close my eyes I see her face, smiling at me, and that slender frame meant to be held. But enough. From now on I shall keep my distance from the rest. No more emotions, and no more losses to my purse.'

. . .

Alyssa slept fretfully, half-waking with every creak of the ship. Twice she thought she heard muffled steps, and twice she hid under her blanket. Gone was her urge to find out what was going on in those shadowy regions. Cold sweat trickled down her brow. She'd never again rest easy until they reached port.

'You look terrible,' Susanna said, slipping next to Alyssa onto the bench at breakfast.

'I didn't sleep much,' she said. 'I kept thinking of Emma.'

Susanna put a sympathetic hand on Alyssa's icy fingers. 'Awful, isn't it? I've done my best to put it out of my mind. The doctor says to let the grief come and ride it out.' She sighed. 'Emma would want us to be happy, I'm sure. The doctor says so, too.'

'The doctor seemed to have a lot to say to you,' Alyssa said.

Susanna took on a dreamy expression. 'Did he ever. And such lovely manners he's got. I can't tell you how nice it was to have someone put my worries to rest.'

Her fawn eyes widened as she heard Alyssa draw in her breath. 'You poor thing, you really are unwell,' she said. 'Have a bite, you'll a feel bit more like it with something inside you. Else I'll tell Matron I'll take you to see the doctor.' Susanna pulled Alyssa's plate towards her and put the slice of bread she had buttered for herself on it.

Alyssa closed her eyes. If only Susanna would stop being so infuriatingly sweet to her. How loathsome it was to be patronised, despite it being in the nicest possible manner.

'Alyssa?'

She gave up. The bread looked revolting, she thought, as grey and stale as paper. She'd be surprised if she'd be able to swallow anything.

'Have another slice.' Susanna held out the plate as if offering a precious gift to her.

'I can't possibly.' She rubbed her temple. 'But you are right, my head throbs terrible, so maybe I should go and see the doctor.' She'd have to come up with an excuse to be left alone with him, though. Now her head really hurt, but that could be cured with a cup of tea and a moment's solitude.

If only there was a way to confer with Mr Kendrick and the doctor without having to use subterfuge. Men didn't know how lucky they were, free to go and do as they choose.

Susanna held fast to Alyssa's arm. 'You'll be good as gold in no time, just you see.' She knocked on the door. A faint pink tinted her cheeks as the doctor waved them both inside his surgery.

'What a charming surprise,' he said. 'I hope you are not too unwell?'

Although Alyssa, with her drooping head, was clearly the patient, his words were addressed at Susanna.

She blushed. 'Not at all,' she said. 'It's Alyssa who needs your help. Her head is troubling her something fierce.'

'Her head, you say?' He clucked his tongue in as false a sympathetic manner as Alyssa had ever heard from him.

'Yes,' she said. 'It hurts.' She softened her voice, to imitate Susanna's. 'Something fierce.'

'She could hardly swallow a morsel,' Susanna said.

'I take it Miss Chalmers is the only one thus afflicted?'

Susanna furrowed her brows with a puzzled air.

He flashed her a smile. 'Would you be an angel and check with Matron if anyone else is out of sorts? I hope it's only Miss Chalmers who has something wrong with her head but I'd rather make sure.'

'I'm on my way.' Susanna picked up her skirt with both hands in her hurry.

'There she flies, your little angel.' Alyssa clapped her hand over her mouth as soon as the words were out.

'Never mind her. Take a seat. Is there really something wrong with your head, or are you simply feeling generally cattish?'

'Very amusing. You know only too well why I'm here.' She sat up as stiff as she could, wincing as she righted her head. She touched her temple.

Mark's expression changed to real concern. 'You are

in pain.' He took Alyssa's wrist before she could protest. 'Pulse rapid, skin pale, and pricklier than usual. No, my dear, don't be offended. You should know better by now than taking my every word too seriously.'

She closed her eyes, for once at a loss for an answer. Instead she said, 'I've been lying awake all night, trying to make sense of it. How could Rosie do that to another girl? And why?' Her voice rose to a higher pitch. 'They were so close to a better life.'

'Don't,' he said. 'Don't give in to hysterics. It's all beastly, but we shall get to the bottom of this. What you need is rest and some brandy.'

He handed her a glass filled with an inch of liquid. Alyssa gulped it down. 'Brr. I prefer the whisky you gave me last time, to be honest.'

He smiled. 'You shouldn't make drinking a habit, you know.'

'Maybe you should then stop plying me with drinks.' This time she made an effort to smile in response, but it didn't reach her eyes. 'We'll have to confront Rosie.'

'Not you. Mr Kendrick and I will take care of that. You won't have any part of this. We'll just say that she's been seen skulking about.'

'But what if she denies everything?' The dull pounding in her temples returned.

'She probably will try, but it won't work,' said Mark. 'People like Rosie hardly think beyond the next meal or whatever it takes to survive.'

The sympathy in his voice took Alyssa by surprise. But then, he'd always shown some compassion for the other girls. Another idea pierced through the mist in her head. 'Oh. Poor Rosie,' she said. 'Have you thought about the fact that she might be just as much a victim as Emma?'

'I'm sorry, but you'll need to enlighten me.'

She leant forward, her elbows resting on her knees. 'We thought that Rosie ran into Emma, and that a fight ensued, because Rosie was jealous of Emma.'

'Yes?'

'But I can't in all honesty see her go further than scratching or hair-pulling, unless something bigger was at stake. Rosie's too cunning for that. You said yourself, she's a survivor.' She paused, waiting for his reaction.

'Of course,' he said. 'Rosie was meeting a man, which would have meant a severe punishment and instant dismissal for him, and ruin for her. They killed her to save themselves, and the man tossed Emma over board.'

'Yes.' Her eyes filled with pain. 'They couldn't afford to let her live.'

He reached out for her hand. It lay limp in his. 'I'm sorry. We'll let you know what we have achieved as soon as we have had a chat with Rosie. It'll have to wait until we've had our dinner, I'm afraid. If we can't come up with an excuse to see you tonight, Mr Kendrick will arrange another game of quoits tomorrow where he'll be your partner.'

He pressed her hand before he let go. 'If you have any more thoughts, write them down and hand him the note. And don't hesitate to call for my help in any way. We don't want you to make yourself ill over this wretched affair.' He took a pen and paper out of his desk and handed them to her. She hid them in her sleeve.

'Thank you,' she said. 'I'm feeling better already. Give my regards to Mr Kendrick. I wish you both luck with your investigation.' She looked straight into his eyes. 'But I needn't have said that. I have faith in you both.'

'This is intolerable.' Harris pushed his plate aside.

Mark shared his feelings. He too had only toyed with his food, and a quick glance around told him that he was in good company, or, he thought, rather not in good company.

Captain Moore's face alone could have cast a band of saints into despondency.

Dawkes cut off a morsel of pork. He sniffed it with distaste. 'I have to agree, Captain. What do you intend to do about it?'

Moore dropped his cutlery and pushed his chair back. 'About what? The girl? There's nothing more to be done, and that's flat.'

'The girl?' Harris' arm shot out, holding Moore back with a grip of steel. 'What are you talking about? Is there something we should know?'

'Let go of me, Mr Harris,' Moore said. 'You seem to be forgetting yourself.'

'Am I now?' The two men locked gazes, rather like alley cats testing each other's determination before they brought out the claws, Mark thought.

Kendrick leaned closer to him. 'My money is on Harris. The captain lacks a certain moral conviction this time.'

Aloud he said, 'Calm down, gentlemen. We have indeed suffered a tragic accident, but Captain Moore did not want to spoil anyone's dinner.'

'Not spoil our dinner?' Dawkes dropped his napkin with every sign of disgust. 'That, Mr Kendrick, has already been done, somewhere in the kitchen.' He reached for his wineglass. 'I take it, then, that this tragic accident has befallen our cook, which is the only possible explanation for the vile stuff that has been forced on our palates? You say there was a girl involved as well? Nothing sordid, I hope.'

Moore shook Harris' hand off.

'Maybe we should all retire to the saloon,' Kendrick said. 'A glass of port will help us all get rid of the bad taste in our mouth. Mr Harris?'

'Another one for me, please.' Turnbull handed Mark his whisky tumbler after hearing out Moore. 'Let me get this straight. You tell us that one of our fellow passengers was unlucky enough to lose her footing on the slippery deck, and fell to her death?'

Captain Moore said, 'Now you see why I gave everyone the strictest warning to stay away from the rail, no matter if you think you're accustomed to the constant moving. It only takes one heavy swell, one good jolt of the *Artemis' Delight*, and over you go.'

'But I don't understand.' Mr Osborne's voice came almost as a surprise. It was easy to forget about his presence, so perfectly did he melt into the background. 'What would that poor girl do on her own up on the deck?'

'We can't be sure, of course.' Mark stepped into the centre of the room, while Captain Moore still struggled for words. 'But you may recall the heavy gusts we had to endure once again, and the effects they can have on a sensitive stomach.' He paused, hoping everyone would conjure up the right kind of picture in their mind.

'You mean that poor girl -' Osborne blinked like a trapped rabbit.

'Stumbled to the rail to relieve herself. Yes, that's what we think.'

'Tragic. Which lass was it? I can't say I'd be able to tell them apart, except your plucky assistant, Doctor, but still one wonders.' Parsons broke his silence.

'Emma Sayce,' Mark said. 'You may recall her, an unusually pretty blonde. She was one of the two volunteers who took over the galley when cook was indisposed.'

'Doesn't ring a bell. Sorry if that sounds callous but there you are.'

'Mr Parsons! Surely you must remember Miss Sayce? Why, she even went to the trouble of making pasties when you wished for them.'

'That's who she was. Sorry to disappoint you, Mr Osborne, but I tend to pay more attention to what is on my plate than to who put it there.'

'That's all very well,' Turnbull said. 'But the question remains, what do we do now? Make up a search party?'

Dawkes sprang to his feet. 'That is an excellent idea. All may not be lost. With a ship of this size, there must be any number of spots that are easily overlooked. Count me in.'

'No.' Moore's voice held a decisive edge. 'We have looked. Believe me, gentlemen, apart from a short prayer for her soul there is nothing more that we can do.'

'What about her family?' Turnbull drummed his fingers on the arm of his chair. 'There must at least be something we can do to lessen their loss.'

'No family, Sir. As you may remember, all our female passengers are unattached. There's not a single one of them who has kith and kin to leave behind.' Kendrick raised his hands in an apology. 'Believe us, there is nothing to be done.'

'We accept that,' Dawkes said. 'Give our regards to Matron, will you? And I do apologise for my uncalled-for remarks about our cook. I did not intend to be callous.'

Moore looked taken aback.

Dawkes raised his eyebrows. 'Well, he was sweet on the girl, wasn't he? From what somebody told me, they were close to what popular literature calls having an understanding.'

# CHAPTER 17

Mark and Kendrick excused themselves after dinner and went to the surgery.

'What now?' Kendrick leant against the wall. Mark envied the ease with which he kept his balance. He still struggled with his sea-legs. 'How can we get hold of Rosie without drawing attention to it? I wouldn't want her accomplice to get wind of the fact that we're on to them.'

'I've checked her medical notes this afternoon. The best I could think of is ordering her here on the excuse that she might have nits again.'

'How credible is that?'

'Very. She had them before, and if she is being friendly with one of those bearded individuals that look after the engine, it's plausible she picked up something.'

'But that would mean that Matron has to accompany her.' They paused.

'Or we could tell her that she'd better keep an eye on the rest and have one of her sub-Matrons accompany the girl. You can count on it, she'll send Alyssa Chalmers.'

'That's true,' Mark said. 'I only hope Matron won't decide that she is well equipped to deal with a minor issue like that on her own.'

'She won't. Not if it is doctor's orders, whispered into her ear by our Mr Wainwright. We'd better put our little scheme into play before the ladies retire for the night.'

Mark didn't have to wait long.

'I've brought you your patient and her companion, Doctor,' Kendrick said in a carrying voice. He sat down in the second chair, while Rosie and Alyssa were left standing.

Rosie looked puzzled. 'What's Mr Kendrick doing here?' She tugged at her braid.

Alyssa took a step aside.

'Mr Kendrick and I just wanted to have a chat with you,' Mark said. 'You may go now, Miss Chalmers.'

Rosie's eyes narrowed. 'Wait a moment, what's going on here? I don't like it.' Her frightened voice was at odds with her belligerent stance. Alyssa put her hand on the handle, but Rosie held her back. 'You're not leaving me, are you? If you go, I'll come with you.'

'No.' Kendrick stepped between Rosie and the door. 'Miss Chalmers can wait outside with Davies, if you prefer that. And keep your voice down if you know what's good for you.'

Rosie glanced around wildly.

Alyssa slipped out of the room.

'Sit down, Rosie,' Mark said. 'I said, sit down!'

She obeyed, staring at him with a mix of truculence and fear.

'You remember, what Captain Moore told you at the beginning, don't you?' Mark stepped next to Kendrick's chair, so they faced the girl together.

'Yeah?'

'We know you've broken the rules, Rosie. You've been seen. You realise what that means?'

She moistened her lips. 'I dunno what you're talking about, Doctor. I haven't done anything. Honestly, I haven't. If anybody says different, they're lying. Mean old jealous cats!' She paused. 'Who was it said so anyway?'

'Do you recall the punishment for disobeying captain's orders?' Kendrick asked.

The blood drained from Rosie's face. 'No! Please...'

'Flogging,' Kendrick continued. 'Or worse.'

Mark felt a prick of pity for the girl.

'Why did you do it, Rosie? Why did you take up with one of the men?' Kendrick asked.

Tears formed in Rosie's eyes. 'What's so wrong with that? That's what we're here for, ain't it? To find a man. One who doesn't just -' She got off her chair and knelt in front of Mark, clasping his hand. 'Where's the harm in that? I told you I ain't done nothing wrong. Don't let them hurt me, Doctor.'

He hated himself, but he had to do it. He prised off her hand. 'Like Emma got hurt?'

'What has she got to do with it? She drowned, didn't she? The poor cow.' Rosie bared her sharp little teeth. 'Wait a moment. She put you on to me. I should have known it was her.'

'Who is your suitor?' Kendrick asked, but the atmosphere had changed.

Rosie sat down in the chair again and crossed her arms upon her chest.

'This isn't helping you,' Mark said. 'If you tell us the truth, Mr Kendrick and I will do our best to make sure you're not punished too hard for what you've done. If not–'

She shrugged, a mulish expression on her face.

'Do you believe he's worth shielding? It's not only the captain's decision you've got to fear. This will go down in your character reference. What man will marry you then?'

She smirked, halfway restored to her usual blustery self, but somehow Mark sensed fright in her eyes. 'I can look after myself, thank you very much. I'll be sitting pretty in my own home long before you think. Who knows, I might hire me a maid if one of my friends here can't snag a husband.'

She tugged at her braid. 'Are we done or do you want a look at my hair, Doctor?'

Mark and Kendrick exchanged a glance. 'I'll take you back now,' said Kendrick. 'And you'd better not talk about our little chat, in your own best interest.'

Another fretful night left her looking like a dog's breakfast, Alyssa decided as she peered into her mirror, and last week's breakfast at that. She twisted her hair into a tight knot, pinning it up with stabbing movements.

'Are you angry with us?' Nancy's eyebrows puckered. 'Only I don't know what we've done wrong.'

She let the last hair pin drop to give Nancy a quick hug, surprising herself. 'It's not you I'm angry with,' she said. 'It's – I don't know. Maybe being cooped up is getting to me.'

Hannah tied her bonnet under her chin. 'Only ten more days to San Francisco, and Canada can't be that much further. I'll miss all this. We have it soft.' She winked at Nancy. 'Even with all this book learning Alyssa is forcing on us.'

Nancy blushed. 'I like it. Back at the orphanage people told me I was stupid when I couldn't figure out the words.'

'Told her?' Hannah muttered. 'Took the strap to her, until she got too scared to try.'

How horrible, Alyssa thought, pity flooding her. She touched Nancy's cheek. 'You're fast becoming my star pupil,' she said.

'Nah, that was Emma for sure. Remember how she would read out every word she could see, down to the writing on the flour sack? She was that proud of her reading.' Her hand flew to her mouth. 'I didn't mean to make fun of her,' she said. 'Poor old Em!'

Alyssa gave her another hug. 'Come on, let's have breakfast.'

At the table, Alyssa's glance wandered repeatedly towards Rosie. The girl appeared subdued, but she wasn't alone in that. Alyssa wondered what had happened the night before, after she'd left the room. With Davies at her side, she could hardly have eavesdropped.

Wainwright interrupted her thought. He leant over to Matron and said, 'The captain wishes you to join us all on deck for a service, madam.'

An albatross flew over their heads, his wings barely moving. Deeper below, a whale raised its head out of the inky water and broke into a monotonous groan. It sounded like a lost soul, thought Alyssa; small wonder that most of the girls and some of the sailors made the sign of the cross. Even the sky looked desolate, with its unrelieved grey.

Captain Moore appeared unmoved as he led them in the Lord's Prayer, over the sound of the whale. He shut the ship's bible and addressed the assembled crew and passengers who had come to pay their respects to Emma Sayce. 'These accidents happen. Anyone who sailed the seven seas can tell you that.' His face softened. 'We all of us have experienced grief and sorrow and loss together.' He let his words resound for a moment. 'We have also experienced joy, happiness and laughter together. Emma Sayce will be mourned by you, Emma Sayce's memory will be cherished by you, and eternal life shall be her reward.'

Alyssa blinked back a tear as she glanced around. Most of the girls cried. Matron dabbed at her eyes, as did Mr Osborne. Mr Turnbull and Mr Dawkes looked suitably grave, and Mr Parsons and Mr Harris stood there with immobile faces.

Mark gave Alyssa a quick nod, while Mr Kendrick touched her shoulder, his eyes filled with sympathy. She gave him a grateful look.

He turned over a new page in his diary.

*'We held a service for a lost girl today. Emma! What a tragic loss and waste. So young, so beautiful, so full of promise. But as I said before, I must not look back.'*

.  .  .

'That was a nice sermon,' Matron said. 'It's a pity we had to sail without the benefit of clergy on board, but Captain Moore's address was all anyone could wish for.' She twisted her damp handkerchief. 'But it doesn't do to dwell too much on the past, girls. Although you've all got to promise me one thing.'

Heads bobbed up and down in eagerness.

'Whatever happens, stay away from that horrible rail. I wish I'd never have to see it again.'

Hannah spit on her fingers. 'Cross my heart and hope to die, Ma'am.'

Alyssa turned her head so no-one could see the sudden sheen in her eyes. Emma hadn't hoped to die. She hadn't deserved to die. Already she could sense the other girls pushing those memories behind them, like sweeping the street to get unsullied across. And like sweeping the streets all that meant was that the muck got transferred to another spot, forming someone else's problem.

Alyssa hands clenched and unclenched at her sides. She couldn't blame the girls. Surviving was hard enough without the support of a family, and wasting time and emotion on things they couldn't change was an indulgence they couldn't afford; whereas Alyssa knew she couldn't afford not to, if she wanted to make her peace with what had happened. Somehow, they had to get the truth from Rosie. It was possible that she knew nothing and her friend had acted on his own accord, to protect himself, but still, they needed that name. Deep in thought she followed the group down into the girls' mess for a lesson.

'Alyssa?'

'Yes, Matron?'

'Are you unwell? I've asked you twice if you feel ready to start your lessons.'

Alyssa duly went to fetch the dreadful tome of Mrs Beeton's. 'We shall now hear about the precautions to be taken before entering a sickroom,' she began, while searching for a way to meet Mr Kendrick for counsel. And the doctor.

Davies came to her rescue before she had finished the recital. 'Beg your pardon, Ma'am?' he piped, poking his head around the corner.

'Oh my, don't say the captain wants a talk.' Matron's eyes widened. 'Did I forget anything? I was sure I had done everything -' Her voice trailed off, her respect for the redoubtable Master visible in her reddening cheeks.

Alyssa stepped up to her.

'No, Ma'am. It's the doctor, Ma'am.'

Alyssa's pulse quickened. 'What does Dr Bryson want from Matron?'

'Nothing.' The boy gulped.

'Nothing?' Matron gave him a blank look. 'Now, tell me. What does the doctor want?'

'It's the young Miss, Ma'am.' A crimson rush to the face followed this statement which made Matron gasp.

The unfortunate Davies turned a deeper shade of red. 'Meaning no harm, Miss, but that's what the doctor said. If Matron can spare you, that is.'

'And pray, what does Dr Bryson have in mind?' Two deep creases appeared between Matron's brows.

'He said as I was to give the ladies my regards,' he performed a quick bow that could have been directed at either of them, 'and if the Miss could help with the medical supplies. Counting and such and writing things down, seeing as how the Miss is real skilful with pen and paper.'

'I see,' Matron said, obviously mollified by the boy's behaviour. 'It could have been phrased better, of course, but I'm sure we'll be happy to oblige. Tell the doctor to expect Miss Chalmers within the hour.'

She waited until the boy had closed the door behind himself before she asked, 'I trust you're not discomfited by this task? I'm astonished that these things haven't been done before we left port.'

'This must be due to all the ailments that have dogged us, dear Ma'am. I think it is very wise to have a proper inventory, and I for one will feel much better knowing that I'll be able to report to you exactly how we are faring in that respect.'

'That is very true, my dear. There is only one thing I feel I should mention to you.' A faint tinge washed over her cheeks. 'It is possible that, undesirable as that may be, you may find yourself,' her voice dropped to a whisper, 'alone with the doctor. I needn't remind you how to behave, but—.'

Alyssa stifled a smile. 'Yes?'

The faint pink blossomed into a deep red. 'You have the most unfortunate tendency to answer back in a manner that borders on the forceful, my dear.' Matron's fingers pulled at the fringe of her shawl. 'Exasperating as men can be, and nobody knows that better than me, I have to warn you that nothing is more unbecoming to a young lady than appearing overly – independent. It is what gentlemen most abhor. Promise me you'll keep that in mind.'

Alyssa crossed her fingers behind her back. 'I promise.'

She gave the unlocked door to the surgery a gentle rap with two knuckles.

'There you are,' Mark said, rifling through a drawer. 'Now where on earth did I put them?' He rifled some more before he pulled out forceps with a small cry of triumph. 'I knew they would be around somewhere.'

Alyssa looked in amazement at the half-spilled contents of the drawer.

'You see, Miss Chalmers, your organisational talents are sorely needed.' His voice boomed in her ears. 'Now let's carry all this paraphernalia behind the screen where you can work without the least disturbance.'

He took her by the elbow, whispering, 'I've put down pen and paper for you. If there is anything you wish to tell me or Mr Kendrick, you can write it down and we'll read it later. I'll go now and leave you to it while I cast my trained eye upon our crew.'

'How long will that take?' Alyssa asked. 'And how shall I occupy myself until then? Or will Mr Kendrick come by soon?'

'I'm sorry to disappoint you,' Mark said, after a brief pause. 'Our esteemed first officer does have other tasks to perform. You'll have to make do with me. But don't you fret, Miss Chalmers. You'll be busy enough to last you a couple of mornings. Believe me, I need that inventory.'

Four pages later Alyssa put down her pen. Matron should be delighted; Doctor Bryson, whatever his personal faults, possessed enough good sense to keep a well-stocked surgery. The only items not listed were the drugs stocked in a padlocked cupboard, as befitted dangerous substances.

All proper and satisfying, Alyssa concluded, with something akin to regret. Not that she'd want to find something remiss, but it would be nice to find the doctor at fault for once. She glanced around. She'd never been here on her own before, and she had rather wondered if the doctor kept another photograph of his betrothed here. Not that it had anything to do with her, but one couldn't help being curious about what kind of girl would be willing to wait for him for what must have been years. But she couldn't see any pictures.

'Hello there,' a cheerful voice said. 'You look as if you've been thrown in at the deep end of the inkwell.' Mr Kendrick pushed the screen aside. He cocked his head to the left, pulling out his linen handkerchief. 'A dab of water will soon set you to rights, Miss Chalmers.'

He dampened a corner of the fabric to give her cheek a quick wipe. 'There,' he said, taking her chin into one hand to scrutinise his handiwork. 'Your old nurse couldn't have done it better.'

'Am I intruding?'

If anyone ever gave out prizes for the most inconvenient appearance, the doctor would win by a mile, Alyssa thought, blushing furiously, while Kendrick said, 'Not at all, old chap. I'm only restoring Miss Chalmers natural beauty, which was sadly marred by a splash of ink.'

Mark raised his eyebrows. 'That would never do, now, would it?'

He wouldn't get a rise out of her. Alyssa pushed the papers towards him. 'Your inventory, Sir.' She put another scrap of paper on top and turned it so both men could read it.

'Who among the crew was Emma friendly with? We still haven't ruled out that a spurned admirer might have killed her, as unlikely as it is,' she'd written. 'Ask Davies;

men will talk. Also, I'd like you to find out if Emma had someone listed as next of kin or a close friend. If there is someone, they have a right to know that Emma is gone. Is it possible to keep a watch on Rosie's doing? I am convinced she will meet her swain again.'

As she had hoped, both men sobered while still in the process of reading. She gathered her skirt with one hand, before she got up and dropped a curtsey.

'I did not have time to finish everything,' she said, hoping her voice would carry far enough to be audible to any one passing by. 'If you wish, I could commence with the inventory after I have finished my other duties.'

'Much obliged, Miss Chalmers.' Mark held out his arm. 'We shall now see you safely back to your quarters. I'm afraid today we can't offer you a turn in the fresh air. It's raining like billy-oh.'

'You shouldn't rile the lass,' Kendrick said after they had seen Alyssa to the girls' mess. 'What has she done to deserve that?'

'You seem to have developed a pronounced fancy for her,' Mark said. 'Joining Mr Parsons in the ranks of her admirers?'

'You have to admit that Miss Chalmers is a remarkable girl.'

'Is she?'

'You don't seem to share my opinion.'

'I admit that she has her good points, but apart from that ...' Mark paused, vexed with himself over his inability to come to a clear decision about her. 'Don't you think there is something morally offensive about offering herself up for marriage to whoever will have her? Anyone with half an eye can see that she's made of different stuff than the other girls. They don't have many choices. But Alyssa Chalmers, with all her flaws, is possessed of character, breeding and education. So why should a decent, lady-like girl demean herself like that, if not for mercenary reasons? Surely you can't condone that.'

Kendrick stared at him as if saw him in a new, and not very flattering light. 'You ought to be ashamed. You of all men ought to know that you do the girl the gravest injustice.'

He crossed his arms upon his chest. 'What choices does she have, when you think of it? Without the benefit of family to chaperone her in polite society? The colonials can be just as snobbish a lot as the rest back home. Or do you think she should hire herself out as a governess or a nanny of sorts? Who'd have someone who is at least equal to the mistress of the house? If you ask me, Alyssa Chalmers is the least fortunate of the lot. If you don't believe me, why don't you ask her.'

He slammed the door shut behind him before Mark could think of a reply.

He gritted his teeth. Time to concentrate on his long-neglected studies. He took the topmost journal from the stack, hoping to shift his attention from human leeches to the more useful ones of the animal kind. Mark congratulated himself that he'd had the foresight to secure himself a nice supply of these fascinating creatures. Since he'd last studied them in medical school, enormous progress had been made in their use for the treatment of infected tissue, especially after amputations.

'Let's see what this chap has to say,' he said aloud, settling down with the journal. Unfortunately, the author mentioned a name that distracted him, in recounting the treatment of one Mr Mace.

It reminded him of the disagreeable fact that all he had done so far concerning Emma Sayce was twiddling his thumbs.

Mark put the journal to the side. Try as he might, he couldn't remember the girl's face. All that came to mind was the impression of something soft and pretty, like the first wild flowers heralding the arrival of spring. Hardly an epitaph, he thought, but honesty compelled him to admit to himself that all his female charges were interchangeable in his mind. Some were rougher around the edges, others more vulnerable, but there really wasn't much to distinguish them in the eyes of a doctor.

Apart from Alyssa Chalmers; no gentle beauty, prickly as she was, but there was a certain air about her. He got to his feet and started marching around the room. Blast Kendrick, he thought, as his sense of unease deepened. A few words floated up in his memory, and a few unobserved looks. He might have been a trifle harsh in his judgment.

He dug two fingers under his collar to loosen it. Maybe Kendrick was right, and he'd been a fool. He took up his journal again.

# CHAPTER 18

'You are muttering to yourself.' Mark dropped the journal as Kendrick addressed him all of a sudden. He hadn't heard the door open, let alone notice his friend approach.

'I've heard that is a sure sign of an unhinged mind.' Kendrick grinned.

Mark picked up the journal and put in on the stack. 'Or of a man preoccupied with weighty matters, Mr Kendrick.'

'Such as? What we'll have for dinner?'

Mark pointed at Alyssa's list. 'Have another look. Have you any idea how we can elicit information from Davies without appearing to do so?'

'That's easy. Miss Chalmers thought we could ask if he knew of anyone who might be able to share a few memories of Emma's last days, as it would seem fitting to write a letter to the orphanage or whoever recommended her to tell them of her tragic demise.'

'Ingenious,' Mark said. 'Shall I do it, or shall you?'

'It would look better coming from you, as you are the doctor and not his superior officer. It'd make it sound more like a request than a command.'

'Consider it done.'

Getting hold of Davies was easy enough. All Mark had to do was corner him when he came to tidy up the quarters.

The boy obviously found nothing unusual in Mark's query. He said, 'I'll have a word with the lads, quiet-like, after we've had our tea, Sir.' Davies lifted the bucket with the dirty water he had removed from the wash-stand with a flourish. 'Anything else you want me to do? Only I got Mr Wainwright's quarters to do now, and he's taking forever to fuss over his toilet these days.' Davies gave Mark a sly wink.

Mark smiled in return. The less intimidated the boy was, the more he loosened up; although it wouldn't do to make fun of his superiors. 'That will be all, Davies,' he said.

True to his word Davies returned in the morning with two names. Emma Sayce, it appeared, had caught the eye of the morose bosun as well as cook's. Both men were rumoured to have courted her discreetly.

'We knew, of course,' the boy said with a hint of smugness in his half-broken voice. 'There ain't much you can keep secret among us, if you see what I mean.' He placed a neatly folded towel on the wash stand.

'So, everybody knew?' Mark enquired.

'Too right, Sir, exceptin' the engine crew but they don't really belong, like. And the brass, of course.' He clamped his hand across his mouth. 'Beg pardon, Sir.'

'It's all right.' Mark straightened his collar in front of the mirror. 'I told you I don't stand on too much ceremony. Only, you shouldn't forget the respect you owe your superiors. There, do I look all right?'

'Just the ticket, Sir.'

'Cook and bosun, eh?' Kendrick whistled under his breath. 'Who'd have thought our surly Mr Smythe to have one romantic bone in his unwashed body.'

'My sentiments,' Mark said, the memory of his last encounter with the man still fresh in his memory. 'Shall we tackle him together in my surgery, me checking up on his troublesome chest and you interrogating him when he can't cry off?'

'I didn't know the lass, and that's flat.' Smythe scowled at

Mr Kendrick while at the same time inflating his massive chest at the doctor's urge. 'So, you get off my case, Mr Kendrick.'

Mark and Kendrick exchanged a glance.

Mark punched Smythe in the back with more force than necessary. The bosun expelled the air in his lungs with a loud yelp.

'Funny, that,' Mark said. 'I've heard a lot to the contrary. You can put on your coat, Mr Smythe. There's nothing wrong with your lungs. Only with your heart.'

'With me ticker? Dead crook, am I?'

Mark smiled, the comforting smile of a doctor intent on soothing only too well-founded fears. 'Let's talk about that later,' he said. 'After we've discussed Miss Sayce.'

The big man shifted in his chair. 'This is going to be between you and me, right?' His tongue slid out, wetting his bristling moustache as well as his thick lips.

'Sure,' Mark said. 'Scout's honour.'

'What about him?' Smythe gave a tiny jerk of the head towards Kendrick as he leaned close enough for Mark to smell ale on his breath.

'Don't mind me,' Kendrick said in an off-handed manner. 'And if it's about the captain's orders to avoid getting friendly, don't mind that as well. At least not now. We don't want to get you into trouble, Mr Smythe, we just want to find out enough about what happiness Miss Sayce found in her last days to comfort her benefactors back home.' His voice was a well-balanced mix of disinterest and joviality, Mark thought, and it did the trick to put the bosun at ease.

Smythe had found plenty of reason to go down to the galley to ask for hot tea to keep him warm during his vigil on the poop. He'd hardly seen Emma's companion, he said, seeing as she was forever huddling in the scullery adjacent to the galley, where she sat peeling potatoes and scrubbing carrots.

'So, Miss Emma and I got talking, in a friendly manner,' Smythe said. 'Nothing wrong with that, is there? The lass was happy enough, singing like a lark and smiling that you'd think you're caught in the shine of the sunrise.'

'Did you two court?' Kendrick asked while Mark still struggled to reconcile the poetic words with the man who'd uttered them. Emma Sayce must have been a special female to affect the fellow like that.

'We might have, in the end. Only then came that bloody swell, didn't it, and carried her away.'

He wiped his nose with his sleeve. 'Is that all? Only I've got other things to do than bleat like a ruddy sheep.' Smythe turned to Mark. 'Now, what's wrong with me ticker?'

Mark listened to Smythe's heartbeat again, before he shook his head as in amazement. 'You're a lucky man. There's nothing wrong with your heart after all. That can happen, you know, when you stop fibbing and get things off your chest.' He nudged the big man towards the door. 'You'll easily see your three score and ten.'

'Well?' he asked, once he'd closed the door behind the bosun.

'He's a possibility,' Kendrick said. 'He's at least eighteen stone. He could lift a girl over the rail as easily as you lift your stethoscope.'

'He seemed genuinely fond of her.'

'That doesn't exclude a lover's tiff or a man spurned, although my money is on Rosie and her beau. We've got no clue as to the why. All we have is a torn necklace'

Kendrick rubbed the bridge of his nose. 'Let's see what cook has to say for himself. I told Davies to send him along as soon as we'd finished with Smythe.'

Sam Plover readily admitted having been sweet on Emma. His voice quivered as he spoke of her, but he acquitted himself with a dignity that surprised Mark.

'She warmed my heart, she did,' he said. 'Most girls don't look at me twice, you see, but she was different. Always saying thank you, always smiling.'

He stared at the pots and pans dangling from their rack, as if they contained traces of his lost love. 'She'd come to me and ask about what to cook and how much to use and things like that right from the start. Or I carried the kettles and pots for her. They're a fair cow to lift and she was only a slip of a girl and not much used to keeping on her feet when the sea got a bit rough like.' His voice trailed away. 'I'd never have been good enough for her, I know that, Sir, but a man can dream, now can't he? Only she is gone and ain't nothing will ever bring her back.' He let a tear slide unhindered down his cheek.

Mark hated adding to the man's obvious grief, but he said, 'You might have been the last one to see her alive, Mr Plover. You were in the habit of walking a few minutes with her when you both were undisturbed, weren't you? It's only natural-'

Plover stared at him, open-mouthed. 'I'd never,' he said. 'What do you think what kind of a girl she was? Or me? I'm not one of that railway lot. Why, if she'd let me court her I'd have asked Mr Kendrick here for permission. I'd have done the proper thing by Miss Sayce, you better believe it.' His voice rang with indignation.

'I'm sorry,' Mark said. 'I am truly sorry for your loss, Mr Plover.'

'Yeah, well, life's a bugger.' He wiped his eyes with his sleeve. 'Better get back to me work, Sir. I got a couple dozen hungry mouths to feed.'

'Do you believe him?' Kendrick asked as soon as they were alone.

Mark lowered himself onto the edge of his desk. 'That he loved her? Sure. But if you mean, did he kill her, you've got to admit he is a possibility.'

'But Cook is scrawny.'

'Anyone who can lift a side of pig the way I've seen him do, could tip a slip of a girl over the side, Mr Kendrick. The question is, does he have the temper for it?'

'A much more intriguing question is, what did he mean with his remark about the railway men?'

They both spoke at the same time. 'Rosie.'

Mark jumped up. 'We'll catch him, if it means I'll have to keep watch over that blasted girl myself.'

A loud cough, followed by a persistent knock on the door, alerted them to someone else's presence.

'It's Miss Chalmers,' Davies said as he opened the door just wide enough to poke his head through the gap. 'Matron told me to wait for her, Sir.'

'Most proper,' Kendrick said before Mark could think of anything. 'And very convenient for us. The doctor needs you to go to the laundry and pick up fresh sheets and the linen for bandages. Let's hope that he doesn't need the surgery anytime soon on this voyage but at least we'll be prepared.'

Davies squeezed past the girl in his hurry to follow orders.

Her face was so pale as to be almost translucent but perfectly composed. 'How long do we have until the boy returns?'

'A quarter of an hour, maybe a bit longer.'

'That will do.' She walked over to the other side of the screen and sat down, folding her skirt around her legs. 'Have you done as I requested, Sir?'

'We have interrogated two men who admired Emma, yes,' Kendrick said. 'But we believe them both to be innocent. What we have found though is another clue. We know where to look for Rosie's friend.'

She let out a deep breath. 'Good,' she said. 'I must confess I had run out of ideas, and the sheer effort to act like nothing has happened towards both Matron and Rosie is becoming intolerable.' Her gaze travelled from one man to the other. 'Do you have a name?'

'Not yet,' Kendrick said. 'But we'll get him, don't you worry.'

She faced them both with an unwavering gaze. 'You will both be careful, won't you? A man who has killed once won't hesitate to strike again.' Another thought hit her. 'Oh God. Rosie is in danger as well, isn't she? If he knows that he's a suspect he can't afford to let her live. She needs protection.'

She swayed. Before Mark could reach her, Kendrick had already put an arm around her shoulders. 'Doctor?'

Alyssa shook her head. 'I'm fine, thank you. It was just a bit much to take in at once. And I haven't slept much lately.' She withdrew from Kendrick's touch.

'Understandable,' Mark said. 'But you don't have to worry. We'll take all necessary precautions, won't we, Mr Kendrick, for our own and for the girl's safety?'

'Your troubles will soon be over, Miss Chalmers.' He peered at her, with considerate affection. 'If it's not too distasteful for you, I'd suggest we carry out our search of

Emma's belongings now to find out about any loved ones she might have left behind.'

She looked at Mark for confirmation before she nodded.

Kendrick fingered his hat. 'Could we entrust that search to you? It is a lot to ask, but we felt it would be more respectful to have a lady touching Emma's private possessions.'

'I will not fail you, gentlemen. Or her.'

He raised two fingers in a small salute. 'I'll leave you two to it.'

Despite her words, it took all the resolve Alyssa could muster to fling open the box that contained Emma's worldly goods. It seemed like a lifetime ago that she herself had written out the inventories. There had been such a sense of excitement then, with all of them eager to start a new, better life, but all that had gone without a trace. Dusty gloom was what the box represented. Alyssa bit her lip to prevent herself from dissolving into tears.

Ten minutes later she fumbled for her handkerchief. Poor Emma. Dead at nineteen, and the only legacy she'd left behind were recommendations from the orphanage about her willingness to work hard and her skills at ironing, cooking, and general cleaning. No wonder Emma had leapt at the chance to find a husband. Toiling for her own family would have been much more rewarding than working all hours of the day in return for her keep and maybe a few meagre coins thrown in once in a blue moon.

'You're crying.' Mark looked up from the pharmacy inventory Alyssa had made out the day before. 'Did the girl leave someone special behind?'

She shook her head, unsettled by the sudden gentleness in his voice. 'No, that's what makes it all so horrible. No wonder she didn't talk much about the orphanage.' She struggled for composure as she gave him the letter of recommendation she'd just read.

'Cheap labour, that's all she ever was for the people in whose care she was given, Doctor. Do you know that there's nothing about her or her gentleness and sweet nature? Every single word in the character reference refers to her abilities to clean out hearths, carry bathwater, and scrub flagstones on her knees without complaining. That's all. They didn't bother to give her more than the most basic schooling.' Alyssa bit her upper lip, until she drew blood, to prevent herself from crying again. 'Twelve years in that horrible place. All she wanted was a chance at a decent life, and she didn't even get that.'

He took her hand and began to chafe it. His skin felt warm, while hers was icy, as if grief and anger consumed all the warmth inside of her. 'We'll find him,' he said. 'We'll find whoever is responsible, and then justice will be restored.'

She brushed away new tears. 'Justice will never be served, Doctor. Nothing can bring her back. She'll never have a home of her own, food she doesn't have to pay for with servility, someone who cares about her.'

'Is that what you want?' he asked with unusual force.

'I?' A sound that was half laughter and half sob escaped her. 'No, Dr Bryson. It's what all the other girls want. Except for me. All I want is to find a place where I can call my soul my own.'

'Which would have been impossible in Australia?'

'Of course. At first, I considered taking up teaching, but there's hardly anyone left who can afford to pay for their daughters schooling, and most of the girls' colleges had to close. That means I'd either have had to rely on someone else's pity, which I could not endure, or marry the first man who'd have me, despite the stain on my family name, to keep my respectability.'

'What stain?'

She folded her arms across her chest, her chin jutting out. 'Didn't you read the references we were given? My papa, high-ranking official of her Majesty, committed the sin of speaking out in public against the horrible conditions on the prison hulk in Port Philips when some inmates attacked and murdered their wardens a few years ago.' She looked him unwaveringly in the eyes. 'Papa didn't condone what happened, but he did present the view that the convicts deserved a humane treatment.'

Her voice caught in her throat. 'After that, invitations ceased. It is one thing to have Christian principles, but another matter altogether to act on them. And in case you think I could have taken in an elderly lady of genteel upbringing as my chaperone, they don't exist in Australia. It's a rough country, wild and untamed.'

She wiped away a tear. 'And no, I'm not taking unpardonable advantage of whoever paid for my passage. It is my full intention to reimburse him and pay the fare for another girl once I have found a way in Canada to board a ship home to England. I'm confident I'll be able to locate my mother's cousins there and find a home with them.' She pushed aside the lingering doubts that crept up on her whenever she thought about her future.

'Wouldn't it have been easier to book your own passage in the first place, even without a chaperone, if you possess the financial means?' he asked. 'Not to mention it would have been much more comfortable.'

She gave him a pitying look. 'How could I? Do you honestly believe there is any captain who would have accepted the booking for a spinster, travelling alone? Believe me, I wouldn't be here if it wasn't the only route left open to me.'

He moved closer to her as Kendrick burst into the room.

Kendrick slammed the door shut with such violence that Alyssa felt herself clasping Mark's hand for support. Something horrible must have happened.

'Damn and blast.' Kendrick thumped the wall.

'What's the matter?' Mark asked.

'Everything. Mr Wainwright and I caught Rosie and her boyfriend drinking and being merry in the small passage of the coal storage, and we tackled them together.'

Mark frowned. 'So, Mr Wainwright ...'

'Yes, he knows. But he'll keep quiet.' He rubbed his neck. 'Stop interrupting me, Doctor.' He shot Alyssa an apologetic glance. 'Sorry, Miss Chalmers, if I startled you.'

'Don't think about it,' she said. 'But please, go on. Did the man confess?'

'Oh, he confessed all right, but only to meeting with Rosie. What's worse, there's no way he could have killed Emma on the night in question.'

He groaned. 'Rosie did sneak out to meet him for a quick kiss and a cuddle,' he coloured slightly, 'but he sent her back before the wind picked up too much, and spent the rest of the night shovelling coal in the company of two other men. They can't all be in on it, which means that he's innocent, although he'll be in a lot of trouble with the captain. And so is Rosie, the insolent little madam.' He shook his head. 'All she had to say was that they were going to marry. Silly girl.'

'Which leaves us with what?' Mark asked.

'Nothing. We are no wiser than when we started.'

Alyssa buried her head in her hands before she knelt next to Emma's box again. Her hands shook as she took out the first garment. Kendrick touched her shoulder for an instant. 'I'm very sorry. I've got to see the captain now,' he said before he left.

Mark kept his gaze deliberately averted as she lifted

out each item separately, shaking them to look for a letter or a photograph, until she cried out. 'Look at this.'

His fingers trailed over the small stack of well-worn clothes. 'What do you mean? I see nothing out of the ordinary.'

She tapped the inventory list he was holding. 'Compare this list of her possessions with what actually is here.'

He studied the paper. 'I'm afraid you'll have to enlighten me,' he said. 'It all seems to be there, apart from what she was wearing when she disappeared.'

'That's what I mean,' Alyssa said. 'She wasn't wearing what she should've worn.'

'She wasn't?' His face was blank.

'She should have been dressed in her everyday clothes, Doctor. But they're all here.' She leant towards him as her excitement grew. 'What is missing is her only presentable dress, the muslin and the lace collar that she'd have put on to go out with a suitor.'

'Yes?'

Alyssa moved still closer, lowering her voice further. 'Don't you see? She wouldn't have done that to go for a walk with someone like the cook or the bosun. Whoever Emma was meeting, he was so far above her own station in life that she wore the only good dress she owned.' She waited to let her words sink in. 'The man we are looking for, Doctor, is to be found among your class.'

∼

'She is right,' Kendrick said when Mark shared Alyssa's suspicions. 'It's the only explanation that makes sense. You see what that means?'

Mark said, 'At least our two suspects are in the clear. The captain will be pleased that his crew is exonerated.'

'You don't think I'll inform him of this turn of events until we've got our man?'

'Why not? You don't suspect Captain Moore, surely.'

Kendrick dropped the gloves he'd been twisting in his fingers. 'Never. He's the most honest man I've ever known.'

'Then you should tell him.'

'Tell him what? That either one of his closest subordinates or, worse, one of the fine gentlemen in the saloon has probably murdered a girl for whom he was responsible? No chance to hush it up then. No, we'll need to find the culprit first.'

'At least you and I are in the clear, with me first on duty in my surgery, removing an iron file from a festering thumb – some of the engine crew really could do with a bit more frequent contact with soap and a flannel – and later being busy making sure that everyone came through without succumbing to seasickness again. Thanks to your assisting me, no suspicion can be attached to you.'

'I presume Miss Chalmers had a few suggestions how we should proceed?'

'Only that we need to establish who might have had the opportunity to strike up an acquaintance with the girl on the sly. Her last rendezvous at least must have been prearranged. Miss Chalmers told me that it would have taken Emma at least half an hour to sneak down to her luggage and get changed into her finery.'

'Don't ask me,' Kendrick said. 'I'm a bachelor, I wouldn't know how long it takes for a female to do all that.' He gave Mark a resounding pat on the back. 'At least you can take heart that no suspicion rests on us.'

# CHAPTER 20

Finding out anything useful without betraying their interest proved to be much more difficult than he had anticipated. Mark cursed silently as he tried to figure out how to broach the subject at the dinner table.

Kendrick caught his glance and lifted his shoulders a fraction of an inch, as if to admit defeat.

Mark opened his mouth as Dawkes raised his hand and sniffed the air. 'Quick, gentlemen, here she comes. What do you think it will be that will tantalise our taste buds tonight? Make your guesses, my friends, then write them down and hand the notes over to Mr Kendrick so he can keep track of our exploits.'

Mark suppressed a grin as he watched the passengers turn their heads towards the passage, sucking in the air through flared nostrils. There were more ridiculous parlour games, and it offered everyone some amusement. After a while, the charms of quoits, darts, whist, and telling tall tales over a nightcap, had begun to wear thin, so competing against each other's nose was a welcome diversion. The captain had drawn the line at allowing them to make book about the outcome though; gentlemen's fun and games were one thing, he'd decreed, outright gambling quite another.

The protest had only been half-hearted at the most; the original favourites, Dawkes and Osborne, were still in the lead and were widening their gap. Tonight, was no exception. They both nodded in agreement as Davies carried in an enormous roast of leg of pork.

'Done to perfection,' Turnbull said as he took a slice of nicely browned meat with just a hint of pink in the middle. 'When cook is in fine trim, he certainly knows what he's doing.'

Mark saw an opening. 'The ladies weren't doing too badly either, were they? I'm starting to feel a bit guilty with hindsight. They could probably have done with a bit of help.'

'I offered my assistance,' Osborne said, a touch of embarrassment colouring his otherwise colourless voice. 'I'm considered quite a dab hand in the kitchen.'

'Which does explain your success in our little game, Mr Osborne,' Dawkes said. 'But in the lead I am, and in the lead I shall stay, you'll see.'

Kendrick smiled at the little man. 'Do I take it then that we have you to thank for some of the delicacies that turned up on this table? The best fare I've ever had on a voyage, albeit dangerous for the waistline. I've come perilously close to growing out of my uniform.'

'My offer was gracefully declined, I regret to say. Miss Sayce, bless her soul, was afraid it might be against Captain Moore's explicit orders to accept my help, because my motive might be misconstrued,' Osborne said.

'I'm glad to hear that,' Dawkes said. 'The question of honour notwithstanding, it would have put paid to our little game here, if you had obtained intimate knowledge of our menu on the sly.' He reached for the wine decanter. 'Speaking of games, can I interest anyone in a round of darts after our port?'

Alyssa had little hope of the men's success. If only she could wander around as freely as they did and mingle, but for a mere female that was impossible. It was most unfair. She knew her own understanding to be much superior to that of most the people on this ship. Why, most of the girls on board possessed their share of good sense, if only they were allowed to use it.

'Alyssa?' Matron peered at her with a worried expression as they sat down for lunch. 'You look tired. I shall insist that Dr Bryson doesn't make too high demands of you on top of all your other chores.'

Unfortunately, Matron's voice carried farther than

she had intended. A snicker greeted her words. 'I bet our Alyssa wouldn't mind that, would you?'

'Nellie!'

'Well, it's true, Matron, ain't it? All the rest of us are stuck here like chooks in a coop, not allowed to have a natter with the men, like, and she goes off all the time to see the doctor. It's not fair on the rest of us, that's all I'm saying.'

Nancy shifted closer to Alyssa. 'Don't mind her, she's jealous.'

'There is nothing to be jealous of,' Alyssa said loud enough to be heard across the table. 'I'd be delighted to hand over my pen to you, Nellie. Matron, will you be so kind as to send word to the doctor that Nellie will relieve me of my clerk's duty, while the doctor does his rounds?'

Nellie's mouth formed a wide circle. 'Me go there?'

'Of course, Nellie,' Alyssa said, beginning to enjoy Nellie's discomfort. 'A couple of hours' work, and the inventory should be done. The hardest part is deciphering those labels on the bottles and figuring out what is what with the scalpels and such.'

She bit with relish into her bread. 'If you see blood anywhere, wipe it off with a bit of alcohol. And mind you don't knock over the jars with the leeches when the ship rolls again. They make such a mess because they get all bloody and bloated once they've fed.'

Nellie turned pale.

Alyssa turned to Matron, a sweet smile on her lips.

'Do you have any other chores for me, now that Nellie is relieving me, Matron?'

'But I don't want to,' Nellie said.

'That's all right, Nellie. It will give me a welcome break, and,' Alyssa winked, 'you can have a natter with the doctor. You won't mind if he makes too high demands on you.'

'I can't.' The girl pushed her plate away, with her bread only half-eaten. 'You know I can't read and write that well.' She looked around defiantly. 'We hardly none of us can, right? Except for Susanna, maybe, and of course Emma.' She looked surprised as she uttered the name as an afterthought. Silence fell across the table.

'Yes,' Alyssa said. 'I've asked for permission to write to Father Pollock about Emma.' She toyed with her bread. 'Only I'd love to be able to share a few memories of her. I'd need your help for that, because I only knew her for a short while.'

She looked around. 'Will you talk to me about her? We could write a letter together later.'

Getting the girls to talk was a bit like digging a well, Alyssa thought. At first the words flowed sparsely, more like dripping, but once whatever obstacle that existed was cleared, they became a constant stream. The picture that emerged was not pretty. Emma had been treated like a skivvy at the orphanage, expected to be grateful for harsh words and constant work because she had been kept on long after she had turned twelve. Alyssa's grief and anger for her friend deepened.

She looked around her. How could the girls be so placid when they talked about that kind of conditions? What horrors lay behind them? A new respect for their endurance grew in her. To go through hardship and abuse, without anyone to protect them and still remain as sweet-natured as Nancy and Susanna or fight back as belligerent as Nellie, was admirable. She only hoped that their future held some comfort. They deserved it, every single one of them. She could almost condone Rosie, snatching at every chance to secure a man.

'I wonder how Rosie is,' she said.

'Don't fret about that one,' Hannah said. 'She'll flounce back in a couple of times and be nice as pie for a bit. She knows the captain let her off lightly, what with only locking her up for a bit instead of having her flogged.'

She grinned. 'When she comes out, Matron says she'll do the laundry for the rest of our trip. That should keep her busy.'

'It was kind of Captain Moore to listen to Mr Kendrick and the doctor when they pleaded her cause,' said Alyssa, 'but what about the character reference? Matron would do for us whatever is in her power, but she can't make a false statement, not for something this serious, and who'll have Rosie then?'

'She still believes her sweetheart will marry her.'

Nellie snorted. 'Not bloody likely, is it? She must be daft to think that she'll live in a pretty house with proper furniture and all that. It's a grog-palace where she'll end up if you ask me, and I told her so, right away when she began to act all stuck-up. Mind, it's where she belongs all right, like her ma before her.'

She shook her head. 'Fancy her thinking she could be a proper lady, like you, Alyssa. As if any of us Tin Pan Alley lot could.'

'Except Emma,' Nancy said. 'And Susanna.' A lull occurred.

Alyssa said, 'I've wondered why Emma didn't go into proper service instead of staying at the orphanage, where she clearly was neither valued nor properly cared for. An accomplished girl like her should have found her services in high demand. I remember waiting for days at the recruiting office to secure us a cook and a maid when my mother got ill, and we offered twice the going wage.'

'Yeah, sure,' Hannah said, 'she thought about giving it a try, but not every household is like yours, Alyssa. Treat you worse than slaves, some of them, and the menfolk pestering every pretty girl. Right, Milly?'

Milly's body went rigid. 'Doesn't matter now, does it.'

Oh no. Horrible pictures rose in Alyssa's mind. She wanted to comfort Milly, but she was at a loss for words.

Nancy gave her a pitying look. 'You don't know much, do you. It's all right for toffs, but for someone like us there isn't much to choose from. At least the orphanage was safe.'

'Mind you,' Hannah said, 'some places were nice. It's just you could only hope to be taken on by someone decent, and with people getting poorer and poorer —-'

Alyssa opened a tin of hand-made boiled sweets and handed it around, letting Milly have first choice.

The girls took one sweet each. A few of them popped theirs straight into their mouth, but Nancy, Susanna, and Nellie held the sweets in their palm, admiring the delicate pastel-hued stripes.

'Nice,' Nellie said. 'I never had this fancy kind before.' She put it on her tongue and rolled the sweet around in her mouth. 'I could get used to that, given half a chance.'

'I'll give you the recipe if you want.'

'You?' Nellie's jaw dropped. 'You didn't make 'em yourself. Stop pulling my leg. Ladies like you don't go near a stove if they can help it.'

Alyssa smiled. 'My mother taught me more than you'd think. She always said, "you'd better be prepared to tackle anything life throws at you because you can't always count on someone else doing for you." And she was right. She'd have loved to open a confectioner's shop herself. My grandpa had one, in Yorkshire, and she grew up next door.'

She handed the tin around again. 'It never hurts to have thought of what else you could turn your hand to, if things don't pan out.'

She picked a lemony sweet, enjoying the tartness tempered by the sugar. 'Who's to say that we all find a sweetheart once we arrive?' She grinned at Nellie. 'You, in particular, had some doubts about me.'

Nellie sucked her sweet with a vengeance. 'Yeah,' she said, 'never mind me. I can be a fair cow, sometimes. You'll do all right.'

'Thanks,' Alyssa said. 'But I might instead go and open a confectioner's shop and you'll all buy my sweets.'

'Or you could become a teacher,' Nancy said. 'You're ever so good at that. I only hope the men will be nice.'

'I'm sure,' Alyssa said with more promptness than sincerity. 'Matron will stay with us until everything's settled. She won't let a bad man court you, Nancy, and neither will I.'

'Yeah,' Nancy said. 'Only how can you tell?' Her small face tightened with worry.

'Keep a hat-pin hidden in your pocket,' Susanna said. 'If anyone gets wrong ideas, he'll soon forget about 'em.' She grinned. 'Worked for me, that one, and for Emma too when one of the orphanage patrons got ideas.'

Nancy said, 'She'd have made a lovely lady, our Em. She'd have looked right at home in a big fancy house. I told her that the day before the accident.' Her face crumpled.

Hannah put her arm around Nancy's thin shoulders and hugged the girl to her. 'She's gone to a better place,' she said. 'It's no use to fret about bygones, love.'

'What kind of man are you hoping for, Nellie?' Alyssa asked. '

'A bloke who's sober and who don't push me around

for starters. If he's got a proper job and ain't an old fogey who wants nursing all the time, that'll do me.' She glanced around. 'We can't all hold out for Prince Charming, right? If you do, you're daft.'

'Don't look at me,' Susanna said. 'If we all waited for our true love, none of us would be here.'

'Emma said it was romantic,' Nancy said. 'She said when things got bad, she'd dream about her knight who'd come to rescue her, and she'd be fine again.'

'Romantic, my foot.' Nellie snorted. 'What about you, Alyssa? Who's it going to be for you? A miner I don't think.'

Alyssa's pulse quickened. This was a question she did not allow herself to ponder, let alone discuss freely. Instead she said, 'Who can say what the future holds? Except for –' she rattled the nearly empty tin, 'these two last sweets which we could offer to Matron and Mr Wainwright.'

Nancy sighed. 'Don't they make a lovely couple?'

Alyssa took more care than usual with dressing her hair. The rhythmic movement of the brush helped calm her mind. It was one of the few moments that belonged utterly to herself. Reluctantly she put the brush down to braid her hair and pin it up.

'It'd look nicer if you left out a curl here and here,' Hannah said, pointing to the temple. 'Softer, like.' Before

Alyssa could say anything, she twisted a strand of Alyssa's hair around her finger and pulled it out of the braid. 'Give it a nice curl like this,' she let the strand unroll gently, 'and you're done.'

Alyssa peered into the mirror. She looked different, younger and more vulnerable.

'Do you like it?' Alyssa turned around to give Hannah's hand a little squeeze. 'You're brilliant, Hannah. Thank you.'

Hannah coloured slightly. 'I enjoy doing hair, and I thought since you're going to see the doctor and Mr Kendrick you'd want to look your best.'

'Hannah!'

'You want to look nice when you're around menfolk, that's all I'm saying.'

Alyssa relented. 'Why don't you go and work your magic fingers on Matron, then? We've been promised another game of deck quoits under Mr Wainwright's supervision, and another stroll around the deck. It's come up fine again.'

'Ooh, she'll be so pretty he won't know what's what.' She ran off in search of Matron.

Finally, Alyssa was alone in her quarters. She glanced once more into the mirror. Yes, the new hairstyle was much more becoming. She'd never be as pretty as Susanna, with her determined chin and too generous mouth, but at least Mr Kendrick didn't seem to mind. She'd more than once caught him gazing at her in admiration, and lately even the doctor seemed to look at her in a different way, betrothed or not. Alyssa twisted a curl around her finger and watched it spring back into shape as soon as she let go.

Before she left the cabin, she slid a hand under her mattress and pulled out her second novel. Since she had already finished the inventory she needed something to occupy her while she sat in the surgery, pretending to work. And the surgery did have excellent lighting.

'Good yarn?'

Alyssa almost dropped her book. 'I didn't hear you coming,' she said as she clutched the book to her chest.

'I didn't mean to startle you,' said Mark, 'but you were completely engrossed. May I have a peek?'

She handed the book over without a word.

'First '*A Tale of Two Cities*' and now Wilkie Collins, '*The Lady in White*'.' He whistled under his breath. 'You have a most unusual literary taste for a young lady.'

'Scores of females do enjoy a well-written mystery, if that is what you're hinting at.'

'Real life can be dreary,' he admitted. 'I'm quite partial to adventure stories myself. And, no, Miss Chalmers, I don't intend to imply that your reading material is giving you fanciful ideas or a feverish imagination.'

'If that's so you may borrow my book once I've finished it. If you return the other one first.' Alyssa kept her words as light as possible, to protect the fragile truce between them.

'Thank you.' His eyes twinkled. 'Although you might let me have the book first. The pretext of you being needed here is running slightly threadbare, and we mustn't start tongues wagging. You lack the privacy to read, and I on the other hand might glean some ideas from Mr Collins about how to separate the guilty from the innocent.'

'Find out their whereabouts.' She put the novel on the desk. 'If you can prove that anyone had company from the time right before the storm, until after it calmed down well into the small hours, he's innocent.'

He ran his fingers through his hair. 'Which, as far as we have established, only goes for the crew, except for Captain Moore and Mr Wainwright. Mr Kendrick and I were, as you remember, busy readying the surgery in case we needed it. I hope you'll accept us supporting each other's story?'

'I never suspected you two,' Alyssa said without thinking.

'No. I realise that.'

'A realisation? Excellent.' Kendrick had a disconcerting way of appearing in their midst like a Jack-in-the-box, Alyssa thought as her face grew warm. He gave her a quick smile. 'Did I miss any startling revelations?'

～

'Character,' Alyssa said finally, after they had compared what they had learned so far. 'It all comes down to character.'

Kendrick nodded. 'If we take it for granted what Miss Chalmers has told us about Emma Sayce, she wouldn't have gone for a moonlight walk with just anyone.' A fleeting shadow crossed his face. 'I wish she'd used that hat-pin. It might have saved her, and it would have been interesting to see who'd have turned up to seek Doctor Bryson's assistance with a nasty flesh wound.'

'She must have believed that he'd marry her,' Mark said. 'Does that exclude anyone? The captain and Mr Wainwright are unthinkable prospects, but as far as I remember all our saloon passengers are bachelors, or, as in Mr Turnbull's case, widowed.'

Kendrick said, 'But he'd also need to be personable to win Emma's favour, don't you think, Miss Chalmers? And he'd be fairly cunning in doing so without anyone noticing.'

'The only one I'd exclude on the strength of this argument is Mr Osborne,' she said.

'A worthy man,' Kendrick picked up her train of thought. 'But maybe lacking a certain dash. All the others are possibilities from your point of view?'

She let the men in question pass muster in her mind. 'Yes.'

'Indeed?' Mark looked at Alyssa as if searching in her face for the clue to a puzzle. 'I'd have thought Mr Harris a trifle on the old side, and Mr Parsons showed a decided displeasure when confronted with our lady passengers.'

'He was taken unawares,' Alyssa said. 'And surely Mr Harris can't be more than forty-five, and he does possess a forceful personality, not unlike Mr Turnbull. That can be appealing.'

'Interesting,' Mark said. 'What do you think, Mr Kendrick?'

'So far I've never been able to fault Miss Chalmers' logic or deductions, and I'm always willing to listen to someone more knowledgeable in any field than I am. If your female intuition says, Osborne is out, Miss Chalmers, then out he is, and all the rest are in.'

He turned towards the doctor. 'I presume our next move will be to deduce where and when our culprit might have met with Miss Emma.'

Alyssa gave him a warm smile. 'Excellent. If you'll excuse me now, it's time I left you gentlemen. Enjoy the book, Doctor.'

'I will,' Mark said as she walked towards the door. 'Oh, one more thing.'

'Yes?'

'Your new hairstyle. It suits you.'

Mark gave the saloon passengers a lot of thought as he sat at his desk, the book unopened in his lap. They were all decent fellows, and none of them was striking him as callous enough to push a girl to her death. Still, the reasoning for throwing suspicion on them was sound.

But were they right at ruling out Osborne? The man seemed mild enough, but he'd be the most likely candidate to be a man spurned. If his emotions were aroused they might run deeper than those of a man who usually got his way or, just as easily, bestowed his affection somewhere else. It was a pity, though. He liked the inoffensive Osborne and he'd hate to see him guilty.

'Getting somewhere, Doctor?'

'Thinking and wondering, Mr Kendrick, that's all.'

'About our little lot here? Who's your prime suspect?'

Mark groaned. 'No one, to tell you the truth. I can't see

any of them luring Emma to a fatal rendezvous. Although I'm beginning to have my doubts about Osborne.'

'You're not serious. He'd be hard pressed to lift a sack of flour, let alone a fully-grown female.'

'Yes, but you must admit that he is the least likely, which, in itself, is suspicious.'

Kendrick looked heavenwards. 'This is ridiculous.'

'Yes.'

'Will you rule out Mr Osborne if we can prove he lacks the physical strength?'

'Gladly. He's a nice fellow.'

After dinner, Kendrick strolled over to Osborne who sat alone in a corner. 'I see you're the only one not playing at darts tonight.'

'Hopeless aim, I'm afraid,' said Osborne. 'It's not my idea of fun anyway. I'd much rather go outside and watch the night sky. It's been a while since I saw the North Star, and this is the first cloudless night in almost a fortnight.'

'Why don't you go, then?'

'Don't you remember, Mr Kendrick? Captain Moore forbade anyone to venture out on deck alone.' He shuddered. 'It makes my blood run cold to think of that poor girl.'

Kendrick gave him a pat on the back. 'If you wish, I'll join you, and maybe we could entice Doctor Bryson here to accompany us? That should ensure that none of us gets pitched over board.'

'Thanks. I'll get my overcoat.'

The stars cast their icy light across the becalmed sea. Waves broke the reflection at odd angles, causing the light to dance as if to the sounds of an orchestra only they could hear. The wind had dropped to a mere hum and the water lapped against the bow.

'Beautiful, isn't it?' Osborne pointed towards a constellation that shone like cut gemstones on black velvet. 'Sirius, the dog star.' He pulled his coat tighter around his throat. 'I'd almost forgotten how cold it can get on this side of the world. And how magnificent the northern sky is. Look.' He pointed towards another constellation. 'The North Star.'

'Every sailor's friend, the most beautiful sight when you're navigating in these waters,' Kendrick said. 'Which reminds me, there's a portable telescope on board, if you'd like to use it?'

'Do you?' Osborne's face shone with eagerness. 'I'd appreciate that if it isn't too much trouble.'

'None at all. Come along, and we'll get it.'

Mark followed them without a word, curious where this was leading.

Kendrick took them to a small storage room between his and the captain's quarters. He flung open the doors of a weathered cupboard, revealing a brass telescope sitting on top of unused ledgers. A gleaming sextant sat on the other side of a dividing partition. The rest of the cupboard was empty.

Kendrick pulled the telescope towards him. 'It's heavy, I'm afraid. Almost a hundredweight.'

Osborne took hold of the instrument. His knees nearly buckled under the weight. Kendrick grasped the metal tube to steady it.

'We'd better carry it between us,' he said. 'If both of you could just hold it for a moment while I lock the cupboard.'

They spent a long time engrossed in the stars. Osborne lost all traces of shyness when asked about the firmament.

Mark shook his head in amazement. 'First your immense knowledge of wildlife, and now astronomy. You are a man of many parts, Mr Osborne.'

'A man must have an interest, Doctor, something to occupy his mind, and there is no finer place in Melbourne than a porch on a summer night, where you sit and watch the sky fill with countless lights, glittering like glow-worms.' He stepped back from the telescope, making way for Mark. 'You should try astronomy, Doctor. You'd be astonished how soothing it is to sit and gaze. There's nothing better to take your mind off trouble.' He rubbed his chilled hands together. 'When my fiancée succumbed to a fever, three weeks from our wedding, I spent whole nights staring at the stars and looking for answers.' He blinked.

'I'm sorry,' said Kendrick. 'Mind you, the captain would have me demoted if I should simply gaze at them, the way you prescribed, Mr Osborne. But I appreciate their beauty as well as their usefulness and reliability. The stars don't lie, gentlemen.'

'Indeed,' said Osborne, shivering a little.

Kendrick said, 'We'd better call it a night. It is getting chilly, and we don't want to cause you unnecessary work, Doctor.'

Mark and Kendrick sat in Mark's quarters, with a drink in their hands. 'I believe he didn't feign weakness when he handled the telescope, you?' Mark asked.

'I was just in time to prevent the instrument crashing down on his feet.'

'That clears Osborne. I'm glad.'

Kendrick nursed the glass in his hands. 'One down, four more to go. Any ideas?'

'Parsons is an unlikely candidate. If anything, he has declared a partiality for Miss Chalmers, and no one else. But if you ask me, he's more interested in your precious steam engine than in anything else.'

'But he's strong, has a logical mind and can be forceful. I can imagine he could be ruthless enough if it suits him.' Kendrick took a sip.

'The big question is, would he have been able to make the acquaintance of Miss Sayce to an extent that she'd agree to meet him?' Mark said.

'Who can say what makes one man more attractive to a female than another man?'

'Apart from money and position, you mean?' Mark thought of the bosun and cook, united in their admiration for Emma Sayce.

'Apart from that.' Kendrick emptied his glass and stifled a yawn. 'We'll have to ask Miss Chalmers about that when she comes to the surgery to see us again. She should know.'

Alyssa was surprised by the question, but, Mark thought, at least she refrained from demonstrating over sensibility; a point in her favour.

'I think what Emma was looking for chiefly was someone she could rely on, someone who'd protect her and take care of her, a knight in shining armour. She'd been orphaned at an early age, if you remember, and she was of a romantic disposition.'

'Someone to lean on,' Mark said.

'And he'd have to have strength of character, and a winning manner.'

'Which fits – whom of our suspects?' Kendrick ran the men through in his mind.

'Mr Turnbull,' she said without hesitation. 'And Mr Harris, maybe.'

'What about the other two, Parsons and Dawkes?' Mark asked.

'Mr Parsons?' Miss Chalmers stifled a smile. 'I'm convinced the only soft emotion he ever had was for all things mechanical. Louisa Jane still almost faints when she remembers how he bore down on her the day we were found out. He is a worthy gentleman but I doubt Emma would have detected any finer feelings in him.'

Kendrick broke into a grin. She coloured slightly. 'I beg your pardon.'

'There's no need to excuse yourself for your words,' Kendrick said. 'We three have become too good friends to stand on ceremony and missish behaviour, I hope.'

'Indeed,' Mark said, 'but I believe Miss Chalmers hadn't finished yet. Pray, go on.'

'It is simply that I cannot imagine someone like Mr Parsons deceiving everyone enough to further Emma's acquaintance without any of you noticing.'

'And our dandy Dawkes?' Mark watched her. 'I'd imagine him to be a firm favourite with the ladies, with his easy manner.'

'Which is why I would rule him out,' she said. 'Surely none of us girls could be led to believe that someone as handsome and well-born would stoop to look at us twice.'

'He's a likeable fellow, but I can't see him exerting himself,' Kendrick agreed. 'He's the type who'd pinch a pretty maid's chin, if you pardon my language, but not more.'

Alyssa said, 'Don't curb your tongue on my behalf. Like you said, there is no need to stand on missish behaviour.'

Kendrick put his hand on hers for a breath. 'Good girl.'

His gaze followed her as she left the room, gently swaying with the rolling ship. 'She's a game one,' he said.

'Miss Chalmers? Yes, you said so before. So, it appears Turnbull is our most likely candidate. What shall we do to determine his guilt?'

They retired to Mark's quarters to ponder the question. He opened the door of his desk, taking out a near-empty whisky bottle. He gazed at it wistfully.

'How likely do you reckon it that we'll get to the bottom of the truth before we've come to the bottom of this one?'

'There's only one way to find out. Thankfully I have something at least as inspirational stowed away in my room.' He kissed his fingertips. 'A reminder of home, my friend. A single malt from the beautiful Isle of Jura. That's in Scotland for your information.'

Mark suspended the bottle in mid-air before he commenced pouring. 'You've held that secret from me? After all the drinks I've plied you with?'

'It's only one bottle,' Kendrick said. 'I've saved it for a special occasion.'

'Like what?'

Kendrick sipped his drink. 'A solved murder, perhaps. Or an engagement.'

Mark sputtered as his drink went down the wrong way. 'What engagement?'

Kendrick traced the rim of the tumbler with his finger. 'I thought we'd agreed that there is some romance in the air.'

Mark opened his mouth, only to snap it shut.

Kendrick drained his glass. 'I'll lay you odds of two to one that Matron McKenzie will be called by a different name before too long.' He pushed himself to his feet. 'Are you coming, Doctor? The captain did agree to another game of quoits.'

## CHAPTER 22

Mark kept an unobtrusive watch on Turnbull. He'd never noticed it before, but the man was certainly attractive to some of the females, judging by the coy glances that followed him when he flung his quoits.

Mark drummed his fingertips on the rail. His gaze flickered towards Miss Chalmers, who stood with her back turned to him, helping Kendrick to keep score. They seemed to whisper. Mark strained his ears to hear what it was, a task that proved impossible because of the shrieking gulls that circled the ship.

He strode towards them. 'Anything interesting?' he asked.

'Mr Kendrick was kind enough to explain to me some of the finer points of this sport.'

Kendrick gave him an amused look. 'It does help with your game plan if you have an inkling of what you're doing, you know. Like he does.'

He nodded towards Turnbull, who also held forth to a handful of rapt girls. He was a well-made fellow, Mark had to admit, with broad shoulders, a relaxed air of authority and a ready smile which he bestowed on the blushing girls. Yes, it would have been easy to see a girl like Emma, who had only youth and beauty to offer, being charmed by a man like that.

He wondered what had happened that fatal night. Had Turnbull been slightly intoxicated, finding it impossible to restrain himself in the presence of Emma Sayce? He displayed a placid temper in public but Mark suspected him to be capable of an impressive rage and passion.

'Are you daydreaming, Doctor?' Harris handed Mark a set of quoits.

'Something like that. Blowing the cobwebs off my brain.' He shaded his eyes from the glaring sun.

'You work too much,' Harris said. 'As do you, Mr Kendrick, and the young Miss. There's a time for everything, and now is the time to play.' He shooed them forwards. 'Make way for the doctor and his able assistants,' he said, winking at Milly and Hannah who made up his team. They giggled in return.

Mark found himself surprised. He'd never noticed Harris to be susceptible to female charms. He flung his quoits with a lack of aim mirroring his state of mind.

'Bad luck,' Turnbull said as Mark's throws missed by a considerable width. 'Maybe your partners can make up for it.'

'But not today. The weather's fast turning,' Kendrick said. Angry clouds pushed their way across the horizon and the crests on top of the waves grew higher. 'It's time to pack up and head inside.'

～

Alyssa found herself getting restless as soon as dinner was over. If only she could come up with a reasonable excuse to head towards the surgery. She missed the easy rapport with Mr Kendrick and, increasingly, the doctor, once he forgot to tease her. Most of all she missed the sense of, strangely, the freedom and comfort their company gave her.

Matron put a hand on Alyssa's arm. 'You'll tear your pretty shawl if you go on pulling its fringes like that.' She lowered her voice. 'I hope nothing has happened to upset you? I realise that you were forced to spend considerable time with Doctor Bryson and Mr Kendrick … But Mr Wainwright promised me I could rest easy about that.' Her left eyelid began to twitch.

'You don't have anything to worry about, Madam. They both conducted themselves as the gentlemen they are.' Alyssa sighed. 'It's only that one does get a trifle bored with being confined for such a long period.'

'Bored?' Nancy's mouth formed a wide circle. 'But there's always something happening here.' She opened her hands. 'Look at us, we've got hardly any hard work to do, and we've got lovely grub and schooling and lessons on how to be a good housewife, and then there's pudding and games.'

'Yeah,' Nellie said. 'If that's boredom for you, I don't mind that. Or more of your sweets. And don't forget as you said you'd teach us how to cook 'em. That'll take your mind off things.' She winked. 'Nothing better than a sweet to catch yourself a honey.'

'You forget yourself, Nellie,' Matron said. 'And as for your shameless begging ...'

'She was only making a bit of fun,' Alyssa said. She grinned at Nellie. 'If Matron says yes, I'll get the second tin for all of us to share, and then we can ask Nancy to tell us how to make that boiled thimble mill pudding we had when cook was indisposed. I can still taste it.'

'It was lovely,' Nancy said. 'But it was Emma who cooked it, not me.'

'But surely you watched her prepare it.'

Nancy shook her head. 'The galley's that small, I sat in the pantry most of the time, peeling spuds and onions and stuff.' She dug her teeth into her lower lip, looking like a startled rabbit.

'Much easier that way,' Alyssa said, reassuring Nancy. 'As long as you were close enough to give Emma a hand with those heavy pots.'

'I didn't have to. You ain't never been on galley duty, right, what with you teaching all these lessons instead.' She grimaced. 'No matter when we only had to do our own cooking, cook always came along to do the lifting. He was ever so nice because it was that hard to keep on our feet with all this rolling going on, without hauling pots around. I got knocked around a fair bit.'

Nancy frowned. 'And I reckon cook sent someone else along when he was too bad. Leastways, I did hear voices a couple of times when we cooked tea.'

Alyssa held her breath.

'Shame,' Nellie said. 'No pudding for us, eh? I reckon we'll have to make do with Alyssa's sweets.'

Matron clucked her tongue in a mild reproach, but Alyssa's spirit lifted. Good old Nellie, she'd said exactly what Alyssa had hoped for. She made straight for the door. 'Another tin coming up,' she said. 'That is, with your permission, Matron? I'll be fine without escort.'

'You may go, but only this once.'

Alyssa drummed on the surgery door. 'Quick,' she said, as Mark opened. 'Can you take me to the storage room, please? I've got permission to fetch something.'

'Sure.' He took the lantern and followed her.

When they entered the storage room, he handed her the lantern and shut the door storage room behind them, wedging a convenient oar under the handle to prevent anyone from disturbing them.

'Well, Miss Chalmers?'

She knelt to fling open her trunk, with a casual disregard for the dust and grease that covered the floorboards. 'Have a lemon drop,' she said. 'And listen to this.'

It took so little time to recount what Nancy had said that the doctor had to push the sweet with the tongue into the pouch of his cheek to be able to speak. 'All we need to do is make sure it was Turnbull who visited Emma in the galley.'

'Yes. Once we've established that he had the opportunity, we'll know. That is, we should better establish the whereabouts of all our suspects during those crucial times.' She pressed the tin to her chest. 'Are you certain you're up to the task?'

He swallowed the remains of the sticky lump. 'You're not the only one who can handle a challenge.'

'I know,' she said, surprising them both. 'I believe in you.'

All he needed to do now was to fulfil her expectations. Mark rubbed his chin, feeling the tiny pricks of the first stubble. He'd have to shave before dinner. In the middle of nowhere they still observed the niceties of society. Well, after all they did have the leisure to retire to their quarters and fuss with their attire. Some of the men spent ages on their appearance. A new thought formed itself… did they really?

Mark whistled as he sharpened his knife on the leather strap. He peered into the mirror, turning his head from side to side as he methodically removed inch by inch the foam that covered his chin. He touched his cheek when he was finished; smooth as silk. Not even Dawkes and Kendrick, with their fastidious grooming, could rival this.

He glanced at his fob-watch. Ten minutes for a wash and a shave, plus at least another ten minutes to change his garments. If Turnbull had taken leave of absence from the delights of the saloon or the deck for much longer than that before dinner on the days in question, he could very well have slipped into the galley to seduce the girl.

Everyone else was already in the saloon as he entered the room.

Osborne hailed him with a wave of his hand, unusual behaviour for that shy fellow.

'You wanted to talk to me?' Mark said.

'Indeed, Doctor. I can't help but notice that some of the young ladies appear strained, especially Miss Chalmers. I've been wondering if they work too hard?'

'What a considerate fellow you are,' Dawkes said. 'It does you credit but remember, these aren't some delicate British flowers but some pretty rough gals bred for an equally rough country, charming as they are.'

He gave an exaggerated shudder. 'I'll never forget the hardships I was forced to endure in Australia. Don't you agree, gentlemen?'

Turnbull said, 'Not for you the call of the wild, then? What about you, Doctor?'

'I can't say that I'll miss shaking out my boots before I put them on in case they hold a venomous guest,' Mark said, 'but personally, I found the country fascinating. There is something about those people, especially on the gold fields, you wouldn't expect. They've got their own code of honour they stick to no matter what, which is more than I can say about some of the gents in our so-called civilisation.'

He smiled at the memory. 'I shall miss that, and the easy camaraderie you encounter once you've proven your worth.'

'But still you're going home.'

'Of necessity, Mr Turnbull. I go where I'm needed most, and that is, unfortunately, as a field surgeon on the battlefields of my own country.'

'I almost forgot,' Turnbull said. 'Please excuse my obtuseness.'

'Don't think of it. But to answer your question, Mr Osborne, rest assured that the ladies all appeared hale and hearty at the morning muster. As Mr Dawkes said, your concern does you credit, but there is nothing to worry about.'

'Would you care to join me for a stroll, Doctor? It's a nice light breeze outside.' Kendrick asked after dinner.

'Gladly,' Mark said.

'Davies, we'd like two cups of coffee please. You'll

find us in the shelter on the poop deck.'

The boy carried the steaming mugs as carefully as if they were eggshells, a tray clamped under his arm. His skin glistened with spray.

'Thank you,' Mark said, watching the boy sway in rhythm with the ship's movements. 'I'm sorry we make a lot of work.'

Davies shrugged. 'You're easy, Sir. It's the other gentlemen which make things a bit tricky, like. If you pardon me saying that, Sir.'

Kendrick waved Davies' apology aside. 'Is there anyone in particular? Or rather, anything? Maybe we could mend our ways.'

'No, Sir, it's just that sometimes some of the gentlemen are cutting it a bit fine like, for dinner, and I have to make sure I'll get it all on the table while it's still hot. And sometimes they all want a bath at the same time, with only me to lug gallons of hot water.'

Kendrick's eyebrows rose an inch. 'I should have thought about that, Davies. My only excuse is that we've never had to cater for a load of fine gentlemen before. We'll make sure we get a few men to give you a hand with that. And we'll ask for more punctuality at meal times. Is there anyone especially tardy? Except for the doctor and me, of course. But that comes under the call of duty.'

'You ain't telling the captain that I said anything, Sir?'

'I give you my word. Dr Bryson and I both do.'

Davies' shoulders relaxed. 'Mostly it's Mr Turnbull

and Mr Dawkes, Sir. Sometimes it's Mr Parsons as well, but seeing as he likes to have a yarn with the engineers, that's only natural, I s'pose.'

Kendrick emptied his mug and put it on the tray, hiding his excitement. 'I'll take care of it, Davies. Now you run along and see that you finish for today.'

'That was quite an interesting conversation, don't you think, Doctor?'

Mark said, 'It's not exactly proof, is it?'

'Not quite, but it should certainly warrant having a quiet word with our friend Osborne.'

'I thought we'd agreed that he's not a suspect.'

Kendrick said, 'Which makes him the perfect man to ask about the habits of the other passengers. Especially since he, for one, shows marked concern for the well-being of others whose lot in life is less happy than his. The only problem is having a word with him alone.'

For once fortune favoured them. Osborne, on waking in the morning, found himself coughing persistently. Only the best interests of his fellow passengers could prevail on him to add to the doctor's burden, and at such an early hour, he apologised as he knocked on Mark's door.

Mark flung off his dressing gown. 'You were perfectly right in doing so, Mr Osborne. If you'll go straight to the surgery, I won't be more than a couple of minutes.'

'Thank you, Doctor.'

Mark hummed to himself as he got dressed.

True to his word, Osborne waited for him.

'You've got a reddened throat, but the lungs are clear,' Mark said after a thorough examination. 'If you take to your bunk for a day or two and get plenty of rest, you'll be in stout health in no time at all. I'll make up a solution for you to rinse your mouth with.'

'I'm much obliged, Doctor.' Osborne coughed into his hands. 'I wouldn't want to spread any infection or cause any other unnecessary trouble.'

'Most commendable. I wish all the men on board were as considerate.' He shook his head in obvious resignation.

Osborne looked surprised.

'I could be mistaken of course,' Mark said, 'but it seemed to me that it would make life for the crew easier if, say, everyone would be in the salon with ample time to spare before the meals are being served. Davies sometimes has to run himself ragged to get his chores done in a proper fashion.'

Osborne nodded. He himself made sure he'd be in the saloon with a book to read or his notebook in which he tried his hand at capturing the life on board, he said – here he coloured slightly, as if admitting a guilty secret – but usually he was there on his own for at least half an hour. Harris also tended to be prompt, and Parsons only rarely came rushing in.

'The captain is not to know,' Osborne said, 'but it seems the engineers are in the habit of calling him when there is some trouble with the steam engine.' He clucked his tongue. 'And of course, Mr Turnbull and Mr Dawkes tend to disregard their watches, although not quite as much of late. I can't approve of tardiness myself, but I am sure they will have a good reason.' He coughed again.

'I'm sorry,' Mark said. 'I shall not keep you any longer. I'll make up the mouthwash as soon as possible and have it sent to you.' They were right after all, he thought. He should feel elated, but instead, a sick taste crept into his mouth. He'd had no trouble casting the hulking stoker who now was awaiting his dismissal in the solitude of a makeshift cell in the role of villain, but dammit, he'd liked Turnbull. They had been through the storm together, when they thought their last hour had come. They had shared jokes and drinks. To unmask him as a ruthless seducer and murderer was a task he dreaded more than anything, and if he knew Kendrick, his friend would share this sentiment.

~

Mark had a hard time facing Turnbull at lunch. He marvelled at the sanguinity of the man, putting on an untroubled air when his guilt must have weighed him down. What an actor that man would have made.

Or would he? Thinking back, wasn't there a hint of a guilty conscience in the excuses he'd heard Turnbull make over belated appearances? How many games of chess had he really played with the captain?

Mark pushed back his chair. He'd go and see Kendrick, who had excused himself with important duties, to decide on which course to take. Sooner or later they'd have to confront Captain Moore with their deductions, and let him come to terms with the fact that his favourite passenger had Emma's blood on his hands.

He found Kendrick in the office, poring over nautical charts. Mark folded his hands in his laps and waited until his friend looked up.

'Not much longer to go until San Francisco,' Kendrick said. 'The ship has made excellent progress, under sails as well as under steam. The captain will be pleased to see how far a ton of coal can take us.'

'That is about the only thing that might cheer him up. I had a chat with Osborne, and he pretty much confirmed our suspicions. When shall we tax Captain Moore with the truth?'

Kendrick fiddled with the sextant. 'If only we had better proof. Turnbull is the only passenger the captain has taken a profound liking to. We all did. He seemed such a decent fellow.'

'That's probably what Emma Sayce thought too,' Mark said.

'We'd better go see the captain.'

'Impossible.' Captain Moore's voice could have sliced through flint. 'Have you completely taken leave of your senses, Mr Kendrick? As for you, Doctor Bryson, I shall say nothing about your utter lack of authority on my ship.'

'Sir, with all due respect,' said Kendrick, 'we have considered every possibility, and circumstances point directly at Mr Turnbull.'

The colour of Moore's face changed from purple to white. 'What circumstances are you talking of, mister? You'd better make your explanation a good one.'

He listened closely, disbelief changing to incredulity clearly showing on his face. 'You're mad,' he said, when Kendrick had ended. 'I wouldn't let a dog swing from the yardarm with this kind of evidence.' He narrowed his eyes. 'That meddlesome girl put you up to it, didn't she? Young Alice whatshername?'

'Alyssa Chalmers,' Mark said.

Moore ignored him. 'I've shown that girl more consideration than she deserved, Mr Kendrick, due to her services during our time of need, but blackening the name of a gentlemen and corrupting my own first officer, that goes too far. Davies!'

The boy came running.

'Go and fetch Ella Chalmers. Hurry!'

'Alyssa,' Mark said under his breath. 'The name is Alyssa.'

'I don't care what her name is. She'll be taxed with her outrageous lies, and then we'll see.'

'You seem convinced of Mr Turnbull's innocence, Sir.'

'I am sure of it, Mr Kendrick. The only thing I am no longer convinced of is of your good sense.'

Davies ushered Alyssa into the room with all the speed he could muster.

Moore took two steps closer, until he was an arm's length away from her, glowering at her in a silence used to beat subalterns into submission.

Alyssa folded her arms behind her back. Kendrick coughed. She turned towards him, relaxing her posture slightly. Mark tried to melt into the background.

'Captain,' Kendrick said, 'maybe you ought to inform Miss Chalmers what you want to talk to her about.'

Captain Moore slapped the gloves he'd taken off in his hand. 'Indeed, Mr Kendrick. You, young lady, have the impudence to accuse my friend, Mr Turnbull, of a heinous crime.'

'Sir?'

The vein in Captain Moore's throat began to throb.

'Don't deny it, Miss Chalmers. You put these two men up to it, which amounts the same.'

She looked straight at him. 'Let me say this. If you mean to say that Mr Kendrick and Dr Bryson did their best to help me see that Emma Sayce's death does not go unavenged, yes, Sir, then I am guilty as charged. But as for accusing Mr Turnbull, you told us yourself that you are the law on board this ship. And I'd rather apologise a thousand-fold to someone wrongly suspected than let a cold-blooded murderer escape justice.' Pain clouded her eyes. 'I am sure you would have done the same in our stead. Every ounce of integrity and moral fibre would demand it.'

He stared at her. A number of expressions chased each other on his face. Indignation gave way to thoughtfulness, and finally something that resembled grudging respect. 'You seem, at least, to have the courage of your conviction, young lady, misguided as you are.'

Kendrick said, 'If we have been mistaken, Sir, we all three must share the blame. But how can you be so sure that Mr Turnbull did not lay a finger on Emma Sayce?'

Moore thumped his fist on the top of his desk. 'Because, Mr Kendrick, he spent most of the time you suspected him of dallying with that unfortunate girl here with me, in my cabin. What's more, he spent it working out ways to amuse the wenches and make their life a bit more comfortable.'

'Are you sure, Sir?' Mark asked.

'If you don't believe me, take a peek at this.' Moore

took a piece of foolscap covered with notes out of a drawer. 'Mr Turnbull has, with my assistance, tried his hands at planning a concert and writing a play to be performed on our way to Canada. This is the list of possible actors, Doctor. As you see, your name appears, as does Mr Kendrick's. You, Doctor, were aptly cast as a comedian. Now if you'll excuse me, I've more important things to do than to listen to your nonsense. And don't forget to restore Miss Chalmers to her rightful place and make sure she stays there. Good day.'

# CHAPTER 24

'Two more days until San Francisco,' Mark said as they stood on the deck. Already the atmosphere felt changed. Gannets dived into the water, emerging with a salmon in their beak. Kittiwakes drew lazy circles in the air. The sailors swarmed up and down the masts with renewed vigour, no doubt anxious to make landfall as soon as possible.

Mark doubted there'd be more than half a dozen of them still sensible at the end of their shore leave. Drink and female company, coupled with a few dollars in their pockets, would see to that.

Not that he intended to judge them. The men had shown remarkable discipline since they set off from Melbourne. He only wished he could be as carefree; or the girl at his side. Alyssa looked haggard. He had hoped that a breath of the salty air would refresh her after the confrontation with the captain, but in vain. That, on top of a long voyage and the unsolved mystery of Emma Sayce's disappearance, had sapped the fight out of her. It disconcerted Mark to see her sudden stillness, when she used to vibrate with emotions.

He felt an impulse to grab her and shake her back to her old self, infuriating and troublesome as it was. Instead he stood beside her and stared at the horizon. 'It feels like a lifetime has passed since we started on this voyage.'

She took a quarter turn, to face him. The sun cast a glow over her, putting the dark shadows under her eyes into sharp relief. 'You're almost home, aren't you, Doctor?'

'That would stretch it a bit, but, yes. San Francisco, then Port Victoria, and onwards towards the battlefields by whatever means.'

He clasped the rail harder. 'God knows I don't want to go there, and it might not make a difference at all. But one has to try. Too many men have died already in the name of bloody glory, leaving only grief, memories, and if they number among the lucky few, they'll receive a footnote in the history books.'

'Yes,' she said. 'That's what it all comes down to in the end, isn't it?' Her voice was drained of emotion. 'But that's still more than Emma will ever get. I've failed her.'

This time he gave in to impulse and touched her hand. 'We won't give up. I promised you, remember?'

She finally looked up, turning her head just enough to lock eyes with him. There was sadness in her eyes, but Mark saw also something else. It was trust and warmth.

'I promised,' he said again, his hand still covering hers on the rail.

'Dr Bryson?'

Mark let go of Alyssa as unobtrusively as he could. 'Yes, Davies?'

'Mr Kendrick wants to see you in his quarters,' the boy said, his voice pitching. 'And I wanted to ask you something as well, Sir.' Even his ears obtained a pink flush, Mark noticed. The boy was obviously embarrassed by his own boldness.

'Don't mind me, Davies,' Alyssa said with a small smile.

'Yes, miss. Only you did say as you'd show me San Francisco, Sir, and them heathen temples, Sir. You haven't forgotten that, have you, Sir?'

'You bet I haven't,' Mark said. 'Not that I would encourage you to take a gamble, of course.'

The boy grinned until every single one of his teeth was on display. 'No, Sir, and speaking of gambling, Sir, and miss, just a word to the wise, as you might say.'

He hushed his voice. 'Mr Dawkes is going around, taking wagers on that game the gentlemen are always playing.' He rubbed forefinger and thumb together in a suggestive manner.

'But the captain said there was to be no book making.'

'He would, Captain Moore would. But that's only half

of it.' Davies' eyes bulged. 'Them bets are rigged, Sir. There's no way Mr Dawkes could lose, with him sneaking in and out of the galley all the time, greasing Cook's hand. It's not what you'd expect from a fine gentleman, would you?'

Alyssa drew her breath in sharp enough to make a hissing sound. 'Indeed not. Since when has he been up to tricks, Davies?'

'Since Cook was crook and the ladies took over, I think. At least that's when I started seeing him creeping into the galley.' He clapped a hand over his mouth. 'Not meaning to be disrespectful, Sir, I only thought you might want to know.'

'Yes, Davies. You've done the right thing, thank you. And I think I'll now see Mr Kendrick.'

Mark took Alyssa's arm. 'You'd better come along as well, in case it's a medical issue and we need another pair of hands.'

Kendrick locked the door behind them.

'We don't want to be disturbed,' he said. 'You two better take a seat. And a brandy.' He pointed at here already filled glasses.

Alyssa sat down as bid while Mark leaned against the wall. 'We've got something to tell you as well, my friend, but you go first.'

'I had an interesting conversation with Bates. That's

the stoker who lost his head over Rosie's charms, Miss Chalmers.' He raked through his hair. 'I only wanted to make sure that he'd be in a fit state to leave us in San Francisco when he accused the captain of having different set of rules for the toffs and poor working blokes like him.'

'He'd seen someone,' Mark said.

'Yes. Not on the night in question, but one or two days before, on his way to meet the fair Rosie he'd encountered a well-dressed man wearing evening dress and a scarlet scarf murmuring something in the ear of a female. He couldn't say who, because the girl's face was hidden and he didn't want to draw attention to himself, but I think we know who it was.'

He paused. 'We have been wrong before of course, but this time I don't think so.'

'No,' Alyssa said. 'It's Mr Dawkes, isn't it, the man with the scarlet scarf. Dr Bryson and I already knew. That's what we came to tell you.'

'Edward Dawkes III,' Kendrick said, watching the light reflected in the crystal of his glass and the amber liquid.

Mark expelled the air from his lungs. He'd hardly noticed he'd held his breath. 'We've got him now.'

'Not yet,' Kendrick said. 'We've got no body, we've got no proof, and I'll be darned if I know how to nail the bastard. Excuse my language, Miss Chalmers, but there it is. It's the only way to protect the other girls. He is a very clever man, and simply exposing him as a cheat won't be enough.'

'We haven't any proof - yet,' she said. 'We'd better go and get it. Before we reach port.'

Both men stared at her in disbelief. Kendrick recovered slightly faster than Mark. 'How shall we do that?'

'We'll have to take him by surprise. Offer him another female to prey on.'

The blood drained from Mark's face as the meaning of her words sank in. 'You intend to be the bait. Are you mad? That man is a ruthless killer, and you expect him to let you live?'

'There is an element of risk involved,' she said. 'But I trust in you and Mr Kendrick to keep me safe.'

'No.' Mark's voice caught in his throat. 'We can't let you do that. Kendrick, say something. Clap her in irons if you have to, but don't allow her to carry out this hare-brained scheme.'

'Believe me I would if I saw any chance of stopping Miss Chalmers. But I know when I'm defeated, Doctor. The only thing we can do is try to come up with ways to keep her safe from harm.'

'Good man,' she said in a slightly unsteady voice. 'Together we can't fail.'

Despite her brave words sleep eluded Alyssa. While her companions filled the night air with snores and snuffles, she had a hard time stifling whimpers. Courage in the presence of two men intent on protecting her was one thing but here in her bunk her own imagination became the enemy.

Alyssa huddled under her blanket. She'd thought of everything she could, but any number of things might go wrong. She'd be a fool not to be afraid of what the evening would bring.

Mark poured himself another nightcap. Long past midnight and still sleep seemed impossible. If only he could come up with a reason to stop her. If only he could come up with an excuse why he should be the one to carry out the crazy scheme she'd concocted. For one whit, he'd tell her to let matters rest; Emma Sayce was long since beyond help. But he couldn't.

He downed the drink in two gulps, forcing himself not to smash the empty glass against the wall. It would be a long night and a longer day.

Ten minutes until afternoon tea would be served in the saloon. Or rather tea, coffee and – Mark wrinkled his nose in distaste – sweet sherry.

He cast a quick glance towards the empty passage before he produced a small phial he'd kept hidden in his waistcoat. The sherry already stood decanted. Mark pulled the stopper off the phial. Ten drops should do the trick. Enough to create queasiness, but too little to cause real discomfort. The last thing he wanted was for Dawkes to take to his bed straight away.

He glanced at his watch. Five minutes. It would take about half an hour for the drops to take effect; and in less than two hours the symptoms should be a dim memory.

Only Osborne, Dawkes, and Kendrick helped themselves to the sherry. Mark's admiration for his friend grew as he saw him refill his glass. As if it wasn't bad enough that Kendrick had to drink with obvious relish a liqueur he detested, he also knew what lay in store for him. Still, it was the best scheme their combined intelligence had produced.

Osborne gave way first. He stumbled out of the saloon, sweat forming on his forehead.

'What's the matter with him?' Harris asked as the small man brushed past him. 'The sea isn't that rough today. Can't be another bout of seasickness.'

Dawkes' hand travelled to his stomach. 'Excuse me, gentlemen.'

Kendrick followed suit, as Dawkes hurried towards the deck.

Mark feigned concern. 'Do any of you feel in need of my attention, gentlemen? Otherwise I'd deem it wise to offer my services to our newly absent friends. Or shall I ask Matron to look after you?'

'Nonsense, man,' Turnbull said. 'We don't need a nanny.'

Kendrick did not show up for dinner. Captain Moore had frowned at the unexplained absence of his first officer but refrained from saying anything.

The soup course was already under way, when Davies rushed in. 'Please, Sir,' he said to Mark. 'If you could please see to Mr Kendrick?'

'What is it, Davies?' Moore asked.

The boy saluted. 'It's Mr Kendrick, Captain. He sends his regards, Sir, on account of his being crook.'

Mark threw down his napkin. 'With your permission, Captain, I'll see to him at once. That is ...'

'Yes, Doctor?'

'How do you feel, Mr Osborne, Mr Dawkes? Fully restored? Otherwise I'd like to make sure that you have a restorative at hand should you need it.'

'Good idea, but you run along now and see to Mr Kendrick,' the captain said. 'You go with him, Davies, and keep me informed.'

Davies knocked at Kendrick's door. 'It's the doctor, Sir.'

Mark took a step back as he saw his ally. Kendrick's hair was dishevelled, and dark shadows accentuated the pallor of his skin. A dressing gown instead of the uniform was the last proof needed that this was a very sick man indeed.

'Davies, I need you to run to Matron and ask her to spare me Miss Chalmers. Take her to my surgery to pick up my black bag and then bring her here. And tell the captain that Mr Kendrick is bedridden.'

Alyssa's eyes widened as she looked at Mr Kendrick.

He grinned. 'Satisfied? I'm quite proud of my handiwork, if I may admit it.' He ran his hand through his hair again. 'Amazing what a bit of talcum powder and some soot will do for you.'

Alyssa managed a small smile. 'You really had me worried for a moment, Mr Kendrick.'

He winked at her. 'It's you we should dworry about, my dear. The only things that get us in my family are accidents or old age. I intend to opt for the latter, and I'll make sure the same goes for you. We both will. Won't we, doctor?'

'Yes,' he said, taking Alyssa by the shoulders. 'There's still time to change your mind, my dear.'

He'd never called her that before. Alyssa's pulse fluttered for a second as she shook her head.

They crept along the passageway, with Alyssa and the doctor supporting Mr Kendrick in case someone saw them. A perfunctory knock at Dawkes's door went unanswered. Mr Kendrick inserted a key from the ring he'd kept hidden in his dressing gown pocket and unlocked Dawkes' quarters. As quiet as a cat stalking a mouse, he slipped behind the painted screen and unlocked the door to a built-in storage space that was masked by the wooden panelling. 'Come along, Doctor.'

Alyssa was alone. Her hands felt clammy. What if her plan failed?

The ship lurched. She put a hand on the desk to steady herself, inadvertently dislodging two books. They fell on the floor. She blushed as her eyes fell on the detailed drawings of a delicate nature that graced the pages of the first book. She laid it on the desk and lifted the second book by its spine. A letter fell out.

She was putting it back in its old place when two words caught her attention. Every other thought went out of her head as she began to read.

'Oh my god,' she whispered as the full meaning of the letter dawned on her.

'What the hell are you doing?'

Alyssa gave a start. She'd been so focussed she hadn't heard the door open.

Her lips were dry as parchment as she said, as primly as she could, 'Please, Sir, the doctor sends you this tonic. He couldn't attend to it himself, because he is still with Mr Kendrick.'

She took the bottle she'd put onto the desk and offered it to Mr Dawkes.

'And how do you explain the letter you're holding?'

Alyssa kept her lids lowered so she could observe him unnoticed through her lashes. 'I'm so sorry, Sir,' she said in a clear voice, 'but I swept it accidentally off the desk when I put the tonic there so I had to pick it up.'

'Did you indeed?' His smile was amused but his eyes were blank. They chilled her. He took the letter and tapped his fingers against it.

'I do wonder, Miss Chalmers, I wonder indeed. You see, I had hoped that you, among all these simpering little geese, were possessed of some breeding.'

He clucked his tongue, displaying a curious mix of distaste and amusement. 'You disappoint me deeply, you know. Intruding on my privacy, reading my private letters. You really shouldn't have done that. Shame, but there it is.'

He moved closer, taking off his gloves as he did so. 'Of course, I knew you weren't a real lady as soon as I set eyes on you. I didn't have to be told that your father made himself common with those murderous brutes you breed in Australia. No wonder no man would have you after that, except maybe for a bit of fun on the side.'

She recoiled. 'If you mean that my father did show compassion for some of the men on the prison hulks, it's true and I'm proud of him. But I wouldn't expect someone like you to understand.'

Her voice rang loud enough in her ears to make itself heard over the drumbeat of her heart. 'Tell me, did Emma read your letters as well? Was that why you killed her?'

Dawkes halted in his step. 'Nothing quite so dramatic, my dear. Although, if you hadn't taught the little pea-goose how to read, encouraging her to get ideas above her station, she might still be with us today.'

'What happened?'

'What happened indeed? What a nosey girl you are. And in case you are wondering, don't bother to scream. My hands would be around your throat before you could cry out.'

He threw his gloves on the bed and stretched his fingers one after the other. 'But I might as well satisfy your curiosity, as one last favour. Do sit down, Miss Chalmers. You'll find it so much more comfortable.'

'I'd rather stand.'

'As you wish.' He closed his eyes for a moment as if lost in a daydream. 'Now, Emma. Pity. A most delightful girl. Prone to prattling, but so eager to please.'

'You arranged to meet her on the deck.' She took a step back, hoping he wouldn't notice.

'You didn't expect me to skulk around in the ship's bowels, did you? There we were, all alone, stars twinkling above us, and I'd just taken off my coat to wrap darling Emma in it to keep her warm, when out fell a letter. She picked it up, and can you believe she had the audacity to boast how well you'd taught her and how she'd prove worthy of my love.'

He chuckled. 'Imagine that. And then, when I was beginning to have a little bit of fun, she acted all coy and demure, saying, "Oh no, Mr Dawkes, please don't Mr Dawkes."'

His voice rose in an imitation of a girl's pitch. 'And then she threatened to scream, although I'd told her she'd soon get used to it. Her sort of girl always does.'

'I presume with that you mean the sort of girl you and your partners intended to sell into white slavery.' Alyssa's voice nearly broke with fury. 'How did you find out about the shipment of unattached girls?

Dawkes smiled. 'I'm a businessman, my dear, and like all good businessmen I have useful connections. The temptation was too big, all these lovely bits of flesh, with no one who'd give a hoot about them. No one does with your kind, you see.'

'You are disgusting,' Alyssa said, sick creeping into her mouth.

'Little hypocrite. What's the difference between selling yourself to one man, as is your intention, or to have several buyers?'

He cast a calculating glance over Alyssa. 'Although I

don't see you bringing in much profit. Emma, on the other hand, would have been a roaring success, had I been able to afford to let her live. But that question, of course, is, in both cases, purely academic.'

Two swift steps and he clamped one hand down on her mouth while the other held her neck in a vice-like grip. Panic rose in her.

'If you want to say your prayers, this would be the right moment.' Dawkes still smiled. His eyes were as cold and shiny as marbles. 'It won't hurt, in case you wonder. Necks break quite easily.'

Alyssa kicked out as hard as she could. Her boot slammed into his kneecap. He let go of her for one split second, and one only, but that was enough for her to cry out.

Dawkes slapped her before he grabbed her throat again. Her vision blurred as his fingers pressed together.

'Let her go. Or I'll shoot you right through the heart.' Kendrick's pistol pressed into Dawkes' back.

'Aim a little bit higher and to the left,' Mark said as he walked out from behind the screen. 'You need to hit him here.'

A second muzzle touched Dawkes' back. 'Otherwise your bullet will pierce the lungs. That's a nasty way to die.'

Kendrick said, 'I'll leave you to do the honours, while I clap him in irons. Captain Moore might want to have a word with him.'

Alyssa's knees buckled under. She sank down onto the bed.

'Are you all right, my dear?' Mark said. 'Unfortunately, I have my hands full.'

'I'm fine.' She took a deep breath. 'Take that letter, Mr Kendrick. The captain will want to read it.'

'He did what?' Captain Moore's eyes bulged.

Mark said, 'Dawkes got wind of your cargo – after all, it was a fairly lengthy process of selecting the girls – and contacted some unsavoury acquaintances in San Francisco with the intention of spiriting the girls away during our stay there. Unfortunately, Emma Sayce caught his eye, and he strangled her and pushed her over board when she resisted his advances.'

Moore sank in his chair. 'Do you have proof?' He ignored Mark, directing his gaze at his first officer.

'Of the murder? No, Sir. But we've got a diary, with pretty conclusive entries, and this letter from his San Francisco accomplice, detailing the plan, including Inspector Johnson's part in abstracting the list of girls from your office. You will remember you saw him going through your ledgers? I'll stake my reputation that he stole the documents there and then.'

Kendrick paused. 'On top of that, both the doctor and I heard Dawkes' confession, and we witnessed a murderous assault on Miss Chalmers, who acted as bait. We were in the nick of time to save her life.'

'You did what?' Moore shot forwards like a bolt.

'It seemed the only possible way, Sir. We had to provoke a reaction to flush him out.'

'Without my permission?' The captain's face turned purple. 'You put that girl's life at risk without bothering to tell your commanding officer?'

'With all due respect, Sir, you told us to find the culprit.' Kendrick held out his hand. 'Your key to the liquor cabinet, Sir. You need a stiff drink, and, truth to be told, so do I.'

Fishing boats darted about, followed by flocks of hungry gulls. In the distance hills curved around inlets of water. Tiny figures milled around, offloading barrels from an anchored schooner.

On board the *Artemis' Delight*, the passengers and girls flocked to the rail with open delight.

'There she is.' The doctor gazed with fondness at the pier. 'San Francisco, jewel of the west. What a sight for sore eyes.'

'Don't forget your promise to Davies, Doctor,' Alyssa said. Spray glistened on her hair and skin, but she didn't mind. 'The boy spends all his time running around starry-eyed just thinking of it, and he has deserved a treat.'

'Do I detect some envy in your voice?'

'Yes,' she admitted. 'It must be wonderful to be free to walk around and see all these wonderful places. It is not fair that men are allowed to do as they choose, and women have to do as bid.'

'If you ask nicely, I'll take you along as well.'

'Would you do that?' For one instant, her eyes sparkled with delight, before she remembered her situation. 'I can't,' she said. 'Neither Matron nor the captain would permit that, and rightly so.'

She managed a weak smile. 'But I'd appreciate it if you and Davies would tell me later what wonders you've seen.'

'Second hand adventure for you? No, my dear, that wouldn't do for you.'

Mark stretched an arm casually out behind Alyssa's back, with his hand at the rail.

It was tempting to lean back into his arm but her good sense made Alyssa resist. 'What choices do I have?' she said. 'I hope to make up for it in the future, though. Maybe I can go travelling with mother's cousin, if I find her, or I'll hire a companion.'

'Are you still set on returning to England? I hoped you might change your plans.'

What did he mean? Her pulse skipped a beat. 'I'm not sure,' she said. 'A lot depends on the girls. I have promised to stay with them in Canada until they have settled. I won't let another man take advantage of their innocence, and neither will Matron.'

'And afterwards?'

She stared at the pier. 'I don't know yet. But I hope whatever happens, we'll part as friends.'

'Just like that? I can't possibly persuade you to come to my rescue, once you are free?' His thumb caressed her cheek. 'I could do with you by my side, although I wouldn't ask you to join me in a field hospital.'

'Wouldn't you rather ask your fiancée?'

'My what?' He slapped his forehead. 'The photograph, of course. I should have told you that I used my sister's picture to protect me from unwanted attention. It was a nice touch, wasn't it? Although I never meant to deceive you.'

He lowered his voice. 'Promise me you'll think about my words, my dear. Unless you prefer Mr Kendrick. Sterling fellow, of course, but you said yourself that, as he is a sailor, you'd be alone most of the time. I hope that at least counts in my favour?'

She glanced at Kendrick who stood less than two yards away from her. For once she was lost for words.

'I won't press you, my dear,' Mark said with more gentleness than she had thought him capable of. 'But whatever you decide, I am sure Mr Kendrick and I will be delighted to show you the sights here in San Francisco, no matter what the captain and Matron have to say to that. What do you say?'

'I'd love that.' She pressed his hand.

A delicate cough made them part. Matron leant forward and whispered. 'This really is not the done thing, Alyssa.' She shot a quick glance over her shoulder. Wainwright and Kendrick stood side by side, indulgent smiles on their lips. 'But I do admit this has been a happy voyage for all of us.'

Captain Moore trod heavily on the floorboards. 'One minute, Mr Kendrick, if you can tear yourself away from the bonny sight in front of us.'

He waved a piece of paper. 'I want you to go full steam ahead to the telegraph office. By golly, the owners are going to get a piece of my mind.'

He folded his arm across his chest and glowered at the world. 'Nothing but girls and murderers on this trip. That's it for me. Give me livestock any day. At least there you know what kind of muck you'll end up with.'


THE END

<u>Coming soon:</u>
<u>Glittering Death (an Alyssa Chalmers mystery)</u>

1862. The brides have arrived in British Columbia, and love is in the air. But their new-found happiness in the prospectors' town "Run's End" is shattered when the hotel-owner is murdered. To make matters worse, something is wrong with the stored gold at the hotel, and an epidemic makes it impossible for anyone to leave.

The brides set all their hopes on Alyssa Chalmers to find the murderer and restore peace in heir new home. But the killer is cunning, and desperate ...

<u>False Play at the Christmas Party (a Jack Sullivan mystery)</u>

December, 1928. Jack Sullivan plans a charity party in his new night club in aid of his fellow war veterans to celebrate his arrival in Adelaide. But some party guests have plans of their own how to benefit ...

## A Matter of Love and Death

Adelaide, 1931. Telephone switchboard operator Frances' life is difficult as sole provider for her mother and adopted uncle. But it's thrown into turmoil when she overhears a suspicious conversation on the phone, planning a murder.

If a life is at risk, she should tell the police; but that would mean breaking her confidentiality clause and would cost her the job. And practical Frances Palmer, not prone to flights of fancy, soon begins to doubt the evidence of her own ears - it was a very bad line, after all...

She decides to put it behind her, but it's not easy. Luckily there is the charming, slightly dangerous night club owner Jack Sullivan. Jack's no angel - six pm alcohol prohibition is in force, and what's a nightclub without champagne? But when Frances' earlier fears resurface, she knows that he's the person to confide in.

Frances and Jack's hunt for the truth puts them in grave

danger, and soon enough Frances will learn that some things are a matter of love and death...

# ACKNOWLEDGMENTS

While writing is a lonely business, there's hardly any book that sees the light of the day without the support of a small legion of people.

For The Case of the Missing Bride, its first champions were the New Zealand Society of Authors who paired me up with the fabulous writer Paddy Richardson. Without her, none of this would have happened.

Last on the list, but just as vital, are the people who cheered me on on good days and cheered me up on bad days: Fellow writers Lyn Towers, Sally-Ann Wilkinson, Lizzi Linklater, Margaret Kaufeler-Evans are chief among them, as is my daughter, who always believed in me.

Thank you, with all my heart.

False Play at the Christmas Party (a Jack Sullivan mystery)

A Matter of Love and Death (a Jack and Frances mystery)

Anthologies:

The Anthropocene Chronicles (science-fiction)

The Singularity (science-fiction)